Memory Can Be Murder

ELIZABETH DANIELS SQUIRE

G.K. Hall & Co. • Thorndike, Maine

Published in 2001 by arrangement with Luna Carne-Ross Literary Agent.

G.K. Hall Large Print Paperback Series.

The text of this Large Print edition is unabridged.
Other aspects of the book may vary from the original edition.

Set in 16 pt. Plantin by Christina S. Huff.

Printed in the United States on permanent paper.

Library of Congress Cataloging-in-Publication Data

Squire, Elizabeth Daniels.
    Memory can be murder / Elizabeth Daniels Squire.
        p.   cm.
     ISBN 0-7838-9408-2 (lg. print : sc : alk. paper)
     1. Dann, Peaches (Fictitious character) — Fiction.   2. Women
    detectives — North Carolina — Fiction.   3. Memory disorders
    — Fiction.   4. North Carolina — Fiction.   5. Large type
    books.   I. Title.
    PS3569.Q43 M4   2001
     813'.54—dc21   00-143888

Acknowledgments

I'd like to thank everyone who has contributed to the further empowerment of Peaches Dann. Sometimes I think she has more friends than I do; what's done right in this chronicle is due to those helpers. Whatever may be wrong is probably due to the fact that Peaches or I couldn't remember.

Special thanks to:

Bonnie Blue, talented sculptor, poet, and puppeteer, who created a wizard puppet that inspired Ann's wizard.

The North Carolina Crime Writers, who organized a trip to the state crime labs, where I learned some criminal ins and outs about plastic bags.

The New York Zoological Society herpetologist who, several years ago, put a rattlesnake through its paces while I took notes. This was originally meant to be used in a short story, but wound up between these covers.

My neighbor, Dan Harwood, for mountain snake stories.

Tom Morrissey, former sheriff of Buncombe County, for material about marijuana growers.

Detective Pat Hefner of the Buncombe County Sheriff's Department, for material about cults.

Carrie Lovelace (whom we shall miss), for mountain herb lore.

Lisa Franklin, for her rosemary recipe, and lots of other help.

Dershie McDevitt, Peggy Parris, Geraldine Powell, Virginia Sampson, and Florence Wallin, my much-valued writing group, for wonderful suggestions.

Robert and Yana Livesay, who also gave useful suggestions.

Worth Squire, the poet, who can always supply the right word.

Pat Dunton, for a few ideas about Jungian analysts.

Monika Wengler and Sue Kensil, who can spell.

Sis Cheshire, my cousin, who has endless memory-trick suggestions.

Laura Gilman, my editor, and Luna Carne Ross, my agent, without whom this book might not have been.

And Chick Squire, my husband, mainstay, and fountain of good ideas.

Chapter

1

Thursday Morning, June 27

"I'm scared." The voice on the telephone wavered. "Maybe I'm losing my mind."

Actually, how not to lose things is something I know a lot about. That and how to find them. Learned the hard way. But I mean objects, like my glasses. Lost minds are not my field of expertise.

"Go away," I wanted to say. "I haven't had my coffee. It's 8:30 in the morning. I have plans for the weekend."

I'd just waved goodbye to my ever-loving husband, Ted, and sat down at the kitchen table. I looked forward to a leisurely cup of coffee and then, after that, I planned four undisturbed days to put the finishing touches on my book: *How to Survive Without a Memory.*

You see, after fifty-five years with unpredictable spaces between my little gray cells, I'm an expert. I have a coping trick for every occasion. I have a publisher and I'm just doing the last rewrite. I want to finish.

Out the kitchen window a robin pulled a worm from the green lawn, which was great for the robin, but not so hot for the worm. Life is like that.

"You do remember me, don't you?" the frightened voice begged. "I'm Cousin Clothilde's daughter Anne, from Winston-Salem. I did a puppet show when you came to visit, back when I was a kid."

The fog lifted a little: I saw a pretty child and puppets that made me laugh, though Cousin Clothilde, this girl's mama, was fierce uptight.

"What makes you think you're losing your mind?" I asked. "You sound sane."

"I hope it's just me being foolish," she said, "but I think someone wants to kill my Sam with black magic." Could I have heard that right?

"I'm Mrs. Sam Newman now." I needed to remember her new name. With her New Man Sam, should she be on the lam or they'd get in a jam? I visualized that. I could remember his name that way. Pictures, rhymes, and puns are a gal's best friends.

"I'm here in the mountains," she said. "Not far. Do you know where Bloodroot Creek Road is?"

"Yes."

"I'm staying at the place right at the end. I'll meet you out on the road by the mailbox. Please come quick."

"I will," I said, "because it sounds to me like I need to hear about this in person." If she was out of her mind, I could tell it better with my eyes helping my ears. Why can't I just say no?

I took my pocketbook with the shoulder strap off the hook where it lives when it's not on my shoulder. (See *Hang-Ons* chapter in *How to Survive*.) I felt for my key ring, which stays snapped inside the pocketbook except when I'm driving. You have to be crafty if you're totally absent-minded or else you spend your whole time looking for stuff. At least it was a lovely day for a ride, sunshiny with blue sky and the mountains shimmery green.

I found Anne standing nervously by the road in a yard full of huge old trees, in front of a strange Victorian house. Half of that house glowed fresh-paint white. The other half was gray with peeling paint. The dividing line was vertical. Even the funny Victorian tower on top was half gray, half white. The front door was bright red with brass carriage lamps on each side. Something wild was certainly bound to happen in a place like that.

Anne was unusual, too. A pretty girl with almond-shaped eyes and arched eyebrows that lifted up at the outer edge. She had long brown hair and an unpainted oval face, like my grandma in her wedding-day picture, and wore a long skirt and a long-sleeved, scoop-necked blouse that would have looked right on Grandma. She put her fingers to her lips and said, "Wait."

She pulled me off into an old springhouse at the side of the driveway. Dark water filled a long stone trough along one side. Thick stone walls were waist-high, with square-cut logs notched together above that. A fine place for secrets. No windows. Slits of bright light shone through the narrow spaces in between the logs. Otherwise the room was shadowy, and cool for June here in the Carolina mountains. Through the wall slits I could smell honeysuckle baking in the sunshine. Nice.

Ted would have asked, "What's going on?" right off. But I figured Anne was shy. The creep-up-on-the-subject type. Glad of the shadows that made her face hard to read.

"I called you," she said softly, "because my mother said that you might help out if we got in any kind of trouble up here. I don't usually do what my mother says. I'm nineteen, and I'm married." She raised her chin as she said that, with plenty of ginger. "But, you see," she said, going minor, "I'm prone to catastrophes. I just naturally have bad luck." She said that with drama, with both hands open as if she held an invisible ball of trouble. "But I was so sure things were going to be better after I married Sam, and they have been — until now. . . ."

"Does Sam think something is wrong here,

too?" I said, encouraging her to get to the point.

"Oh, that's part of the problem," Anne said, hugging herself like she was cold. "That's why we can't leave. Sam thinks the greatest chance of his career is here. Sam's an artist, and he wants to paint Revonda Roland. That's the woman we're working for. And I want Sam to have his chance." She raised her chin again. There was spunk in this girl, scared or not.

"Where does black magic come in?" I had to know that!

"Revonda's son, whose name is Paul, has books about magic." Anne's voice wavered again. "He told me so, though I haven't seen them. He keeps his room locked. Plus he told Sam something bad would happen if we stayed here. He said this place killed people."

Well, a girl with imagination would certainly see black magic in all that.

I noticed two large black spiders lurking in webs in a corner as if to give the right atmosphere. Another ran across the floor. I try not to be scared of spiders. Scared. Did Paul want to scare off Anne and Sam?

"Sam's a genius." Anne's eyes shone with pride. "He just hasn't been discovered yet." She paused and stared at the spiders. "Sam paints what's wrong with the world. He paints the kind of portraits that show what people are really like, how they're trying to impress other people — stuff like that." Anne began to walk nervously up and down, making the springhouse seem

11

even smaller than it was.

"So they don't like his portraits?" But certainly nobody would threaten death because of that.

"Oh, sometimes they do like his portraits!" she cried. "Because Sam paints so exactly what they're trying to pretend to be that they don't see what's wrong with it. It's only if they find out what other people think of the portrait that they get mad."

She stopped. "There's Sam."

I heard footsteps on the gravel drive outside, and somebody whistling gaily.

"Anne," a man's voice boomed, "where are you?"

She smiled like Christmas morning, stood tall, stuck her head out the door, and called, "Right here, Sam."

Almost immediately a large, cheerful man exploded through the doorway, and I thought Aha! Exhibit Number One. The black-magic target. Maybe. Sam was stocky, about six feet tall. Muscular, not fat. Casual, in jeans and a white T-shirt. His reddish hair and beard burst forth with wild exuberance. The springhouse seemed five sizes too small for him.

Sam reached out his hand and beamed. "You must be Cousin Peaches." I liked him right away. Charm, I thought. He turns the world golden as soon as he walks in the room. Even for a fifty-five-year-old cousin on his wife's side.

12

"This is Sam," Anne said, in a tone that said, "This is my darling." He put his arm around her shoulders, and I could feel electricity shoot through her. Feel attraction between those two till it crackled.

He turned his whole attention to me. "I understand you've written a book."

"*How to Survive Without a Memory*," I told him. And felt foolishly important. Well, of course I was pleased that my book was going to be published, but he made me feel like Margaret Mitchell and Agatha Christie rolled into one. Such a nice man!

"We all need a book about how it's absolutely O.K. to be imperfect. I'm for that," Sam said.

I was startled. "I never thought of my book that way," I said. "But I guess it's about how to get around what you're *not* good at by using what you *are* good at, like remembering things by rhymes and other tricks if you can't just remember them neat. I guess that *is* about the art of being imperfect." We laughed together. I felt a little drunk. Super-charm affects me that way. And as for Anne, her eyes were full of hero worship, like an actress in an old silent-movie love scene.

"That's wonderful, to accept being imperfect," Sam cried, "because the bad thing is to lie to yourself. This rotten world is full of people who do that!" He beamed and brushed away a swinging spider.

"And you paint people exactly the way they

lie to themselves — that's what Anne tells me. I'd love to see your paintings," I said. Was it Sam's paintings that enraged this Paul until he implied threats?

"I'd love to show you my work!" Sam led us out into the blinding sunlight, waving toward a small weathered building across the driveway from the big house. "Come over to my studio!"

"We have a great deal here," Anne told me. "We get a studio and half the day for our own work, and the other half of the day we work for Revonda Roland. She grew up around here, then went off and made it on the Broadway stage. Now she's come back and is fixing up this place."

Revonda Roland, I thought. Vonda was a little like wander with a German accent. I pictured Hansel and Gretel wandering. They were German, right? I put the witch in the picture — scary things are easier to remember. And Revonda was vondering again: revondering. I'd get the last name next time.

Sam pointed toward the house: "That's my first job here."

"I can imagine!" I said. "I never saw a house half-painted quite like that."

"Paul did it that way," Sam laughed, "and then announced he wouldn't finish the job. That's part of why we're here."

We crunched down the white gravel driveway. On the left, before the curve to the house with its wide front porch, stood the studio, with a

14

two-car garage downstairs — a bright red car in one side and a white pickup truck in the other. A brown van was parked beside the building. Above the garage the studio had big windows. A huge old tree on one side of the building drooped branches around it like protecting arms. Sam led us up the stairs on the side of the building and into a room paneled with pine.

He strode past a small table with four bentwood chairs around it, and past a big work-table with puppets sitting at the back: a red-haired grouch, a wizard in a pointed hat, even a goldfish. Sam hurried us past an empty easel, set just right to catch the light, and led us to the end of the room where paintings leaned against the wall.

"Here's one I like," he boomed. He picked it up and set it on the easel.

My first thought was: What perfectly lovely colors. A beautiful design. Then I realized it wasn't an abstract design but a trash dump. On the edge of a pond, oozing some poisonous-looking green stuff into the water. I felt tricked.

He threw his arm around me. "Gotcha!" he cried happily. "Some of my things are not that subtle." He pulled up a painting of a circle of scrawny, hungry-looking children with large frightened eyes. "I started to call this *Hunger,*" he said. "But I decided to call it *Eyes.*"

I could see what Anne meant about his pictures. I wouldn't want that one in my house, with the hungry eyes following me around. How could the man who painted that picture be so cheerful?

"This one is my mother," Anne said in a voice like a challenge. "It's not finished yet."

I was shocked. I know Cousin Clothilde pretty well. Pop, my eighty-five-year-old father, is fond of her. She drops by when she comes to the mountains. And there was the time when my first husband, Roger, and I went down to the beach and spent the night at Clothilde's house in Winston-Salem on the way. That's when we'd met Anne as a child.

Cousin Clothilde's house looked like a photo spread from *House Beautiful*. Except more elegant and less practical. The living room was all in shades of white and gold. Pop said that Cousin Clothilde's father was a pig farmer, and she was working to get away from the pig image. It made me feel tired, just looking at her, with her every hair teased into place. Somehow Sam had got that into the picture. He caught her attitude by the way her lips were pursed: Only perfect would do for Clothilde.

It was the only portrait I ever saw that I wanted to talk back to. Listen here, I wanted to say, who gave *you* the right to decide how I should behave?

"Does your mother like it?" I asked Anne.

"So far," she said, "it's the only thing she does like about my marrying Sam."

I was amazed.

"Mother felt I should marry a rich man who

16

could look after me." Anne made a face like she had a bad taste in her mouth. "She doesn't think Sam will ever be rich." She threw Sam a loving glance, and he threw his arm around her and gave her a bear hug. "But Sam *is* rich. He enjoys life. We enjoy life."

I knew I wouldn't want the judging eyes of that portrait of Anne's mother in my house any more than I'd want the eyes of the starving children hanging in my kitchen. I'd get an ulcer.

"Really remarkable pictures," I told Sam. "They get me in the pit of my stomach."

"Because they are about the state of the world." He threw his arms wide with enthusiasm. He seemed too large even for this big, bright room. "My pictures are about the way we pretend that everything is beautiful while the world falls apart."

"But we don't!" I couldn't let that pass. "Don't you watch television? We constantly criticize. We carp at every little thing any public figure does. Why —"

He interrupted. "But that's the same thing. The opposite side of the coin. We tell ourselves we all ought to be perfect so any little flaw should be magnified and pecked at. The world has cancer, and we carp about zits." Why did he radiate joy when he was telling me that?

"I believe I have talent." He paced around the room, pleased with himself. There was even something naive and charming about that. "And I have a great opportunity here. I am painting Revonda Roland's portrait, and it's going to be the best thing I've ever done."

"Why?" I asked.

But he looked at the clock over the worktable. "It's noon!" he cried. "I have to run. Revonda gets upset if I'm late. Cousin Peaches, it was great to meet you!" Sam gave me a quick hug, then exploded out of the room with as much speed and energy as he'd exploded into the springhouse when he first appeared.

"Do you have to go?" I asked Anne as soon as I caught my breath. She was standing by the picture of her mother. I noticed they had the same bow-shaped mouth. But Mama's was rejecting. Anne's was merely tense.

"I can be a little late," she said. "It's Sam that Revonda likes most. Here, sit down." She waved at the bentwood chairs by the small table, then pulled one out for me.

"You called me," I said, "because . . . ?" She walked over to the worktable and picked up the wizard puppet in his pointed black hat. He was a large puppet, with a head that was almost life-size. She slipped her hand into the body, held him in front of her, and suddenly he grabbed my eyes. Anne all but disappeared.

"Revonda *is* trouble," the Wizard said in a deep portentous voice. "She's a retired actress who never retired." He nodded wisely. "She wants what she wants. She wants Sam. That can pull Sam and Anne both into danger."

"But she's seventy-five years old," Anne's

18

voice said as she reappeared, frowning. "She doesn't want Sam for a lover. She wants him for a protégé, almost for a son. She can help him. What's wrong with that?"

"She already has a son," the Wizard said darkly. "And a twisted bad relationship. Be careful of the son. He wants to hurt."

Anne slipped her hand out of the puppet, and suddenly he was only cloth on the table again. "I'm sorry," she said, "but I think better if I talk with the Wizard. It's silly, but it works." She patted the empty black puppet.

I'd never been warned of danger by a puppet before, I'll say that. But Anne did look upset. Kind of pinched around the face. "Could you meet Revonda and Paul and tell me what you think?" she asked. "When I'm so scared, without any real reason, it makes me feel crazy. But," she added quickly, "don't go now. Revonda doesn't like surprises. I'll work it out for you to come when she expects it." She smiled. "I feel so much better knowing you're going to help."

"O.K.," I said. "Call me when I can meet them. I'm mostly home working on the book." I gave her a hug. "I like your Sam," I said.

I drove home feeling lonesome. Ted and I usually handle things together. We're a new team, only married for a year and a half. But when you work with somebody who just naturally pings when you pong, whose strengths and weaknesses dovetail so well with yours, you get spoiled. And since I had this ominous feeling, I wished he was here to talk this strange situation over with before things got worse than just the premonitions of a nervous cousin.

Ted was only away for a few days at a newspaper symposium down east. But I knew from experience that all hell can break loose in a lot less time than that.

Chapter

2

SATURDAY MORNING, JUNE 29

I got back to my own work — rewriting the chapter on machines that help memory. Funny the simple bits you don't think of unless somebody tells you. Like the answering-machine trick. If you're out and you have to remember to do something first thing when you get home, what's the best way? Why, call yourself up. Leave yourself a message on your machine. Actually I insulted Ted by mistake the first time I tried that out. He picked up and I said, "I don't want to speak to you. I want to speak to the machine."

The phone by my desk rang. It was Anne. "I haven't called you back," she said, "because Revonda's son Paul has been away. He had a big blowup with his mother and stalked out. Not long after you were here. Revonda's been too upset for you to come meet her. But now" — her voice got more intense — "Paul's been gone for two days. Nobody knows where. He simply vanished. Revonda's in a terrible state, but she won't call the sheriff. Perhaps if you could offer to help Revonda find him . . ." Her voice trailed off.

"I've never done missing persons," I said. But by now I was so curious that I said, "I'll be over later this morning, as soon as I check on my father. He's not in good health." I didn't add that Pop always bore watching because he could make more trouble sitting still in a wheelchair than three-year-old quintuplets in a china shop.

"We'll be in the big house," she said. "The room on the right with the door onto the front porch. That's Paul's room. Revonda is getting us to paint the woodwork while he's gone."

What? Painting woodwork didn't sound to me like a thing you'd worry about if you were in a terrible state about your only son. It made me even more curious about this Re-wonder Revonda, who went to pieces and thought about woodwork all at once.

Pop would know something about Revonda if her people came from these parts. I could kill two birds with one stone when I went by to make sure he was O.K. I would not mention magic. Pop's imagination could take off enough without extra help.

But Pop wasn't O.K. He was bored. He'd rolled his wheelchair over to the glass door that looked out on the garden, where the phlox and roses and foxglove were in full bloom, and was staring into space. He turned around balefully when I came in from the kitchen, where I'd stopped to speak to Bessie, his new house-keeper.

"Even the birds hide in the woods," he said accusingly. He managed to look so frail under his fine white hair that I might have let myself forget what a force he can be. I knew he was angry because his favorite sitter had married a rich Texas oil man and quit her job. Fortunately, Pop is loaded and can afford sitters around the clock. But he couldn't compete with a Texan who was rich, young, and sexy.

"I have a puzzle for you," I said. "What do you know about a woman about eight years younger than you named Revonda, who grew up in Bloodroot Creek and went off and became an actress?"

"Revonda Glenn," he said. "Her married name is Roland. Hot dog! She did what she pleased." He rolled his chair back over to the round mahogany table where he usually sat and waved a hand for me to sit, too. "She wasn't an actress when I knew her. But she knew how to get people to help her out. She did summer the-ater when she was only fourteen. That's how I met her. Some gal! Folks like Revonda and me made a point to know the summer people. If you want to make money, it helps to know money." He winked at me. "Later she went off and worked for one of them after her father drank himself to death. Her father was talented and no good."

"Talented how?" I asked.

"He could carve little animals that almost came alive. But mostly he just drank."

"What became of Revonda?"

"I heard she married a summer person's rich cousin and got to be a star on Broadway but under some other name. Elvira Lane, I think it was. She was a second-string star. That was in the fifties and the sixties."

Pop was having one of his good days, remembering all that.

"I'd like to see Revonda again," he said. "She was never dull. Have you met her?"

I was glad I could say no. Pop getting in touch with Revonda while trouble brewed was not what we wanted. I said a friend of mine had asked about her, then managed to change the subject. A little later I set out for Revonda's.

It's strange and wonderful how every single mountain valley is unique. Bloodroot Creek Valley is long and broad with low mountains along both sides like the backs of sleeping dragons, and far mountains visible beyond that. The fields by the road are a patchwork: row-crops, tall grass, cows, and a bigger patch where new houses seemed to grow in rows, too. In one field a tractor was cutting hay, and children waded in the creek by the road. Revonda's place was at the far end of the valley. Beyond her house the road took a new name and rose sharply toward the pass over to Mitchell Creek.

I drove in her driveway, past the springhouse on my left, up to the big, old Victorian split-personality house. I heard dogs barking, but nobody came to the door to check out why. The red car was missing from the garage. I went straight to the room on the right with the door that opened directly off the front porch, where Anne said she and Sam would be painting woodwork.

I knocked and Anne called, "Come in." I walked right into a cracked mirror — or at least that's how it felt. There were mirrors in front of me, above me, to both sides of me. Mirrors of all shapes glued to cover the wall and, in between them, black. Except around the door at the far side of the room. Sam and Anne, each with brush in hand, were busy painting that woodwork white. They stopped and said, "Hi."

I wanted to say, "Let's get out of this place." There was something about that room that made me dizzy. I get quite dizzy enough with no help at all just trying to work some strange machine, like a new computer. Or having to fill out a tax form. But this was much worse.

The mirrors were all sorts of odd shapes, as if Paul got them from a junkyard and then made a crazy quilt to cover the walls and ceiling. All I could see in every direction was me, reflected from every angle and in every size. I'm not bad looking, but once is enough! Actually, it wasn't just me, but me and everything around me. I felt queasy.

"I feel like these mirrors could swallow me up," I said. "How do you stand it?" Mirrors and more mirrors reflecting mirrors. "When one of us moves," I said, waving my arms to see the effect, "everything moves like we're all inside a dern kaleidoscope."

"It helps if you deliberately look at something else," Sam said. "Look at one of us."

I looked at him, and it did help. He was the same as the day before, hair and beard still electric, grin still enthusiastic.

"This room could be helpful if you forget what you look like," I tried to joke. To keep my balance. "Except I'd like to remember myself right side up, not upside down and sideways and every which way."

"We never came in here until yesterday," Sam said. "Paul never invited us in, and he'd lock the door when he left."

"Revonda says he used to be a stage-set designer and a costume designer, and I can believe that," Anne said, rolling her eyes. "Maybe for horror films. Revonda went off to the liquor store. She'll be back."

Just looking at this room made me feel drunk. At least the floor didn't reflect. It was black and bare.

The French doors I'd come through didn't reflect because they were curtained on the inside with some white opaque stuff. Paul didn't want anybody to see in. Paul has kinky sex here, I thought. That was it! What a place for an orgy. Well, evil is in the eye of the beholder. Remember that. But this room encouraged the eye to expect something bizarre.

I noticed the poster on the door from Paul's room into the rest of the house. That door was closed, all but a crack, and hanging on the back of it was a picture of a naked man, about half life size, spread out on a five-pointed star. He seemed to be standing in the air between Sam and Anne.

"What did you say about strange books?" I asked.

Anne pointed to a bookcase. "Mostly about Medieval magic. We were looking at his books yesterday, after we measured to see how much paint to get." She folded her arms across her chest and hugged herself. "I'll tell you, those books make me nervous. Some of them have curses in them."

"But some of those books have magical cures, and some of them are very funny," Sam said. "I opened one book at random, and it said that in order to cure a cold you should kiss a mule." He began to laugh.

Anne's smile was forced. "I guess I feel like if you're prone to bad luck, then curses are more catching," she said. I noticed she had picked a spot to paint that was far from the bookshelf.

Suddenly I was grateful that all I have to fight is a bad memory. Hardly ever has it occurred to me that I was prone to bad luck. "It seems to me," I said, "that to a large extent we make our own luck by looking life straight in the eye and doing whatever has to be done."

"I guess when I'm in a place like this," Anne said, "I half believe in demons."

Demons. I didn't even like hearing that word in this kaleidoscope room. This was not a room to be rational in. This was a room to foster dreams — no, not just dreams. Nightmares. Be sensible, Peaches, I told myself.

I started over to look at the books, to see for myself what could be in them that scared Anne. I kept my eyes on the black floor so the mirrors wouldn't make me dizzy. Whammo. I bumped into a chair. And what a chair. It was a dark wood rocker with a grotesque face carved in the back. Because I'd bumped it, the chair began to rock, and the face looked up, down, up, down, almost alive. I looked away from that grotesque face into the mirrors, and I saw the face on every side leering at me, and moving this way and that. I was seized with terror. I screamed, and shut my eyes to stop seeing that demon face. This place really got to me.

Sam rushed over and put his arm around me. Anne cried, "What is it?"

I pulled myself together. "I suppose there is some little corner in me that half believes in demons, too," I said shakily, "especially when that dern chair face rocks and I'm already feeling dizzy."

An angry voice said, "Only a fool ignores demons." I knew it must be Paul. He stood in the doorframe where the poster of the star-man had been a minute before.

He clicked on the light by the door, making the room twice as bright. Paul was odd enough to fit the room. He wore black jeans and a black T-shirt and a pair of scuffed high-topped hiking shoes that looked like they'd walked a long way. And yet he didn't look like a man who'd like to hike. He held a cigarette in the long pointed fingers that would have seemed just right for a pickpocket or a saint, except his fingernails were bitten. A curl of smoke wafted past his face. He was good looking, with dark curly hair and even features and a sensuous mouth. He had intelligent eyes. Around his neck a medal hung on a black cord, a strange antique medal with letters and numbers on it glimmering in the light. Paul, the costume and stage set designer. I made myself remember that.

He raised the cigarette to his lips, took in a puff, and blew a perfect smoke ring in Anne's direction. "You have absolutely no right to be in my room, but you assume you have the right to read my books," he rasped. "And to condemn them." He looked Anne up and down as he said that, as if he liked her bra size and had contempt for her soul. He was so contemptuous he was like a burlesque of himself. He fascinated me and made me angry.

I wondered how long he'd been listening at

the door. He turned toward Sam. "After a single glance you feel you have the right to laugh at my books."

Sam said, "Why do you care so much?" He was so eager I suspected he was composing Paul into a picture.

Anne was flushed with anger. She tried to answer Paul back. "I was interested in what you like to read, Paul. I wondered why you stay in this place you seem to hate, why you come back." That was a challenge. Good for her.

"Why I come back?" His voice hit two notes at once, like a kid I used to sit near in the sixth grade. "Where would I go? I can't live forever in the woods." A vein stood out on his forehead. "What did you think I'd do — work for an old woman like you and Sam do? I'm not like you." Now he was shouting at Anne, ignoring me. "You came here for my mother to use against me. You and Sam." He swept them both with hot black eyes. "Where did my mother know you before, Sam?" he demanded.

"Your mother? Revonda never knew me. We came here through an ad in the Asheville paper."

Paul's sneer reflected round and round and round us. Very ugly. "An ad? Bullshit. My mother never hired anyone without fifteen references. She never asked Sam for a reference, did she?" He wheeled on Sam.

"Or me," Anne added.

"You?" Paul laughed. His teeth were shiny

white. "Revonda doesn't care about you. You are an appendage. My mother knows Sam from somewhere" — he glared at Anne — "and she lies about it." Paul was trying to upset and scare Anne. I was sure of that. Anne was wide-eyed. She seemed dumbfounded.

I heard a car in the driveway.

"You know why my mother wanted to hire you?" Paul snarled at Sam. "She did it to make me look bad. Because I don't finish things fast enough to suit her. She did it to prove I do a bad job of whatever I do and you can do better." His face was bright red. "Why the hell do you think you have the right to paint my room without my permission," he demanded, "even if she told you to do it? I damn well ought to have the right to say O.K. or not O.K."

He turned to me. "You don't have any excuse for being in my room, whoever you are." This was not a man who would be easy to like.

His words had run together so fast nobody had a chance to say who I was. "What the hell happened to privacy?" he demanded.

I heard the outside door of the room open, and there stood a white-haired woman in a bright red pantsuit, a great deal of skillfully applied makeup, and gold jewelry by the ton.

"When you leave and don't tell anyone when you're coming back, what do you expect?" she said archly. "I say you lose your rights, Paul. This *is* my house."

She turned to me, smiled with great charm,

31

and said. "You must be Anne's cousin she said was coming over. I'm Revonda Roland."

"Now you're going to ignore me, aren't you?" Paul cried out. "You get upset when I vanish, or so you say, and when I'm here you treat me like shit." There was anguish in his voice, as if he were a child and his mother had rejected him.

"Paul, dear," Revonda said condescendingly, "we'll discuss whatever upsets you later, when our guest is gone." Her red and gold stood out in the mirrors.

"No," he said. "That won't make it right." He turned and his eyes hit Anne. The paintbrush was still dangling in her hand. She seemed to have shrunk. He held her in his gaze and said: "So you've noticed there are curses in my books. There are, and I'd like to put a curse on all of you." He scanned us all with his angry eyes. "Because you're putting a curse on me by the way you treat me."

Revonda laughed like ice cubes tinkling. Just listening made me cold. "But you've told me what to do about a curse, Paul," she said. "I know what it says in your books and that you believe it. If a man or woman refuses to accept a curse, it boomerangs and hurts the sender. If we all refuse to accept your curse, it will come threefold back on you."

I thought: When this Revonda is angry, she doesn't know how destructive her words sound.

I watched Anne. She seemed too upset to hear what Revonda said. Still worried by Paul's threat.

I thought: This Paul has spotted Anne as more vulnerable than Sam. He's spotted her weak point. Her fear of bad luck. He's going to use that against them. Because he doesn't want Sam *or* Anne here. He wants his mother to himself.

"Get out, all of you!" Paul yelled.

Anne started toward the outside door. The mirrors must have confused her. She walked briskly toward what she must have thought was the door, and crashed head on into a long piece of mirror.

She let out a small cry, staggered back, and Sam rushed to put his arm around her. "You'll be sorry for this, damn you!" he said to Paul. His voice was calm but strong. I would not have wanted anybody to look at me with the rage Sam had in his eyes as he looked at Paul.

My intuition told me this was not the time for me to learn more about these people. This was the time for me to get out.

Chapter

3

SUNDAY, JUNE 30

Ted called Saturday night, and I told him a little bit about the wild family my cousin and her husband were working for. But not much. Why worry him? He wouldn't be back till Monday afternoon.

Revonda called and invited me to lunch at noon on Sunday. I figured she was as curious about me as I was about her and her son. If she was embarrassed about the scene I'd witnessed, she didn't say so.

"I've heard so much about you," she said when I arrived. "How you've almost been killed several times and so cleverly managed to outwit the killer. I understand you've also written a book."

She was dressed to the nines in a tiger-print pants-and-blouse outfit and tiger's-eye earrings.

I don't mean that semiprecious stone they call tiger's-eye. Her earrings were made out of glass eyes, which must have come from a taxidermist. They looked smashing, as if Revonda had taken on the spirit of a big cat. Her own green eyes were just as bold, which fit with what my father said about her as a young woman: "She did what she pleased."

But her manners were super-civilized. She shook my hand and welcomed me and said how she enjoyed meeting a cousin of Sam and Anne's. "They are so talented," she said. "They answered an ad. But I had hardly hoped to find such high-quality young people who I'd want for friends as well as helpers."

She ushered me into her living room, where light streamed in from windows on two sides and brought out the vivid colors in this great big red-and-blue Oriental rug that covered the whole floor. In the middle of the room were two red cushiony couches, back to back, as if to dramatize that sometimes there were people in that room who didn't want to speak to each other.

Big fringed red-and-blue pillows were plumped just right on the couch facing us. Polished silver ashtrays sat on the coffee tables. No newspapers or books out. I felt as if there ought to be a velvet rope in front of the whole sitting area, like a museum.

Tiger Woman strode right over to a bar, where she poured us both glasses of sherry. She led me around the couches, past some chairs, past a stool with a coat of arms in needlepoint, and stopped by a group of pictures on the wall.

"That's where I came from." She waved toward black-and-white photographs, all enlarged. They were out of place with her rich-actress furniture, but I could see by her high head that she was proud of them.

In one photo a mountain man in an old felt hat and high work shoes held the hand of a little girl. She had Revonda's determined face and sharp deepset eyes. The man reminded me of some of my folks on Pop's side. In another picture the same man had on Sunday clothes and stood by a tree with a tired-looking woman and the little girl. A third picture showed the man, still in felt hat, holding a dead snake by the tail. He had to hold his arm high to show the whole length. The man had angry eyes like Paul's.

Revonda leaned against the back of a high-winged oversize, overstuffed chair with a jungle print on it: red and blue tropical flowers plus a lot of lush green leaves. The colors were so electric I'd have almost been afraid to touch that chair. Something might crawl out of the leaves and bite me. But Revonda leaned and pointed to another part of the wall in back of it.

"You saw where I came from. This is what I was able to do!" she crowed as she waved at framed theater posters. Here was Revonda grown up, but still young and pretty, playing all sorts of parts. I could recognize Joan of Arc with her sword and Lady MacBeth staring at her damned spot and Queen Elizabeth with her ruff.

I noticed a silver-framed picture on a dark wood table next to the jungle chair: Must be Paul, at about ten, dressed up in a suit and a necktie and holding hands with his mother. Paul and Revonda smiled as if they didn't need a thing but each other. "I was a good mother," Revonda said. "You can see that. You must forgive Paul his temper tantrums. He has such an artistic temperament."

My eyes couldn't find a picture of her husband. Why did she care if I, a newly met stranger, thought she was a good mother?

Queen Revonda Elizabeth of Arc led me through a dining area with huge Audubon prints on the wall, through a pleasant kitchen with a stone fireplace, out onto the side porch, where Anne was setting a table for lunch, putting wineglasses on a glass-topped table surrounded by five wicker chairs. Revonda nodded. Not a lot of warmth between those two.

Then here, to ruffle the peace, came Paul around the corner of the house. His black eyes under his tousled dark hair said he still thought we were rats carrying plague. He was smoking just as he'd been the day before. Mephistopheles complete with his own hellfire smoke, I thought, that's what he meant to look like. Complete with hounds of hell. Twin black rottweilers came running down the porch behind him, growling. I backed up and bumped into

Revonda, who had lingered behind me.

"It's all right," Revonda said loudly, stepping forward. She patted the dog nearest to her. "You can see they're good watchdogs. They obey. They are friendly as long as I say, 'It's all right.' " She smiled encouragingly at me, but my left leg was thinking about the time a dog bit me in the third grade.

"This one is Hound," Revonda said, continuing to pat the dog. "The other is Baskerville. Baskerville likes Paul better than she likes me. Hound obeys me better. She's a good dog."

Paul glared at her. "I don't answer your commands fast enough."

I could see he had come to lunch in order to be difficult. I began to suspect that was what he enjoyed most in life.

"You remember Peaches Dann," Revonda said to Paul.

He bowed. "How could I forget the interloper friend of your new helpers, who will replace me." So friendly.

Sam was coming up the porch steps to join us. Revonda turned and smiled radiantly at him while Paul plunked himself down at the glass-topped table.

Paul shrugged. "You'll all learn to hate this place as much as I do." He still wore the strange antique medal with numbers and letters in a spiral on it, which swayed against his black T-shirt. He glowered at his mother, ignored the rest of us, and smoked.

Revonda just went on with the next act: elegant lunch. She got Sam to carry it out on a tray from the kitchen at the end of the porch: crab salad and chilled white wine and rolls and butter.

She slipped into a seat next to Sam and looked up into his face and fluttered her eyelashes. "My son is very talented." I figured she was saying that for Paul's benefit. "He's tried painting, not to mention designing stage sets, and tried real estate."

"And failed at all of them — at least, by your standards." Paul blew a cloud of smoke. My eyes watered. I was sitting next to him. Anne was in the seat at the end of the table between Paul on one side and Sam on the other. Sam watched us all like he enjoyed the show.

Revonda went right on sipping her wine and acting like everything was O.K.

"Sam is painting me," Revonda turned to me, smiling. I refrained from telling her to watch out. Certainly he'd catch that predatory look she gave to Paul. Like no matter what Paul did, he was still her possession. Perhaps she'd be blind to the truth.

Paul is disappointed in us, I thought. He hasn't managed to make us miserable or furious. But he'll keep trying.

Anne was fidgeting. She put her fork down, reached into a black bag she'd brought with her, and pulled out the Wizard, black pointed hat, black robes, and all. "How do you do," he said,

39

bowing, "I am at your service." He wore white gloves, and Anne's hand was in one of those gloves holding a big book marked *Spells*.

"Ask me a question," he said, "any question. I know everything. It's all right here in my book of spells."

Revonda raised an eyebrow, which said the Wizard had not been invited.

Paul laughed. Not with us but at his mother. "Ask the Wizard what to do about snakes, Ma. You haven't told these people about killing two rattlesnakes the day before they came, have you, Ma? You haven't told them this is a big year for snakes. Maybe you need a spell to keep these people safe."

I shivered. I'm afraid of snakes.

Anne must have been, too. She let the Wizard's book slip. Her wineglass teetered on the edge of the table, then plunged. I gasped. Revonda cried, "My Waterford crystal!"

But Sam had already caught the glass in midair and put it back.

The Wizard waved his wand and said, "My magic can do anything. I can even make a wineglass fly."

I laughed. Anne was trying to break the tension.

Revonda did not laugh. "Perhaps you have a puppet that deals with reality. I might like that." She looked at Paul. "I don't care for magic."

Paul jumped up in his cloud of smoke. "You don't care for magic because it interests me," he snarled. "You don't care for anything that interests me. You'd like to throw out all my books. And don't start telling me how you gave me braces and piano lessons and my own shrink. To hell with that. I'm leaving. Just give me some money, damn it. It's my money."

Revonda put her hand to her throat, and I thought: Mary, Queen of Scots, sentenced to beheading.

"I won't give you money to use for drugs and liquor, or to spend on that girl. I won't help you to destroy yourself the way your father did."

I was embarrassed to be sitting there sipping from her Waterford crystal, looking out over the blue-green mountains and hearing all that. Paul began to yell so loud the neighbors could probably hear, too, and the nearest neighbors were out of sight.

"You got your money from my father. Who drank because he hated you. His money will curse you."

Revonda stayed calm, chin high. "Weak people shout."

Paul stalked off the porch and around the house. I noticed Anne had put the puppet away and turned pale. She'd meant to help.

Revonda looked sick, and a tic by her left eye made it appear to keep winking. Her hand on the table clenched. "I'm so sorry about this," she said to me. "I simply get so upset at Paul I'm not myself." She said that without humility. Her head was still high. She can't help acting

41

proud, I thought. My mother used to say, "Pride goes before a fall." I read somewhere that the Greeks called it hubris, which brought the anger of the Gods.

Maybe if Revonda actually saw herself in Sam's portrait, she could begin to change. Maybe Sam would be doing her a favor after all.

Maybe you're lucky in this life, I thought, if you have some very obvious fault that helps you to avoid hubris!

"I hate to leave you folks, but I promised to go pick up some plants from Revonda's friends who're moving," Sam said calmly. Good moment for an exit! He thanked Revonda for the delicious lunch, which he'd eaten in double time, winked at Anne, and went off down the porch steps. He drove off, waving goodbye. I thought he was lucky.

Anne and Revonda and I finished our crab salad in uncomfortable silence. Then Anne took the plates into the kitchen, and Revonda showed me where the bathroom was. She led me back through the kitchen, dining room, and living room to a small hall with doors off both sides. A bookshelf stood against one wall of the hallway, with all sorts of knickknacks on it. My eye fell on an old-fashioned pearl-handled pistol. That didn't go with the family pictures on the wall. Wrong style. Just beyond the shelf a door on the right was painted black and had a brass door knocker on it. I thought: That's Paul's room. It must be.

Revonda hesitated by that door as if she wanted to look inside, and I was curious myself. Was Paul in that room, raging? Or had he taken off again? But she raised her head even higher and didn't look. She led me to the end of the small hall and pointed out the bathroom door.

Like every other room in the house, the powder room was eye-catching with wallpaper that had wonderful dreamlike birds and animals among green leaves. The venetian blind matched the leaves in the wallpaper. I pushed it aside and looked out the window and saw a young boy wandering past the house. I didn't think much about it. Country people wander through each other's yards, looking for lost dogs, taking shortcuts, or whatever. I put the blind back squarely in place. Revonda's house had that effect. You felt everything had to go just so. I got my lipstick out of my shoulder bag and touched up my face. Then I returned to the table where Anne and Revonda were waiting.

Anne left us and in a little while came back with a chocolate cake. We made polite conversation. Anne said her family were going off on a cruise. Leaving that afternoon, in fact. Her mother had finally persuaded her workaholic father to take a few weeks off and go to Bermuda.

Revonda told us how this house had once belonged to her great-grandfather. It had passed out of the family, and she'd been so pleased to be able to buy it back. Maybe that was Great-grandpa's pistol on the whatnot shelf.

We spoke politely. We had the air of three people in remission from an illness; Paul's outburst was still with us. Finally Revonda got up and asked if I'd like to see her theater scrapbooks.

She opened the white door across from Paul's black one and led me through into a small study with blue and red flowered curtains, blue and red flowers on the wallpaper behind an old-fashioned rolltop desk. Cheerful.

Anne joined us shortly, and we all three ended up looking at scrapbooks together. We spread them out on a table and drew up chairs.

That was the first time I saw a picture of Revonda's husband. Always in pictures of her. At after-performance parties and such. He was a moody-looking man, pale with brown hair. Generally looking at his drink, not at Revonda.

Finally I glanced at my watch and was surprised to see it was three o'clock. I thanked Revonda for the lovely lunch and was standing just inside the front door saying goodbye when the doorbell rang.

Revonda opened it to a woman who could have been in that theater scrapbook, done up for a comedy. She had inch-long false eyelashes, hair piled up like a modern sculpture, a swishy flowered chiffon dress, and three-inch heels. She had on enough makeup to frost a cake, which didn't hide the fact that she must have been about seventy years old. Funny, the effect was kind of nice. Now, how did she fit in?

"So here I am," she said to Revonda, "cheering myself up with a new dress. My godson doesn't answer when I knock on his door, but you have some nice company for me to meet." She stuck out her hand to shake with me. "I'm Marvelle Starr," she said. "Actually I'm both Paul's godmother, and the theater's gift to Bloodroot Creek. Because I'm too old to do face-cream commercials any more, and those were the best parts I got. So I'm retired. Sometimes it depresses me that I'm retired. I come down to talk about old times with Revonda here."

Paul had a godmother! That didn't fit any better than the pistol. But, hey! I thought: Marvelle Starr. What a stage name — designed so you'll remember not just the name but what she wants to be!

"This is Peaches Dann," Revonda said formally, keeping her hand on the doorknob. "She and Anne are just leaving."

I wanted to go home and jot down my impressions. As we started down the gravel driveway, Anne turned to me and begged, "Don't go. Come by the studio for a minute," and I remembered how I'd wanted to look at her puppets.

I spent about two hours, admiring her handiwork and talking. I sensed she was nervous and wanted company. The air was heavy. Even indoors. I walked over and looked out the window toward Revonda's house. Marvelle Starr in her swishy chiffon was just getting into her silver

Ford and saying goodbye to Revonda. She zoomed out the driveway. "That Marvelle doesn't let this heavy weather keep her down," I said to Anne.

I picked up a puppet in the shape of a mischievous little girl with red hair. "That's Me Too," Anne explained. "About all she says is 'me, too.' " My watch caught my eye. I said, "Good grief, it's after five, I'll have to go."

That's when the scream hit us. I was so startled I dropped the puppet. Yet some part of me wasn't surprised. The scream seemed to come from Paul's side of the house. Anne and I both rose instantly and ran toward the porch of the big house. We dodged through the white rattan porch furniture so fast Anne knocked over two chairs. She seemed O.K., so I ran ahead, around the corner of the porch, drawn by the scream.

Revonda stood in the outside door to Paul's room, mouth so screaming wide I could see down her pink throat. Not like herself. Not like Joan of Arc or Queen Elizabeth. Her eyes were round with fear, and she was clutching the doorframe.

She grabbed me and pulled me into Paul's room among the crazy mirrors, Anne following close — the three of us reflected every which way. Revonda pulled me into a small room off the mirror room — Paul's bathroom. The walls in here were black. Against them were a shining white sink, a bathtub, and something strange sticking out from the wall.

Revonda kept on screaming. She waved wildly at that whatever-it-was built in the wall. And then my eyes grasped it. It was a pull-out laundry bin. My grandmother had one like that with a chute right down to the basement. A pair of bare feet stuck out the top, seeming totally unreal, like monster flowers. Clear plastic ruffled round them. Only, the flowers were two hairy legs and bluish bare feet sticking out of rumpled black pants. Also a hand, twisted so you could see the gray-white palm. Black spirals were painted on that palm and the soles of those feet — spirals like the one on that medal Paul had been wearing.

"Help me pull!" Revonda begged. Then I understood why she hadn't pulled this body out alone. It was stiff. Stuck in the bin. As I pulled, I asked myself: Could this awful wooden thing be Paul? We'd seen Paul alive and angry just — I glanced at my watch — five hours before.

Chapter

4

SUNDAY, 5:15 P.M.

We tugged the body out of the laundry bin and laid it on the black-and-white tile bathroom floor. Paul's face was blue and moist, with the thin plastic stuck to it, like plastic wrap over something hot that had cooled. A black spiral was painted in the middle of his forehead. Green leaves were inside the bag, stuck to his face. Something thin and hairy that could be dill. My grandmother used dill for making pickles, but, dear God, not in the bathroom. Not as decoration for the dear departed dead. And near the dill some other green I didn't recognize, with little pale flowers on spikes.

Revonda cried out, "Oh, Paul!" She sank down onto the floor next to him and began to sob so hard I was afraid it would tear her lungs.

I felt sick, but I also felt a kind of awful calm.

48

Because I was sure I was looking at some deliberate and terrible creation. Something devised to send a message, either by Paul if he killed himself or by the person who killed him. I searched for a suicide note, scanning the black-and-white floor and the white enamel fixtures. Nothing in the room but Paul wrapped in plastic and a white washcloth and towels hanging on a rack and a cake of white soap on the white basin.

Through Revonda's sobs I could hear Anne in the next room on the telephone. "Come quick. A man is dead." I heard her describing the way we found Paul. Surprisingly calm.

"You must come sit down," I told Revonda. "You need to keep your strength to help when the sheriff comes." That galvanized her. She raised herself up from the black-and-white tiles. "That Harley Henderson's an old fool!" she cried out. "I've known him all my life. He won't know what to do."

I heard a car outside on the gravel. I heard Anne say, "Oh, Sam! Thank God, you're here," and then a mumble I couldn't make out. Revonda pulled herself up to her feet, holding on to my arm, still shaky, makeup running all over her face, but her voice was suddenly firm: "Sam will know what to do."

I reached in my pocketbook and handed Revonda a tissue to wipe her face before helping her into Paul's room, where Sam took her arm and led her toward the face chair. I went back and reexamined every inch of the bathroom, beginning with poor Paul. I put on the reading glasses that always hang around my neck on a chain and looked more closely at the feathery herb near his poor blue face. Yes, definitely dill. I took out my notebook and made a sketch of the dill and the other herb or whatever it was. I read the words on the dry-cleaning bag, which was what was over Paul's head and body — an ordinary flimsy-looking dry-cleaning bag. Three winter dresses in my closet were stored in bags like that. Down a side of that twisted bag, small white letters against Paul's black shirt said WARNING: TO AVOID DANGER OF SUFFO-CATION, KEEP AWAY — I had to lean around sideways to see the rest — FROM BABIES AND CHILDREN. DO NOT USE IN CRIBS, CARRIAGES, OR PLAYPENS. THIS IS NOT A TOY. I shuddered. Not a toy. I wrote the words in my notebook.

I looked down into the laundry bin. The bottom was narrower than the top. In the very bottom a black hole opened onto the cellar floor below. It was not wide enough for a body to fall through.

I tried to imagine Paul stuffed into that bin with plastic stuck to his face. His arms would be pinned to his sides. He must have struggled violently to get loose. Blacked out before he could get out. Or suppose he deliberately dived into that hole, deliberately stuck himself there. I had to be calm and keep my mind clear.

The top of the bin was pulled as wide as it

would go and splintered where we had forced Paul's stiffened body out. Nothing else in the room seemed to be out of the ordinary.

I left the bathroom and entered Paul's hall of mirrors. Revonda was sitting in the chair with the face carved in the back, rocking. Sam was kneeling next to her. I thought how the darned chair face must be sticking out its tongue at the middle of her back and almost began to laugh, but this was not the time. At least Paul's wooden face wasn't reflected all around us. Revonda's face was bad enough. It had collapsed. She looked a hundred years old.

Sam's broad artist's hand was covering her long slender hand on the arm of the chair, and he was saying, "I'm right here," just like my mother used to tell me when I was scared of the dark.

Anne was still holding the phone. "They want me to stay on the line till someone gets here," she said to me. I was getting used to the mirrors, more able to ignore them, to treat them like television wallpaper.

"I'm alone now." Revonda's whisper was hoarse and forced. She turned to me.

I said, "I understand," because I could see she needed me to so badly. I didn't understand this kind of being alone. Alone with ugly memories of fights. Alone with sad reflections. The mental kind. In some of the real physical reflections, she must be able to see Paul's body, as I realized I could, through the bathroom door. I wished I

51

hadn't noticed that.

Poor Anne, anchored to the phone, was watching Revonda with tears in her eyes. I could see Anne felt she had to say something, to do something. She couldn't bear the pain that radiated round Revonda. Revonda hardly moved except to rock. The pain crackled. I could feel it, too. Ungrounded.

Anne said, "Revonda, we'll help all we can. We'll be here with you. We won't leave you. I promise."

Because Revonda looked so low, I was glad Anne said that. Or at first I was. Then it worried me. I looked at Anne's gentle, old-fashioned face. She was the kind to keep a promise. What if something more was wrong here? If poor Paul was a symptom of something out of whack? In his family? In the valley? Whatever. Then Sam and Anne ought to get out.

But now, I suspected, it was too late for that. So what next?

I needed somebody to talk about this with, to try to unravel what was happening here. Somebody who was not mixed up in the horror. I needed my journalism professor husband back from his symposium. He's good at facts. I'm good at intuition. Oh, how I missed Ted.

Chapter

5

Later Sunday Afternoon

The sheriff's deputies didn't take me seriously. But they didn't let me leave, either, on the chance that I might be more than I seemed.

There were three men: tall, medium, and short. Those men must have been used to some chilling sights, but they looked at Paul and his mirror room with wide eyes. "By damn," said the shortest one to the tallest. "Don't this beat all?" He pulled himself straighter in his tan uniform, as if he was remembering to be as professional as possible. He pulled up a chair next to Revonda and began to ask her questions. Her face was blank, as if she didn't hear. Her eyes were red rimmed and glazed.

Meanwhile, Medium-Sized had detached Sam from Revonda and was towing him out of the room. "I wasn't even here," Sam was saying loudly. "I need to know what happened, too."

The tall deputy made sure Paul's outside door was locked, then asked Anne and me to go with him. He walked briskly, with shoulders thrown back, indicating he wanted us to go in front of him. "All the better to see you, my dear," the Wolf would have said to Little Red Riding-Hood. Why did I feel like he was a wolf? Because I knew his job was to suspect us all. Because he had a spring in his step like he enjoyed suspecting.

He led us down the hallway from Paul's room, through one end of the living room with its big couches and pictures of the past. I turned my head and saw Sam and Medium-Sized sitting at the far end of the room in two chairs. Sam was talking, and the deputy was taking notes.

I would have loved to hear what Sam was saying, or what the other deputy was asking Revonda. But I was so glad to get out of that mirror room, reflecting Paul's body, that nothing else seemed crucial.

The tall deputy told us his name was Ron Brank. Ron, I thought. I'd like to *ron* away from this place. I pictured that, with him running after, waving a gun. Vivid pictures help. Brank? Well, you might say we were at the brink of being suspects, and *brink* is almost like *Brank.* Or you might say that *Brank* rhymes with *yank,* and he wanted to yank us in for questioning. Also he was a lawman who would never rob a *bank,* which rhymes with *Brank.*

54

"I'm actually a neighbor," he said, neither chasing nor yanking, but leading into the dining room. "Revonda didn't recognize me, so she must be in a bad state." He shook his head. "Of course." His brown-black eyes seemed kind, at least at that moment, even if his black curly hair put me off. His hair was as coal-black as Paul's. He glanced at his wrist. He wore one of those watches with circles and hands to tell everything: tides, seasons, day, month, altitude, pulse. Expensive. He was obviously willing to pay to know. His wrist under that watch was thick and muscular. Sexy.

Anne is going to confuse him. I thought. Precision & Muscle meets Imagination & Grace, and — let's face it — my cousin Anne seemed spacy in her state of shock. But charming. Maybe more charming because she looked so helpless.

Precision & Muscle was polite. He held a chair for me at the dining room table. He told me to sit there and wait, then he took Anne into the kitchen to question her. He left the door open, to keep an eye on me, I suppose. I couldn't hear exact words. This Ron what? Ron-on-the-brink, yank me to the bank. Brank.

Sun shone in the kitchen window, turning Anne's hair blonder. Better than that eerie mirror light in Paul's room. Ron seated Anne at the table in front of the fireplace at the far end of the kitchen. Her back was to me. He sat on the opposite side of the table, holding his notepad and a small black tape recorder. Boy he didn't take a chance on forgetting. I could see his mouth moving.

More men arrived, including an extra-tall gangly one. I'd seen his picture in the paper. He was the sheriff. I'd never dealt with him because we live in the city. We deal with the Asheville police. But in the county, he's in charge. "What have you found out here?" he boomed at Sam's interrogator.

The next thing I knew, Revonda appeared with her deputy trailing behind. His mouth was half open in surprise. The deputy gripped his notes and followed close, as if he wanted to make it clear that Revonda was his witness to question even if she did seem to be getting away from him.

Revonda marched right over to the sheriff. He was standing near her theater posters. Even compared with Lady MacBeth, the real Revonda looked haggard, but her head was back at that proud Revonda angle. "Harley," she said hoarsely, "I've known you a long time." She didn't say it like a compliment.

"I've known you just exactly as long." He spit out the words and clenched his oversize hands into fists. Not friendly. These two had fought before.

"Somebody killed my son," she said, "and I expect you to find out who." She said that like a challenge.

All it took to pull Revonda together was rage.

Rage that this man, whom she did not respect, was in charge of finding out what happened to her much-loved son. Rage was her tonic. She was going to be all right. I wasn't so sure about the sheriff. His face turned red, and I hoped he wasn't prone to heart attacks.

"I intend to investigate every angle," he said. "Murder, suicide, and accident."

I almost laughed, except this was so grim. How could you possibly suffocate by accident in a plastic bag with spirals painted on your hands and feet and forehead, and sprigs of herb beside you?

"My son did not kill himself!" Revonda thundered. More noise came out of her than I would think could fit inside. Short Deputy and Medium Deputy opened their eyes wide again. Ron Brank in the kitchen glanced up briefly.

"If you don't discover who killed my son, I will." She was hissing. What versatility. "I have a friend," she said, pointing to me, "who has solved two murders, and I'm going to get her to help. This is Peaches Dann."

The sheriff looked me over. "This is no place for anyone who thinks solving crimes is a hobby."

He had a nerve! I didn't say anything. I wanted to help Anne out. If Revonda thought I was working to help her, fine. The sheriff was a paper tiger. Revonda was a real leopard. Ready to sneak through the bush, so to speak. She leaned on that chair with the jungle print. I half expected her ears to grow pointed and a lashing tail to appear on her rear. Given a choice, I was better off on her side.

Chapter

6

SUNDAY, 7:30 P.M.

"What was it that you didn't tell the deputy?" I asked Anne as we drove along. She bit her lips.

"What makes you think —"

"Maybe I can help you in this mess," I said, "but not if you don't level with me."

So, O.K., I had jumped to a conclusion. If you can't remember details, you have to do that. Develop your intuition. Maybe my intuition somehow feeds on those details I can't retrieve. At least not when I want to.

The deputies had let the two of us go, saying they might have more questions later. Someone was still interrogating Sam, and the sheriff himself was working on Revonda. I had suggested that Anne and I go for a ride and maybe get something to eat at McDonald's back nearer town. I was hungry. Anne had said she wanted to go to the studio and wait for Sam. So I'd whispered, "I need to talk to you in a secure place."

She wrote a note to Sam and fastened it to the door at the bottom of the stairs to the studio. Upstairs, lights were on. The deputies must still be searching. Her note said we'd bring back chicken sandwiches.

I imagine some of the crew swarming over the place had already searched my car because they let me take it. Also, it seemed that my usual in-case-I-need-it junk was better organized than when I left it! Anne and I rode past the springhouse, out of the driveway, in silence. We rode down the long valley with the green mountains on both sides, green fading to blue dusk.

"I trust Sam," Anne said tensely. "I know he tells me the truth. But he does things that other people don't understand."

I waited for her to tell me more.

"That man rattled me," she said. "I mean, Ron Brank. First, I felt better because I could tell him all the awful things that happened. He seemed to understand that it felt like being dipped in poison. Like maybe it *was* part of some curse. He made me feel safe."

At best, Precision & Muscle is a balance for Imagination & Grace.

"And then," Anne went on, "he began to ask questions about where I came from. He asked me where I met Sam."

Long silence. She held her hands clamped

tight together. The feel of rigor mortis came back to me.

"Why were you afraid of that question?" I asked.

She gave me a nervous glance, but she'd gone too far to stop. "I told him I bumped into Sam in Boston, which was true. I was living there and doing kids' parties with my puppets. I was doing O.K. even if my family didn't think so. But I just naturally get into trouble. One day I took the wrong subway and ended up in a tough part of town, and I was thinking about how I might do a puppet show about a character who got lost in a dangerous place. And there, right next to me while I was looking the other way, a girl was stabbed."

She turned her eyes to me, amazed. Those green eyes under the lovely curved eyebrows. Somehow those eyebrows added to a haunted look in the eyes. Not good.

"In a dangerous part of town was that so strange?" I asked. "But I admit getting lost and ending up in a dangerous place would have rattled me."

Anne went on reliving Boston. "I never saw the girl" — she sighed — "until she brushed against me as she fell. She lay so still on that dirty sidewalk, bleeding. The knife was still in her back. A kitchen knife. I don't like to remember that. It's like I'm right there again. Near trouble. Like always." She hunched her shoulders.

"What did that have to do with meeting Sam?" I asked.

"Afterward, when the cops let me go, I bumped into Sam on the police-station steps." She paused, looked at me searchingly, crossed her arms, and hugged herself.

"Look," I said, "I know what it's like to get lost and feel dumb about it. And I've come across several bodies, though I don't feel jinxed like you say you do. What happened to me was part chance, part knowing lost souls and maybe, partly, that after you do something once, it's more likely to happen again. People pull you into it. The important thing is to figure out why it happens and do something to try to stop whatever is wrong. So, now you need to talk. I'm here to listen."

She took a deep breath. "I got to talking to Sam on the street in front of the police station. I told him I'd been questioned as a witness to a crime. Sam told me he'd been questioned as a suspect in a crime that hadn't happened and would I like to have a cup of coffee." She gave me a pleading glance. "There's just something about Sam that made me know he was O.K."

It seemed to me I'd heard somewhere that was the way a number of women had reacted to that famous Victorian Englishman who drowned them in bathtubs. On the other hand, Sam did seem as trustworthy as a great big puppy.

Anne sat up straight, uncrossed her arms, and smiled. "It never occurred to me that Sam had committed a crime. He isn't the type. He's too alive."

"What was he accused of?" I asked. We had arrived at McDonald's. Good. I could see the time had come when I needed to write down any names or dates she mentioned. We each got some chicken fajitas and Anne got an orange juice and I got coffee. We parked, and between bites she told me the rest of the story. Trouble didn't hurt her appetite.

"Sam and I went to a coffee shop, and he told me he'd worked for a ninety-year-old woman named Margaret Lansing, a real honey, he said." Anne took a gulp of her juice. "Sam promised this old woman he'd let her die at home in bed, not in the hospital on machines." She bit into her fajita, swallowed the bite, and went on: "He sat with her and held her hand while she died." She turned to me. "There was nothing wrong in that."

We were parked, windows down, next to a small dogwood tree with thin leaves. A brown bird sat on a branch near the top and watched us. Anne threw him a crumb of tortilla, and he jumped down to get it. She went on slowly.

"He said the woman was in pain and ready to go. I guess I'm good at listening. Sam needed somebody to listen and to believe him."

"Who was it who didn't believe him?"

"The police," she whispered. Then she raised her voice. "Because it turned out she'd changed her will to leave Sam six hundred thousand dollars." She frowned and sighed. "She'd cut out her only nephew, who never came to see her." Oh, boy! She finished her fajita and her orange juice and wiped her hands on the napkin. She went on in a sudden rush. "So the nephew accused Sam of using undue influence to get her to change her will. He accused Sam of deliberately letting her die of neglect in order to get the money sooner." She turned to me angrily. "You know Sam would never do that! He told me he didn't care about money except for enough so he can paint what he pleases. Sam didn't want to waste good painting time in court."

"And so?"

"That's why he offered to let the nephew have the money if he wouldn't press charges." She sighed. "Just like that. Six hundred thousand dollars, gone. I'm not sure I could have done that. But Sam didn't care."

"I bet your father was horrified," I said and then wished I hadn't said it. Anne's father was an accountant. Losing even a dime struck him as a mortal sin. I lost some change once when I was visiting him years ago. He made me keep looking till finally I found it where I'd dropped it out on the lawn. I spent an hour and a half looking for thirty-five cents, which was considerably less than the minimum wage.

"We didn't tell my father about it," she said. "I couldn't tell this deputy Ron Brank about what happened in Boston. So I told him Sam wanted to paint me, and that's how we met.

Which is partly true. Only that was later."

"But what will happen if Sam tells about the woman who died in Boston?"

Her eyes filled with tears. "I had to guess what Sam would do," she said. "I think he'll follow my grandmother Ott's advice."

"Why?" How did her grandmother get into this?

"My grandmother loved Sam right away. She was the only one I told about what happened in Boston. She stood there right by her window box full of red, white, and blue petunias. She's a flower person. She said. 'You and I know Sam is a wonderful, irresponsible artist who doesn't care about money, but most people wouldn't be able to understand that.' Mainly she meant my parents. 'So I just wouldn't tell anybody about that money,' she said. 'It's none of their business.' "

"Let's hope," I said, "that Irrepressible Sam remembered that. Your grandmother may have been right, but it's easier to tell the truth. You have to remember yourself every minute to tell successful lies or even half-truths, which I guess is what you've done. *I* couldn't carry it off." I gave her a hug. "I'll cross my fingers for you."

Chapter

7

SUNDAY NIGHT AND

MONDAY MORNING, JULY 1

Ted called late Sunday night. He said he'd been worried when he couldn't get me on the phone. I told him the whole ugly story. "I'll have to tell Pop what happened to his friend Revonda," I said to Ted, "or else somebody else will make it sound worse. I tried to call him just now, but he was asleep already."

"I can't imagine how anybody could make what happened sound weirder than it was," he said grimly. "The papers and the TV will have a field day. I could start home now," he said, "if that'll help."

If I knew Ted, he'd listened so hard and taken so many notes and networked so long at his conference that he was exhausted. "I'd rather have you home later, rested and full of good ideas."

"Good," he said. "I'll get home early to-morrow afternoon."

Amazingly, I was able to sleep. Paul's strange death left me feeling stunned, but I had to be on my toes the next day. Anne was going to need moral support. Pop was going to need calming down.

I was at Pop's before he woke up. I found Ella Marie, the sitter on duty, in the kitchen reading a romance novel with the door into the hallway open so she could hear Pop call. Ella Marie: blond, about thirty-five, with blue baby-doll eyes and plump hands.

"It's important for you to keep your voice down when I tell you something that may upset you," I said quietly.

"What?" she whispered. Her eyes seemed to double in size.

"There's been a strange murder near Blood-root Creek," I said. "The victim had books about magic, and he was the son of an actress. The television and the newspaper will be play-ing this up. Have you brought in the paper yet?"

She shivered with anticipation. She licked her upper lip. With all the Ella Maries out there, of course the media would be playing it big.

"The dead man's mother was a friend of my father's when they were young."

"A friend of your father's!" Ella Marie cried out as loudly as if she'd been stuck with a pin and won the lottery at the same time. I could see a personal connection with the murder really got to her.

Pop rang his bell. He has radar ears.

"I'll go," I said firmly. "Stay, please, and cover the phone."

I hurried through the dining room into the living room, past the sliding glass doors overlooking the garden and down the short hall into Pop's room.

"What's happened?" he asked hopefully. "What's wrong?" He looked so innocent, lying there under his fleecy white blanket which matched his silky white hair. Innocent as dynamite.

No point in putting this off. "You remember we talked about your friend Revonda Roland?"

"Of course. She was never dull. What trouble is she in now?" He clutched the blanket, like he was ready to throw it off and jump up.

"Yesterday she found her only son dead."

"Oh, I'm sorry," he said. He eyed me thoughtfully. "You're mixed up in this somehow, aren't you? That's why you asked me about her the other day!" He sounded triumphant to have figured that out.

"Our cousin Anne is staying with her," I said resignedly. "Cousin Clothilde's daughter from Winston-Salem." Keeping him out of the middle of this was going to take all my ingenuity.

"Tell me what happened!" he demanded, and I did, trying to play down the dramatic parts, like the eeriness of that mirror room. "You were there!" he cried. "You have a talent for these things, Peaches!" Pop just loves to be in the thick of things, which is hard for a man who can't walk and occasionally is not even sure where he is. "We must call Cousin Clothilde and offer any help we can give!" he said eagerly. "Call Ella Marie. I want to get up right now!"

"Cousin Clothilde and her husband are off on a cruise," I said firmly. "Anne has asked me not to bother them till they get back, no matter what."

He began to ring his bell again.

What Anne actually said was that she was grateful her parents were away. They tended to get hysterical when she got in her messes. I would hardly have called this Anne's mess, my-self. It was Revonda's tragedy.

Pop rang his bell like the house was on fire. It's a brass bell with a wooden handle that makes enough noise to wake the dead. We couldn't wake the dead. But maybe we could find out what it was the dead man knew. Pop might actually help with that.

Ella Marie arrived, waving the newspaper and smiling happily to be called where the action was. "It was a man named Paul Roland they found dead — right?" She handed the paper to me, and I was surprised how little the paper had discovered by press time. None of the lurid de-tails, except that Paul was found dead in a plastic bag. Good. That gave me time to regroup. I left fast and got myself a cup of coffee from the pot in the kitchen. Pop didn't like family members hovering while he dressed, anyway. He liked his most helpless moments to be private except for the sitters. He couldn't manage without them.

I took my strong hot coffee and sat down at Pop's table in the living room. He had a shelf of his books and mementos behind him if he sat on one side of the table and, if he sat on the other side, the glass doors onto the garden right where he could look out.

In nothing flat, Ella Marie wheeled Pop's chair next to me on the side of the table where he could look out on the roses and lilies. "A good day for action," he said. Ella Marie hovered hopefully, hungry for details.

That gave me an idea. "Let's get Ella Marie to go buy some Danish pastry from the Blue Moon Bakery," I said. The Blue Moon down the mountain in Asheville had ovens imported all the way from France, and Pop couldn't resist their baked goods — I knew that. Ella Marie would be gone at least three quarters of an hour.

"Get a loaf of raisin-pecan bread," I told her. That was her favorite. I could see she was near mutiny to be sent off while we discussed Paul's death.

"What do you think is going to happen next?" Pop demanded as she disappeared out the door.

I told Pop about the sheriff and how Revonda didn't trust him.

"The sheriff thinks it could be suicide or murder or an accident?"

"I think he put in that accident part to upset Revonda," I said. "Though I did read about a man who apparently hanged himself by accident because he found it sexy to *almost* hang himself, and one day the almost didn't work."

Pop considered that with relish. "People are very strange. What can we do to solve this case?" He leaned back in his chair importantly. He calls me the Absentminded Detective, and I think he figures that means that if I can be a little bit like Sherlock Holmes, he can be like Watson. Of course, once you get the reputation for being able to help when something goes wrong, you get called. Especially by relatives. Because we claim kin in these mountains, we have enough to sink a battleship.

"I think the sheriff is leaning toward murder," I said. "He may suspect Anne and Sam. Sam is Anne's new husband."

"The bastard!" Pop said. I could tell he meant the sheriff, not Sam. His eyes sparkled with anticipation.

"So the more I know about where Revonda is coming from," I said, "about anything in her past that could be related to this in any way, the better. After all, this happened after she came home to the valley where she grew up, and where you knew her."

"Revonda liked me," he said, then sipped his coffee. "She liked anybody who looked like they

71

were going to have the gumption to get off the farm and get over being poor. That was in thirty-three, when we were both in this amateur theater group. I just moved the scenery, but she was in some of the plays. She could see I was going somewhere." Pop preened. "She was right, too!"

Pop was born in 1910. He would have been twenty-three then. He used to be a looker. "Just how close were you and Revonda?" I asked.

He smiled enigmatically, sipped more coffee, and went on. "She had this grandfather she talked about a lot. He was rich. People saw him coming, and they smiled. He was generous. He told Revonda she was smart and she'd marry a rich man." He stopped and considered. "Maybe she was being kind, letting me know it wasn't going to be me. Because I wasn't rich in those days."

Good grief. Imagine if Revonda had been my mother! Thank God Pop hadn't been rich. But if Revonda had been my mother, I wouldn't have been me.

"Her grandfather died in a fire and didn't leave anything. He'd spent it all. Her father was dirt-poor. He drank. Revonda said she was glad her grandfather never knew how bad things got."

"Revonda has pictures of relatives around the house. Nobody looks like a grandfather. That's odd."

Pop shrugged. "He died when his house

burned down, and maybe the pictures burned. Revonda's father wouldn't let her mother have a picture of the old man. They hated each other. Revonda's pa and grandpa."

"Not a happy way to grow up," I said.

"The fire was set," Pop said. "Somebody getting revenge. Her grandpa was a lawyer, you see. Maybe somebody thought he didn't get them off when he should have. Or he got their enemy off when they wanted revenge. His house burned with him in it when Revonda was a kid."

In some families, tragedy stalked from generation to generation. Somehow it seemed to happen a lot out in our mountain coves, where the hard times and the fierce family loyalties had meant revenge was O.K., even to later generations.

"You must have known her well for Revonda to have told you all that," I said.

He gazed out at the garden. "She was some gal."

"So what happened after her grandfather died?"

"Revonda asked me not to tell," he said defensively.

"Pop," I said, "it must have been over sixty years ago when she asked you not to tell. Unless her son was murdered and it's relevant, I'll keep mum."

He poured milk and sugar in his empty coffee cup and stirred them up.

"I won't tell you what I know if you don't tell

73

me what you know," I said. He sipped the sweet milk. I waited.

"Her father kept drinking and he beat her," Pop said.

I whistled. "Revonda wouldn't want anybody to know that, even now. She's too proud. If you hit her, she'd hit back. But I suppose as a child she couldn't stand up to a grown man."

Pop nodded. "He only beat her when she tried to take his whiskey away. So she stopped trying. She told me it made her feel bad that she couldn't do anything to help him. He drank himself to death. That's one reason she left the county. She couldn't bear for everyone to know. You see, she found him down on his knees, leaning over the privy. Maybe he went there to puke. He was dead, with the bottle still in his hand."

I could see him. "How did anybody know?"

"In a valley like Bloodroot Creek, news travels," he said airily. "The sheriff had to know, to rule out foul play. He was the father of the sheriff they have now — the one you met. As soon as Revonda could, she left the valley. Damned if I can see why she came back." Pop paused and thought. "To show us, I suppose, that she wasn't like her pa, that she was like her grandpa said she'd be: Rich. Damn it, I'd like to see her. We need to go offer to help."

"Pop," I said, "the last time you decided to get mixed up in what looked like foul play, you were poisoned. Thank God you're so tough you're still here. Trust me, this is not an appropriate time to visit."

Pop mixed up with Revonda and maybe black magic was more than I could cope with, I was sure.

"Like it says in your book, it's important to do it now!"

That stopped me. Pop had asked to read my manuscript. That meant, of course, that he got a sitter to read it to him. He's legally blind, even if he can recognize people and see colors and movement. The fact that he wanted to hear my book had amazed me. He doesn't believe anybody should admit a fault.

"I do have a chapter called *Do It Now*," I said, grudgingly. "It certainly does not apply to rushing off half-cocked to see Revonda."

"Yes, it does. I just read it," he crowed and reached in back of him and took the top chapter off a facedown pile. He thrust it at me.

"Read the part about putting off what really matters. Go on, read it!"

O.K., I thought. Get it over with.

Don't put off a thing that's crucial. Do it now. *By doing something right away, you leave less chance to forget.*

"But —" I began.
"Keep reading," Pop thundered.

I ought not to have to use my own book to testify against myself. The Constitution should outlaw that. I read:

I like the Serenity Prayer: Dear God, grant me the serenity to accept the things I cannot change, the courage to change the things I can, and the wisdom to know the difference.

(I'd never change Pop, for sure.)

What that has to do with Do it now *is this: if you always did everything you meant to do immediately, you'd be either compulsive or a saint. So I find it helps my wayward psyche to put off a few things that don't hurt. Then I feel better about remembering to do the things that really matter. The trick is, like the prayer says, to know the difference.*

"Exactly," I said, "and therefore . . ." Pop glared at me. I went on reading.

If you put off doing the laundry and forget to do it until you need the clothes, that may not make a difference. If you put off storing the winter clothes until the moths eat them, that does.

If you put off calling a friend who is twenty, she will probably forgive you. If you forget to call a friend who is ninety-seven, she may have departed for the Promised Land before you call. You'll feel bad. That's a difference.

"A-ha!" Pop cried out. "And Revonda and I

aren't spring chickens!" I ignored that.

If somebody could get hurt if I don't do it, I do it now. Immediately.

I made that rule after I read the newspaper story about the coed who got raped. She wasn't sure if she locked her door. While she lay in bed debating, she fell asleep. In the morning there was a man in her room, who said, "If you scream, I'll kill you," and proceeded to rape her. She needed that rule the night before. Do it now.

I had thought about deleting the rape bit — it didn't really fit with the upbeat quality of the book. Naturally, Pop loved that part.

"Now, you'll admit," Pop said, "that someone may have been murdered at Revonda's house under very strange and suspicious circumstances. If you ask me, a crazy man did it. He may be about to murder Revonda and Anne and her husband at any moment. We need to get there right away!"

After that outburst he leaned back in his chair, out of breath, and shut his eyes.

I reached over and touched his hand. "You look exhausted from the strain. Let me go right now and come back and report to you about what happens," I said.

He sighed — hating to give up, I figured. "I guess that's best. If you're sure you'll tell me *everything.*"

"In the meantime," I said, "I wouldn't talk about this too much. I think it will bring us good luck if we just keep it to ourselves."

"Of course," he said. "And in the next few days, we'll have Revonda and Anne and her new husband over to lunch. It's the least we can do, don't you think?"

Ella Marie arrived with a bag of wonderful-smelling baked goods before I could answer. God bless her.

I left quick before she could ask questions, leaving her and Pop happily eating fresh-baked Danish. I went down Pop's front steps, past the boulders my mother had made into a super rock garden, to my car, waiting in the driveway. At least it was a lovely day. The road side of Pop's house faced woods and a near mountainside, cool and shadowy.

I was not even out of the driveway when a van came careening up and Anne jumped out. She ran to the window of my car.

"I went to your house. . . ." She was breathing hard. "Your neighbor said you might be here. Something terrible has happened. A folder of Sam's sketches has vanished."

That didn't sound so terrible, compared to finding Paul dead.

She clutched my arm. "That folder could incriminate us."

Chapter

8

MONDAY, 10:45 A.M.

"Sam copied magic marks out of Paul's books, and he copied some pages, too," Anne told me. We'd pulled our cars into an overlook on the Blue Ridge Parkway and sat on the low stone wall to confer. "Those things were in a folder of Sam's sketches in our studio before . . . you know . . . and the folder was gone when we got back after . . ." She kept hesitating, trying to decide how to describe Paul's death. "The sheriff's people searched our studio before they let us go back there." She looked out across the valley of trees to the far mountain, swallowed, and went on: "The sheriff asked us questions this morning. I think he's decided Paul was murdered."

"He told me it might be murder or suicide, or even an accident. How can you tell he thinks it's murder now?" I asked firmly.

"It's not what he said. It's just a feeling I have."

Two buzzards were soaring out in the valley in front of us.

"While the deputies were searching our studio, they must have looked at Sam's pictures." She flushed. "If my father was shocked, what did the deputies think?"

"Describe the pictures you think would have shocked them most."

"The worst is the one of the old man's body under ice. Sam didn't show you that picture. My father said you'd have to be crazy to paint something like that." She sounded hurt.

"Actually, it's a beautiful picture if you don't look close. There's a lovely pattern, silver and white, with other colors glinting through." She hesitated as if she wanted to stop there, swallowed, and went on. "But if you keep looking, you see what's actually there." She frowned. "You know how Sam says he likes to paint man's inhumanity. And, boy, did he hit the jackpot in that one." She got a faraway look, as if she were seeing the picture in the distance.

"And what's in the picture?" I nudged her to go on.

"You see, this old man lived by himself, and he ran out of stove wood, and by the time his neighbors noticed there was no smoke coming out of his chimney, he was lying on the floor frozen. The pipes near him froze and burst, and then the pipes thawed and gushed water all over him. His body froze again, all covered in ice. That really happened. The newspaper clipping that told about it was part of the painting." She turned troubled eyes to me. "And when the sheriff's men searched our studio, what do you suppose they thought when they saw that picture?" She stared into the distance again, and then her voice thinned to a whisper. "They didn't *say* anything, but a dead man under ice is almost like a dead man in a plastic bag. And furthermore, right now, while he's upset, Sam is painting something else that has a real plastic bag in it. I can't be sure what it is yet."

I put my arm around her. She needed the warmth. "We must focus our minds on what we can do to find out what really has happened."

She nodded. "Yes. I know. I'm trying. That's why I came to get you."

"Here," I said, "we're getting cramped. This wall is too low to sit on." I walked her up and down the stone-walled overlook, as she pulled herself together.

"Yesterday, you told me you were afraid Sam told the deputies one thing and what you said didn't match," I reminded her. "What happened? Did Sam tell them he'd been accused of helping an old lady to die in Boston?"

She winced when I asked that. Then she broke into a smile. "No! He didn't tell them. And, of course, he didn't do it!" she said hotly, but then she broke into an even bigger smile and stood straighter. "Thank God he didn't mention it, and neither did I."

I prayed they'd done the right thing and the accusation wouldn't come back to trip them up later.

"So," I said, "things often turn out better than you expect!" But that bit about Sam even then painting a picture with a plastic bag in it did bother me.

"Sam just doesn't think about appearances," she said.

She was so right.

"And I trust him completely," she said, "but when I'm scared, I'm not positive I trust myself in who I pick to trust."

Maybe I'm lucky. If you have a bad memory, you *have* to develop a good sense of who to trust. Because you often need to ask someone what happened. I thought I trusted Sam, but I wasn't absolutely sure.

"Let's go talk to Sam," I said.

Chapter

9

MONDAY, 11:30 A.M.

We passed an old woman walking down Blood-root Creek Road, dressed in about five shades of red: skirt, socks, blouse, overblouse, and even a cloth hat, all swearing with each other. In the sunshine she positively shimmered. She wore high-topped work shoes and clutched a bunch of wild flowers. She waved with her free hand. When we got out of our cars near the studio, I asked Anne who Ms. Mismatched-Reds could be.

"That's Knowing Agnes." Anne frowned, as if this Knowing Agnes didn't make sense to her. "Revonda says she wanders up and down the valley and goes to visit wherever she wants to, and people look out for her. They got her to wear red so the cars won't hit her."

"That sounds kind."

"You have to be careful when she's around," Anne said. "She repeats what she hears. Without even knowing what it means. Otherwise, Revonda says, she's harmless."

Interesting, that they let her be. Town people would have locked her up, maybe had to. But how intriguing — that she could repeat what she heard and not know what it meant. I wondered if people used her to repeat what they wanted heard. Well, this was not the time to worry about Knowing Agnes. It was the time to worry about Anne and Sam.

We found Sam at his easel, painting away at something I couldn't make out, except there was a glint like clear plastic or ice in it. I asked what it was, but he said he was just fooling around to see what would come. He began humming to himself some spiritual I half-remembered. "Nobody Knows the Trouble I've Seen." Not his kind of song, I would have thought. I felt a dent in his confidence. His movements were tighter. He wasn't laughing, even with his eyes.

"Let's go for a walk," Sam said, giving me a significant don't-talk-now look. Did he expect the place was bugged? He cleaned his brushes and put them away while Anne and I each ate some cheese crackers and drank a glass of milk. Instant early lunch.

The three of us walked up the road past a field of cows, past several houses, and finally we came to a field that appeared empty. Sam spread the rusty barbed wire, and we slipped through the fence.

"There's a nice private nook, where we can talk." Sam led us around a big boulder set against the side of a hill. A lower rock was almost like a bench. I was just about to say he'd found a great place when a brown bull with a white face appeared.

He came out from behind a clump of bushes on the other side of the field and lowered his head and stared at us. His tail swished.

"Not to worry," Sam said cheerfully. "Bulls aren't fierce like they used to be. They've bred them to be milder."

Sam sat back on our rock, perfectly at home. He turned to me, and without any preamble he said: "What would Paul be trying to hide in that room with the doors locked except for what was in his magic books? He had place markers in them! I figured if he had any crazy idea that could be dangerous, the books would have a clue to it." His eyes were eager for me to agree. But I waited.

"If there was any real kind of danger here, I didn't have any right to ask Anne to stay here. So I needed to know. Paul might have come back before I had a chance to look over his books."

"He did it all for me." It was the first time I'd heard Anne be sarcastic. Her eyes glinted with anger.

"Did what?" I asked.

"On Friday," he continued, "when we measured his room for paint and went out to do errands, I put the marked books in a bag and took them with us."

"And copied the marked pages at the library." Anne's eyes were still angry. "I didn't realize what he was doing." One of her hands was picking bits of grass nervously, though she kept the rest of herself still.

"I knew Paul would be mad if he found out," Sam said, throwing his arm around Anne, "and I didn't want you mixed up in something like that."

She pulled away. "I'd rather know all along what we're mixed up in," she said in a low voice and ducked her head.

"I put the copies of magic stuff in one of my envelopes of sketches where no one would ever have a reason to look."

"You thought," Anne said unhappily.

"All on Friday?" I asked.

"Yes. Then I was busy and didn't have a chance to look at the stuff, and on Sunday we found Paul's body, and when we got back to the studio after the sheriff's people searched it, the envelope of magic stuff was gone. If they found those magic spells, they must be wondering why we had them." He stopped and frowned. "I had even copied a page with marks like the ones we saw on Paul's body."

Bingo. We'd come to the jackpot.

Annie winced. I whistled. "And you think the

deputies found your stuff and took it?"

"This morning they don't act like they took it," Sam said in a hopeful kind of way. "People like that think of magic as like strange kinds of sex," he said, becoming more cheerful. "Off-limits and therefore fascinating, and dirty at the same time. The thought of it tends to make them smirk. They're not smirking."

Anne nodded.

"So," I said, "our best hope is to explore the possibility that you somehow misplaced the stuff." The bull raised his head and ambled toward us. I made myself sit still. Bulls chase what moves.

Sam stared at his feet and said, "Oh, hell. I didn't mean to make trouble." He looked as glum as Anne did.

"O.K.," I said, "if you lost something, you came to the right person. I happen to be an expert at losing things — in fact, I have a whole chapter in my book about it. I may know more ways to do it than anybody else you ever met." I made myself sound cheerful. I had to rev them up.

Sam threw his arms around me. "I knew we could count on you!" He acted as if I had announced I could turn straw into gold. "Let's go over all the ways of losing things you know and we'll see what fits." A strange way of looking for Sam's envelope — but why not? It's always pleasanter to talk about something you know well, than to get up and walk past a bull of doubtful disposition.

"Obviously, this was more than *elementary losing*," I said, slapping a bug that bit my arm. "It wasn't just that you put it somewhere and you don't remember where."

Sam shook his head. "We'd have found it by now if that was all."

"And *wrong-size losing* is out? You didn't look for a large envelope when you should have been looking for a small envelope because you forgot you moved the stuff?"

He shook his head no.

"Did you put it in a dangerous place, like on the kitchen counter where one of you could sweep it into the trash with an elbow and not notice?" I seemed to remember a tan trashcan next to the counter. "I think of that as *two-stage losing,* and maybe it should be three-stage or even four-stage, because it isn't serious unless you put out the trash and the trash man takes it to the dump."

"*My* envelope was too big for the waste-basket," he said firmly. He slapped a bug, too. This field was not my favorite place after all, except it smelled good, like new-mown hay. The bull began to rub his back against the apple tree. Two small apples fell.

"I specialize," I said, "in *sandwich losing*. I'm usually smart enough to find something if I've merely dropped something else on top of it. Know thyself, they say, and I know myself well enough to know I may have put my sweater on top of the cookbook. Though you might call that *open-faced-sandwich losing*."

I knew myself well enough to know I was mainly putting off passing that bull. "But *sandwich losing* can be sneaky," I continued. "You put a paper down on a pile of papers the same size, then later absentmindedly put another pile of papers on top of that. Especially dangerous for writers.

"And then there's *purloined-letter losing*," I said. "That fits with Poe's famous story about the blackmail letter carefully hidden in plain sight. Suppose the envelope you've been looking for has been altered to look exactly like something you would hardly notice, like a grocery list. Perhaps you inadvertently wrote on the back of it. Ted and I have an expression when we find something we lost that way. We say we Edgar-Allan-Poe-'d it. But again, your envelope sounds too big for that."

"I have searched every scrap of paper the right size, believe me," Sam told me earnestly. Anne shrank more into herself as if she was cold. The sun had, in fact, gone under a cloud. The mountains around us had turned from green to blue-gray.

"We haven't run out of possibilities," I said. "Stop looking hopeless. Next, we'll try a variation of what everybody's mother always tells them."

Anne glared at me. "You mean: 'Stop and think where you had it last'? We did that. But we can't remember *where*."

"Let's try an expansion of that." I felt I was on to something. "Go through the day. Because we want to remember what else you may have done that may have contributed to some complicated or compound way of losing." Hey, that might work.

"We'll try anything," Sam said. He picked a long piece of grass and began to chew it.

"We can make a schedule of everything that happened even if we don't find those papers," I pointed out. "We may find other clues to what killed Paul so soon afterward." That revived them a little. "O.K.," I said, "you got up on Friday morning. Then what?"

"We had cornflakes and orange juice," Anne said, almost belligerently.

"And you said that we were running out of food and toilet paper and we'd better go to the grocery store," Sam reminded her. "Then Revonda knocked at the door."

"You see, it was right after you left on Thursday that Revonda had a big fight with Paul, and he ran off," Anne said. "She acted like it was the end of the world and went to her room, sobbing. So on Friday morning we were relieved to see her asking for something and acting more like herself."

"That's when she told us that she wanted to paint Paul's woodwork. I was curious to see Paul's room." Sam's voice came alive.

"Revonda gave us the key, and we went over

and measured to see how much paint we'd need," Anne said. "At first that room seemed more bizarre than anything else. I thought what a great scene the Wizard could do with a backdrop like that. Wow!"

"I was the one who went and looked at the books first, but Anne looked, too," Sam said. "Then we knocked off to do errands, but we went back to the studio, and Anne fixed us some sandwiches for lunch before we left. I said I'd forgotten something in Paul's room. I parked the van in front of Paul's door and put the marked books in a canvas carrying bag in the van for us to take with us."

"You should have told me." Anne gloomily waved away a fly.

"No," he said, "you would have talked me out of it. You'd have been afraid I would get in trouble."

"And you have!" she cried.

"Not yet," Sam said. "And if we find the copies of the pages Paul marked, I'll bet they show us what went wrong, and why he died." Sam raised his chin as if he dared us to disagree. The sun came back out from under the clouds, lighting his lion mane.

"So you put the books in the van," I said, "and then what?"

"When we went to do errands, I took along one of my big envelopes that has sketches and clippings for picture ideas."

"While I went for groceries for us and for

Revonda and to get some things for Mert next door," Anne said, "Sam went to copy something at the library. Something for his idea envelope, I thought."

"Anne didn't notice when I took the bag of books out of the van." Sam glanced at her sheepishly. "I was a little sneaky," he said with a wink.

"You used the library copying machine, I assume," I said. "Anybody see you?"

"I doubt it," he said. "You see, there were a lot of schoolchildren having a story hour, and the reader was making noises like all kinds of animals. Moo, baa-baa, bow-wow. Attention was on her.

"Then," Sam continued, "I put the magic pages in between the larger sketches, in the hopes that if anybody ever looked in my envelope they'd only see the sketches. Because Paul would have had fits if he knew. After our errands I put the books back in Paul's room."

"While Sam was copying pages, exactly what were you doing?" I asked Anne.

"I was off getting some birthday wrapping paper for our neighbor Mert at Roses. One of her grandkids is about to be three."

"What kind of a bag was the wrapping paper in?" I asked.

"Oh!" Anne cried. "It was in a big flat brown paper bag. It was the size of Sam's manila envelope." Her face lit up with hope. "And after he got in the car, I threw that bag, which had been in the front, into the back of the car." Her eyes became huge. She pressed her fingers over her mouth, then pulled them back. "I could have picked up that bag and the envelope together. I've done that before. Picked up two things at once by mistake when my mind was on something else and not even noticed. I could have taken them both together into Mert's." She caught her breath, then broke into a big grin. "So maybe the sheriff doesn't have that stuff!"

"Pickup-and-delivery losing," I said. "I hadn't thought of that."

Sam grinned, too. "Sometimes it pays to make mistakes."

Then Anne frowned. "Mert would have noticed. She doesn't miss a thing. And she calls herself Mert the Mouth!"

"Did you take anything else into her house?" I asked.

"I picked up her newspaper in the driveway," Anne said. "Sam went right back to the studio, and I took the bag to Mert. I carried the bag and paper together."

"Now try to remember every move you made," I said.

"I stopped on the front porch a minute and talked to Mert. I pulled out the paper and Mert said she guessed the paperboy left her two newspapers because she already had one. She said that boy was so vague she wondered why he didn't walk off a cliff. I guess I gave her the bag of her stuff and came home."

"Didn't you wonder what happened to your envelope?" I asked Sam.

He threw out his hands. "I thought it was between two canvases that I brought in." He laughed. "I was so busy not calling anybody else's attention to the envelope that I didn't check it myself." He raised an eyebrow at me. "Revonda called me and diverted me. She can be demanding."

Now, there is another way to losing I hadn't thought of: *Super-hiding*. I've done that. In fact, I never have found the wallet I got to surprise Ted for Christmas last year.

"Maybe I was foolish to take those books and copy those pages," Sam said. He didn't say it like apology. He was smiling like a friendly pirate. "But now that something or somebody killed Paul, we absolutely need to look at what he marked in those books."

He had a point. Anne sat up straighter and said, "I'll go see Mert. She called this morning and asked if there was anything she could do to help. I'll tell her I need to talk. She'll be dying to know what I saw yesterday." She jumped up, ready to start. Thank goodness the bull's back was turned, tail swishing flies. I stood up, too, ready to get out of there. Anne turned to me. "You come, too, Peaches, and help look and listen. There's not much that happens in this valley that Mert doesn't know — and tell."

"If that envelope is at her house, Edgar-Allan-Poe-'d, or sandwiched or whatever," I said, "the

94

two of us will find it."

"Say, this could all be a lucky break." Sam jumped up and threw his arms wide. He rushed over and hugged Anne, who hugged him back this time. Then he hugged me again. Which was kind of nice.

The bull was still hind-end toward us, but he flicked his ears. "Please," I said, "can we sneak out of this field while the bull is busy?"

Chapter

10

MONDAY, 12:30 P.M.

"Notice Mert's lilies," Sam called after us as we
set out across the road.

"Yes," Anne said to me, "she has the prettiest
double yellow lilies I ever saw, all in bloom at the
side of the house. That's like Sam," she added.
"If he was about to be hanged, he'd notice yellow
lilies." She said that with rueful pride like maybe
it was a mixed blessing. What? No hero-worship?

Whoever built Mert's house liked to make
wood paper dolls. Near the lilies was a wood
cutout of the rear end of a woman leaning over,
presumably weeding. Around the top of the
porch was the kind of fancy scalloping that
people call gingerbread. The waist-high rail
around the porch had fancy-cut spokes, too,
and the supports at the corners of the porch
roof had the cutout silhouettes of birds. Even

the front door had a cutout of a soaring eagle applied at eye level. To the left of the door, a large plastic throw covered a pile of something Mert evidently didn't want the rain to blow onto. Before I had time to look underneath the plastic, the front door opened.

"I saw you coming!" cried a small woman with freckles, her gray hair pulled back in a bun. She threw her arms around Anne and cried, "Oh, Lord, I've had you on my mind!"

She turned to me and said, "And you must be the smart cousin who is helping out!"

"Peaches Dann," I said. "I hope I can be smart."

"Well, come right in." She grabbed us both and pulled us inside. She led us right through the living room past a brown couch and a recliner and a coffee table with a bunch of the yellow lilies and some blue irises. Except for the flowers on the table, all the surfaces were bare. No manila envelope. She led us on into a bright kitchen full of strawberry smell, talking all the time. "Just imagine. Just imagine me, yesterday when you found Paul, me taking all the neighbors to a revival. And it isn't even the usual time for revivals." Her broad mouth twisted up into a wry, kindly grin. "We went off just when you might have wanted to yell for help. And now what can I do? Besides pray?"

Anne said coffee would help.

"I'm freezing berries," she said. "You won't mind if I finish."

She sat us in two chairs at the kitchen table, handed us each a cup of coffee from an electric pot, and sat down to hull more strawberries. "Have a few from the master supply," she said, and I noticed she'd also put a saucer of powdered sugar on the table to dip them in. She picked up a particularly plump red strawberry by its green cap, dipped it in the sugar, and held it out for me to bite from the cap. I did and we all laughed.

"Good, huh?" she said, and then shot us a searching glance. "Now let's get serious. You know, the sheriff treated me like we went to that revival yesterday just to spite him. Every outside witness gone when you found Paul. And imagine me missing the only murder I may ever have across the street, if it was a murder. The folks I've talked to are fifty-fifty on whether it was." She cocked her head. "Now," she said, handing Anne a strawberry, "I want to hear the whole story."

Anne told it well. She got across the feel of what happened. How, in a way, it seemed unreal and, in a way, predestined. She even told something I hadn't heard yet — Revonda had persuaded the Reverend Moore, who had known Paul, to give a memorial service right away, even before the medical examiner gave back the body, in order to lay to rest all the talk that Paul was a heathen. I wished Revonda luck. Of course, Anne left out the part about Sam, and how he kidnapped magic books.

"I suppose they asked you a lot of questions," Mert demanded. She'd left the strawberries to get herself a cup of coffee.

"That deputy named Ron Brank asked and asked," Anne said. "He said he lives just up the hill."

"And sharp as a tack." Mert sat back down. She took a sip of coffee and peered at Anne over her cup. "Likes excitement. And likes the girls. Watch out."

While we talked, I'd been busy looking around the kitchen, trying to see any place where a big manila envelope might be. But the counters were bare except for a mixer and a few canisters.

"Do you think those marks on Paul were coiled snakes?" I turned back to hear Mert say that.

Snakes! In my mind I saw those whorls again through clear plastic, and in my mind they came alive, and they were snakes about to strike. My imagination is almost as good as Anne's.

Anne looked spooked.

Mert leaned forward across the table, eyes narrowed. "Some folks say those marks were magic, meant to call the devil." She closed one red-stained hand into a fist. She stared at the fist like it surprised her, opened her hand, and laughed. "If you ask me, this magic stuff is silly, just a lot of playacting to pretend to be important. That's what I think." She said that like a challenge. "Some people around here see the

99

devil everywhere. They found a satanic cult at the high school last year. Maybe you heard. Just kids trying to say: 'Look at me.' That's what I think," she said scornfully.

So if Mert found Sam's copies of the spells and stuff, she might not take them too seriously. But the people she told might.

"If you ask me, what hit Paul had to do with Revonda," she said. "Somebody getting even with Revonda. Lord knows they couldn't pick a better way. Revonda is strong. What that woman's been through would fell an ox. Paul was the lost one. I wonder if anybody would bother to kill Paul, just for himself — if it was murder."

Mert turned to me. "I suppose you know about the preacher who mailed Revonda a snake?"

"Revonda?"

"In a shoebox," Mert said. "A dead copperhead. There are a lot of good Christian people in this valley, but there are a few nuts. Jeeter Justice, up the hill, is one. Jeeter sent a note with that dead snake, calling her the snake temptress, coming back to this valley as a bad example to the young'uns. They put him in the state asylum at Broughton for a year."

"For mailing the snake?" That sounded extreme.

"Well, not just that. He took to going into banks, and he'd yell and harangue about how they were lairs of greed all full of sinners. When

100

he was on trial for trespassing and disturbing the peace, he began to scream at the judge and call him a sinner and a hypocrite, and the judge had him committed to Broughton. Now he's out, and if he takes his pills, he stays calm. His wife is a fine woman. Related to most folks in the valley."

Anne was bug-eyed. "Revonda has never said a word about anybody mailing her a snake!"

"Revonda won't say what makes her look bad." Mert began cutting up the strawberries she'd hulled. She looked first at Anne, then at me as if she was about to say something important. "I'm truly sorry for Revonda. I'm sure she is really a good Christian woman, but she brings trouble on herself." Mert tucked the loose hair back in the bun at the nape of her neck as if she wanted to set the world right. "Revonda likes to own people." She shook her head. "Paul got away from her into craziness. That's what I think. Like Paul's father got away into drink. And finally drove into a tree, poor man, and that killed him."

"When?" I asked.

"A couple of years ago, just after they moved back here. I never did see the man sober."

Mert stopped with a strawberry in one hand and small knife in the other. Her fingers were red with juice, which reminded me of blood. But her face was still kind. "I knew Revonda when we were kids. She had a hard time. Then she's had a bad time with that boy. Even when she got back here. But she didn't want to throw Paul out. If Revonda could just try not to put on such airs, not to be so arrogant right out in front of God and everybody. Then she'd have more real friends." Mert still paused, knife in the air. "And now Paul's gone."

"You say the vote is fifty-fifty suicide or murder," I said. "You believe Paul could have killed himself? You think he could have marked himself and put that bag over his head and jumped into that laundry chute?" I had my doubts.

"I do." Mert said that firm and clear.

"Ron said it was possible," Anne said, eating another strawberry, "because of the way thin plastic bags cling. I asked him about that. Except I noticed there wasn't a marker by his body. And there were those whorls" — she squirmed — "or maybe snakes."

While I sat there and tried to sort out suicide and snakes, Mert got up and began to sugar the cutup strawberries. "Never waste time," she said. "Our pioneer ancestors in these parts were Scots-Irish. I guess the Scots stuck on me. Now, Revonda's grandfather came here from South Carolina. A three-piece-suit oratorical county lawyer. No way Scots. He died in a fire."

"I understand Revonda grew up dirt-poor," I said.

"Her father was a charmer with a run-down farm. All that piece of land was good for was to hold the world together. And like I said, he drank. She found him dead of it, frozen solid in the privy. She'll not tell you about that."

But Pop had.

"Of course," said Mert, "her father spoiled her best he could when he was sober. He let her act like a boy. She was the first girl in this valley — and I guess the only girl — to win the Fourth of July contest to catch a greased pig — greased with lard. We don't do that now. We think it's cruel to the pig. She was a sight when she finished, but she won. She always won. Except with her men.

"Revonda went off bitter. Her father insulted people when he was drunk, and he wouldn't let Revonda's mother go to church. When he drank himself to death, the folks in this valley didn't come to the funeral. Revonda resented that."

"It seems like too much," I said. "And her husband killed in an accident. Now this with Paul."

Men nodded. "Otherwise she's done so fine. It's a study."

"You mean on the stage?"

"And marrying money. But money didn't help Paul." Mert put a freezer container of sliced strawberries in the refrigerator, and began to fill another.

"When I was a girl," Mert said, "we knew families that feuded. Mostly over in the next county. Mostly related to making whiskey. Bad blood lasts a long time in these mountains.

103

Some said Revonda's grandfather got in the middle of that, as a lawyer. Some will be saying that there's bad blood down to now. I don't hold with that."

Bad blood and bad luck. We had to allow for both or either. But above all, we needed to find the envelope with the magic symbols in it.

"This is a wonderful house," I said. "I love the way the shelves have Victorian curlicues to hold them up. Could you show me the rest of the house?" Mert took me into the two bedrooms, one with a sewing machine set up and pieces for a quilt on the bed. But no stacks the envelope might be in. The closet door was standing open, but the shelf stood empty except for a black straw hat and a pair of black medium-heel shoes. I'd left Anne back in the kitchen where I counted on her to look in every cabinet and nook.

The second bedroom was full of pictures of grandchildren. "I stay in here," Mert said. "The front room is for kids who spend the night." I opened the closet door and said, "Oh, that's the wrong door," as if I'd opened it by mistake.

No sign of our envelope.

I asked to use the bathroom. At least I could search there with the door shut. A brown bathrobe and a plastic shower cap hung on a hook on the back of the door. The bathtub was a nice old one with claw feet. Nothing under it. But don't give up, I warned myself. A pencil and a shopping list lay on the counter near the toilet.

The list said, "recycle newspapers." Hey! That was it! The tarp on the porch covered newspapers! A sandwich-loss possibility.

I came out of the bathroom and found Sam had arrived and was telling Mert how he loved her kitchen. He had his arm around Mert, like she was his long-lost mother.

While Mert was diverted, Anne shook her head at me. She hadn't found anything. I smiled and winked at Anne.

"I couldn't help seeing 'recycle newspapers' on your Do-It list," I told Mert. "Sam tells me he's about to recycle his and Revonda's. Should we take the ones under the plastic on the front porch for you?"

Sam hardly even blinked. "Yes," he said. "Revonda called and wanted me to take the dress she's going to wear to the memorial service to the cleaners. And we're going to recycle papers on the way." He was so casual. What an actor.

I prayed to God my guess was right and our envelope was in that pile. Where else was left?

Mert led us to the porch, took off the plastic throw, and reached to help us move those papers into the van. "You girls just relax," Sam ordered. "Let me show you how strong I am." He picked up a big bundle of untied papers from the top of the pile.

We couldn't stop Mert. "I'm used to being handy. I didn't grow up to sit," she said. But Sam and Anne and I worked so fast, we moved most of the papers. Nothing odd in my piles. We got in the van, me in the backseat and Anne with Sam now in the front. He didn't say a word until we were way down the valley. He whooped: "Hooray. You were right! I found it!" What a break. What a relief.

"Anne, I know what you did with that stuff. You must have put the bag and envelope down on top of Mert's pile of papers." He laughed and turned to me. "There must be a whole category for people who have a special talent for creative ways to lose things." He turned back to Anne. "You absentmindedly handed Mert the bag and put the newspaper down on top of the envelope. Did the phone ring? Obviously something diverted Mert. She left that paper there because she already had another one."

Anne laughed. "Mert or one of her neighbors put more papers on top and didn't notice. What incredible luck."

Sam turned and winked at Anne. "The best mistake you ever made. So now we can study the stuff Paul marked in his books, even while the sheriff has the books."

They both began to sing: *"We'll recycle all the papers when we come, when we come."* And then: *"We'll study all the magic when we come, when we come."* Singing to celebrate.

"Sam," Anne sang, "you *are* changing my luck!" That look of worship was back in her eyes. She loved him partly because he sang all-out like a mad pirate, or a mad saint.

To make everything fit our fib, we went back to Revonda's to get her papers to recycle. One of the sheriff's department cars was there, and a deputy, who seemed to be studying Revonda's front door, nodded at us. Because I needed to visit the plumbing, I went into the studio. (Last bathroom visit had been research.) Sam carried the precious envelope hidden in a newspaper. He carried in some other stuff from the backseat. I wasn't paying too much attention to what. Anne went ahead of us, so she didn't notice, either.

I heard him open the closet door and the rustle as he hung something inside. I turned and saw him put the envelope flat on the closet shelf, still under the newspaper.

I noticed a glimmer behind him. I heard Anne start to scream and shut her mouth on the sound before it could get out and be heard outside. She leaned on the round table as if she could hardly stand. "Sam. There's a plastic dry cleaning bag in that closet. With something black in that bag. It wasn't here before."

"Oh, yes," he said. "Not to worry. I just put it there. It's only Paul's black suit. Actually, I already got the cleaning while you were at Mert's."

"Paul's suit is in a bag like the bag that killed him!"

"I should have thrown the bag away," he said casually, "but to tell the truth, I want to paint it.

I can do it by memory but not as well." That was Sam. If it upsets you, paint it. I could see Anne wanted to burn the thing.

He pulled the hanger out of the closet, whipped the bag off the suit and folded the plastic bag up. She just stood stunned as he put the bag in the top bureau drawer with his socks.

"Paul wore this in a dinner-theater play, and someone spilled soup on it. One reason Revonda wanted me to go right to the cleaners was to get this suit. She's comforting herself by being picky."

"And the detective let you walk right in with a bag like the one that killed Paul?" Anne had her hands on her hips, outraged.

Sam seemed surprised. "They don't care what we bring in, only what was here when Paul died."

"Why get Paul's suit today, for him to be buried in, when there's only a memorial service coming up. Why bring the suit here?" she asked.

"I know you won't like this." He pulled on his beard and looked sheepish. "But this is important to Revonda. This suit isn't for Paul. Revonda has asked me to wear it to the memorial service. He and I are the same size."

Anne gasped, and her eyes went so large they hardly seemed to fit in her face. "Why would she want you to do that?"

I wondered myself.

"She's obsessed," he said, "by wanting to be sure each of us will look right at the service. And you know I don't have a suit."

Anne shook her head no, but Sam ignored that.

"Revonda's friend Marvelle is finding a black dress for you, Anne," Sam said. "Revonda needs any comfort we can give her. And just because Paul owned this suit doesn't mean we have to be superstitious, does it?"

He should have known Anne *was* superstitious. Even I could remember that.

"It's a dead man's suit. It could be a murdered man's suit, a haunted suit. Please don't wear it!"

I wished that girl didn't have such a good imagination. I wished Paul hadn't said he'd put a curse on us. I'd repressed that. It had gone right out of my head. It came back now.

Anne deliberately straightened herself. "Maybe I'm being silly," she said. She clenched her fists and took a deep breath. "If I'm hysterical, that won't help."

She forced her face into a tremulous smile. "At least Sam won't walk in Paul's shoes," she said, turning to me and trying to joke.

Now it was Sam who looked horrified. "Did you have to put it that way?" he said slowly. "Because now I've promised and I really can't go back on my promise." He picked up a brown paper bag from the closet floor. Slowly he opened the bag and took out two black shoes, both glowingly shined, and with the laces neatly tied in bows.

Chapter

11

MONDAY, 5:30 P.M.

I came home to find Ted's car parked in front of the house, and hurried inside so fast that the door banged shut. I ran through the living room and found him in the kitchen leaning on the counter near the electric coffeemaker, leafing through the mail, and waiting for the coffee to finish dripping.

I threw my arms around him. He felt so normal. He felt like the center of the familiar world. And our nice sunshine-yellow kitchen was a part of that world. No mirrors. No black candles. No paintings of disasters. Nobody saying Help! I kissed Ted like he was the most wonderful man in the universe.

"Bad stuff you're mixed up in, huh?" he said into my hair, hugging me back hard, then holding me out where he could see my face. His eyebrow's were raised in a what-now? expression.

"I sure do need you to bounce this around with. I need you to be sane like you always are," I said.

"That bad?" he said. "Let's get some coffee and go sit down. Boy, I never learned so much in four days. Really good stuff about computer reporting for my journalism classes. I'll be telling you about it for weeks, but let's hear the disaster now."

We went and sat in the two big armchairs that are catercorner in the living room. I started at the beginning, to make sure I told all. I explained how Revonda had been with her friend Marvelle, and how Anne and I had been together most of the time — but not all — during which Paul either killed himself or was killed. But Sam had no one to vouch for him. And how that could be bad because he had been accused of murder in Boston, though the sheriff might not know that since charges weren't pressed. I told Ted about Sam kidnapping Paul's books, and about the sketches that vanished and how we'd just found them, and I even threw in the bit about Sam having to wear Paul's shoes at the service.

Ted ran his fingers through his hair: sign of deep thought. "You realize," he said, "that you've allowed family loyalty or whatever to put you in a bad spot. You've kept things to yourself that you should have told the sheriff, and probably you'll continue to keep mum, if I know you."

"But Anne *is* my cousin," I said. "And those two kids don't know diddly-squat about taking care of themselves."

"Which means," he said, "that they are even more likely to let the cat out of the bag about your part in this."

He was right. I'd been thinking so hard about helping those kids I hadn't thought about myself. Old One-Track Mind.

"I'd advise you to get out of this and stay out," he said, sipping his coffee thoughtfully. "But I know you'd rather spend a year in prison than stop now."

"That's true. I have a feeling Anne and Sam are going to need all the help they can get."

"Be very careful," my husband said, grinning like that was a joke. "I'd miss you."

"We need your logical mind in this," I said, encouraged by his grin. "You need to come look at these copies of the pages Paul marked. I told Sam I had to come home and ask for your help. He suggested we come back this afternoon."

"One of us mixed up in this is already too much," Ted said. He drummed his fingers on the arm of his chair, considering. "But I certainly don't want you in trouble by yourself. He was good at logic, but he was also good at rationalizations. We finished our coffee and set out before he even unpacked.

As we got into Ted's car, I felt drops of rain. By the time we reached Bloodroot Creek, the rain almost overwhelmed the windshield wipers. Thunder boomed. Revonda's house looked pretty dramatic in the lightning flashes. Especially the tower. There's something horror-movie about a tower on a dark house. The electricity was evidently off because both Revonda's house and the studio were dark except for one flickering light in each — a candle or an oil lamp, I figured.

We parked, ran through the rain to the door, and felt our way up the dark studio steps. We called out, and Anne opened the upstairs door for us, holding a candle. "Sam's over with Revonda," she said. The candlelight made her lovely face downright exotic. She had on a caftan of some wine-red Indian fabric with a big paisley print — comfortable, no doubt, but adding to the exotic effect. Underlining her natural grace. I introduced her to Ted, and I could see appreciation in his eyes. Ha! I thought. Gotcha! Ted wouldn't pull out and leave such a pretty girl in the lurch.

She took our wet raincoats and hung them on a peg to drip. I could tell by the way Ted immediately darted his eyes around that he was itching to look into every corner of the studio and especially at Sam's paintings. But Anne waved her hand toward the bentwood chairs around the round table and made it clear, as she hurried us to them, she wanted us to sit right down and look at the magic stuff.

We sat in three chairs, and Anne put a large envelope on the fourth chair. She pulled out some papers and held the top one in the candle-light. She knocked the others on the floor, said, "damn," and picked them up, nervous, as if she was afraid they'd fight against her.

"Sam and I have had a chance to just glance through these," she said. "I'll begin with the only place he says was marked with a red ribbon, which must be the one Paul thought was most important of all."

She held out a picture of a round-headed, half-bald man wearing a loose overblouse and a shirt with a ruff collar. His right hand was on the handle of a sword with a word on it: *Zoth*. Behind the man was a window, and through the window were books and manuscripts scattered on the ground near a tiny human head, which seemed quite cheerful considering it had no body. Strange. "And here's the opposite page." Anne pointed. I read Mr. Ruff-and-Sword's name: Paracelsus, 1493?–1541.

"A physician, astrologer, mystic, and magus," Ted said, studying the text. "His motto was *'Be not another if thou can'st be thyself'* "

"Well, I'm for that," I said. "That's not magic."

Ted was already digesting what the page said. Talk about reading fast. "Because Paracelsus thought for himself, he made enemies and dis-covered things, it says here." He read further. "Paracelsus discovered a cure for syphilis that worked."

"Yes," Anne said, "and because he laughed at

the bigwigs and went by what he saw with his own eyes, Sam thinks he must have been great. That article about Paracelsus explains how he thought magic worked."

Good grief, on this one page could there be an explanation of magic? No wonder Paul put a red ribbon there.

Ted read aloud: " 'Imagination is like the sun, the light of which is not tangible but which can set a house on fire.' " Did he mean like the sun's rays could set fire through a magnifying glass?

" 'All depends only upon a man's imagination to be sun — that is, that he wholly imagines that which he wills.' "

"That doesn't seem so strange," Anne said. "Giving a good puppet show works the same way — imagining wholly." She glanced at the puppets hanging against the wall, shadowy in the candlelight. "Which is why I'm glad I have a good imagination." Her face softened. She glanced back at the page, and her frown lines deepened again. "So why did Paul need black woodwork and crazy mirrors if plain imagination does the trick?" she asked. "Why did Paul put his red ribbon to mark this place?"

That was a good question.

"Perhaps the other pages Paul marked tell more about how he thought," Ted said. "How did he mark them differently?"

"Sam says all the rest were marked with scraps of torn paper, like he just did it on impulse," Anne said.

We passed the pages around between us. There were all sorts of strange charms, even one for becoming invisible. Oh, come on!

But these charms were all knocked right out of my mind when a black symbol caught my eye: three marks, a little like a Chinese word. Points of ink made parts of the symbol rise like flame. It was labeled "Charm used in cursing an enemy."

Revonda had said Paul was into *good* magic. A curse couldn't be good magic. I shivered and turned to the next page — and that knocked my socks off, too. "Here's the charm with lines in a spiral and magic symbols like that thing that Paul wore round his neck!"

Anne nodded. "Yes, I know," she said. "Paul told me it was a charm to bring him protection."

"So what did Paul need protection from?" I asked.

"From his own imagination, perhaps," Ted guessed. "Or maybe from someone who wanted to manipulate his imagination to scare him to death. Or maybe from someone he suspected wanted to kill him."

"But who?" I asked.

A throaty dramatic voice answered from the doorway: "Someone wanted to destroy him, and they succeeded!" I jumped an inch. Revonda! There she stood, holding a folded umbrella. She was so white her makeup was like a wrong-color picture painted on her face. She wore a white shirt and black pants. Sam was a dark shadow behind her. I hadn't heard them come up the step — maybe due to the storm noise or maybe because we were concentrating on the pages. And, oh, boy, what would she think when she saw we had them?

"I saw your car," she said to Ted. "I'm Revonda Roland — you must be Peaches' husband." She came forward and held out her hand to Ted, who stood to meet her. Even her hand was unnaturally white. Yet, in her despair, she could still look up at Ted through her eyelashes, almost like a flirt. "If you've come to help, I thank you. I don't expect much help from the sheriff."

Sam came in and stood behind Anne's chair with both hands on the bentwood back. His hair was pointed with wetness.

"You see," Revonda said, "Harley was once a shy kid who asked me to marry him. He was a lot younger than I was, so I thought it was funny. I laughed at him. I was too young to understand how that could hurt his pride. Now our sheriff will do whatever is guaranteed to hurt me most."

"But certainly he'll have to behave like a professional," I said. "He is the elected sheriff of the county."

"I wouldn't trust him as far as I could throw a two-ton truck full of lead weights," said Revonda. "He's slippery as a greased snake. We're on our own."

Then Revonda turned to Anne. "Those are pages from Paul's books, aren't they?" The

Paracelsus picture was faceup on the table in front of Anne.

"I copied pages before Paul died," Sam spoke right up, "the ones he'd marked. I was afraid that something was wrong here. I wanted to know what he was mixed up in. And now we *need* to know."

I waited for Revonda to get mad. But she went around to Sam and put her arm around him. "Thank God you did," she said, hugging him. "Because the sheriff has taken Paul's books, and we all need to look at these for clues." She took the envelope of papers off the fourth chair and put it on the table. She sat down in the chair. "I've looked through Paul's books," she said, "but not at a time when I thought . . ." She hesitated. "I didn't expect to find him dead."

She took a deep breath. "There's a lot about mirrors." Revonda's voice was hoarse, but she began to read us about some man named Pretorius in the seventeenth century, who said a boy could see the future by staring at a mirror in a basin of water.

Sam was looking over her shoulder: "He thought the devil helped, of course."

Revonda bristled.

Sam patted her arm. "Why should the devil have to help?" he asked. "Look, here it says a person can stare into a shiny shield to see the future. Or stare at a shiny fingernail. If anyone stares at something shiny long enough, he can hypnotize himself, right?"

"You mean" — I leaned forward — "you could hypnotize yourself into seeing the future? Listen!" I was getting excited. "In Paul's room I could almost feel demons and until I got used to those crazy mirrors, I did feel hypnotized. So the members of a cult trying to raise demons could certainly have stared themselves into some altered state of mind." I felt the hair on my back and arms rise.

Revonda leaned forward. "And that altered state of mind could lead to murder."

She put her hands over her face. "I can't look at these anymore now. I can't stand the strain. Tomorrow I'll look, after we pray for poor Paul. But don't think for one minute," she said, raising her chin, "that because I'm not studying these now I won't do everything in my power to find the killer."

I wouldn't want to be a killer that Revonda decided to track down. She had the most determined eyes I ever saw in my life. Even candlelight didn't soften them. "We *will succeed,*" she said, seeming to beam her whole will through her eyes.

I had the oddest feeling that some kind of magic was on her side.

Chapter

12

TUESDAY, JULY 2, 12:30 P.M.

So Sam wore Paul's black suit. I almost laughed. The suit was so strange with Sam's lion-mane hair. He was like a mad, long-haired scientist dressed to win the Nobel Prize. But I could see Anne struggling desperately not to be superstitious about that suit — to say nothing of those black shoes.

We were all in Revonda's living room, ready for the service, though we didn't have to leave for fifteen minutes. Revonda had put on black with pearls and held her head high. Trembly brave. She sat in her jungle chair, sipping a Scotch for the road, the dogs at her feet. Sam sat close beside her in his mourning suit. I was on the other side. Anne looked at a bunch of red roses and blue delphinium. "I like these best," she said, looking at the card. "From Tam."

"Let me see," Revonda demanded. She examined the flowers. "My cousin Mat could have afforded better than that," she said in a prissy schoolteacher voice. "He's a lawyer."

Ted winked at me. Yes, Revonda was uptight. Ted had just come back from taking something out to the kitchen to the cousin in a too-tight dress who was rearranging the fridge, fitting in the offerings of food that friends and neighbors brought.

Someone knocked hard on the front door. The dogs began to bark, and Revonda had to shush them. The sheriff opened the door and stuck his head in. The rest of him followed uninvited. This was hardly the moment we needed for him to turn up, with those half-closed, speculating eyes. He walked in so determined, yet light and quiet on his feet: a stalker. "I have something important to tell, Revonda." He stood tall on her oriental rug in his fancy boots.

Sam got up to give the sheriff his seat next to Revonda and stood behind her, leaning on the back of her jungle-print chair. I bit my lip. By gosh, Sam was like an Amish elder rising from a dreamscape — like a guardian angel in deep mourning. But he didn't seem funny to Anne. Her scared eyes kept repeating: Sam in a dead man's suit.

"Revonda, honey," said the sheriff, pulling his chair around to face her, not far from me but ignoring me. "I know you don't want to see me right before the service. But the media people have been after me so hard. I need to tell you what I told them before you hear it on the news." He shifted in his chair, leaning toward her. "I think I owe you that." He turned and stared at the rest of us. "I'd like to be alone with Mrs. Roland."

Revonda held her head like a statement: A woman with real pearls gets what she wants. "I want my friends to stay right here. They can be helpful." She reached up toward Sam behind her, and he put his hand over hers and patted her hand.

The sheriff's square jaw firmed up even squarer. But he also squirmed, all gangly six-feet-plus. Queen Revonda had him pinioned with her magic stare. Whatever he'd come to tell half stuck in his throat.

He began to talk about the ways Paul could have died. He kept waving with those big, clumsy hands. Medium-wide-apart when he said: ". . . rumors of a cult." Wider when he said: "It could have been a crazy person." Twisting together when he talked about drug killings. Revonda had told me she thought drug dealers could buy him off. Harley Henderson wouldn't even charge much, she'd said — he didn't have enough sense.

Revonda spoke: "You said you'd come to tell me what you told the media. You said you let yourself be pressured into a statement. Well, I'm waiting."

Ted was watching her with a little pleased

smile. He likes a woman who knows her own mind.

Even the rottweilers saw something was up and sat at attention, ears perked.

The sheriff leaned forward and paused. "Now, Revonda" — his eyes were steady on her, but his hands held each other as if he was nervous — "honey, you're not going to like what I say."

"I never have."

"The coroner found cocaine in Paul's system. That didn't kill him. But it sure could have twisted his thoughts. And as for his body, there were no lumps. No broken bones. No sign of a struggle."

"And so?"

"And, honey, the most likely thing is that Paul killed himself."

I was relieved. That meant the sheriff couldn't possibly suspect Sam or Anne.

But the jolt hit Revonda like she'd been shot. She pressed back in her chair. She blinked.

The sheriff just plowed on. Either that man was thick, or else he really meant to hurt. "If there'd been a note, we would have decided right away. But people don't always leave a note."

"Cowards kill themselves. I didn't raise a coward." Revonda was rigid as glass. Her eyes glittered. Maybe the glitter was from tears, but she didn't let them fall.

"Well, honey, there were no latent fingerprints in his room from anybody but you and Sam and

Anne and your friend Marvelle — and your play detective here." His voice went heavy with sarcasm when he got to me. "No recent footprints from anybody we couldn't account for. First, we thought there were, but, Revonda, you have so many kinds of shoes, we found a match for the extra prints by studying your closet." He managed to make it sound like it was all her fault for liking shoes. Like maybe she was Imelda Marcos in disguise. That big mouth half smiled, like he was glad it was her fault.

"Now, about the plastic bag. The bag that killed Paul was next on the roll from the one on a dry-cleaned pair of pants in Paul's closet. Little faults in the plastic matched. That bag must have been from the same batch of cleaning. You might say he had the means right at hand to kill himself."

Revonda seethed with fury. I could practically feel the heat from where I sat. The sheriff had reactivated her. Pushed the emergency button. "So you're too stupid to catch a killer in gloves," she hissed, "or a killer who borrowed a pair of my shoes."

I had visions of a crazy Killer Cinderella. We'd catch her with Revonda's slippers.

The sheriff shook his head slowly, as if he didn't know what to do next. "We'll keep looking, honey. Good Lord, we go way back, you and me. I'll do all I can." Mock soothing voice. "But I still believe Paul killed himself."

"Why?"

"He was depressed, honey. When Henry Williams at the Box Elder gas station told him to have a good day, Paul told Henry it was a good day to be dead. Now I ask you! He killed himself."

"I suppose you think the devil made those marks on Paul. Some fools think so. I hear Jeeter up the hill says that. And it's his daughter, Jinx, who ran after Paul. Told the world she loved him. Little fool."

Jeeter. Men said someone named Jeeter mailed a dead snake to Revonda. The name was so odd it stuck in my mind. And his daughter was after Paul? And named Jinx? How horribly appropriate! To love Paul would sure be a jinx. Revonda said this Jeeter's name like poison.

Revonda was practically breaking her pearls from twisting them. But still pink-furious. "You know there was nothing in Paul's room that matched those marks on his body. Nothing he could have used to paint himself like that. You told me that yourself."

"But you didn't see him come in, did you, Revonda, honey? He could perfectly well have put the marks on someplace else and then come home and killed himself." Now, that was far-fetched. We'd seen him just a little while before he died, and the sheriff knew it. But the sheriff sounded pleased he'd thought of it.

Revonda's fingers pressed into the chair until I thought the fabric might tear. Sam reached down over the chair back and put a hand on each of her black shoulders. "We have to get to the church," he told the sheriff. "The service is at one, and it's ten of one now." Sam was almost holding Revonda down. But it didn't work.

She jumped up and screamed at the sheriff: "You don't know about Paul. All you have is a mouth as foul as a garbage truck. You don't care who killed Paul. Or somebody has bought you off."

The sheriff turned bright red, and his eyes became even narrower. He stood up, too, so he looked down on her: "Revonda, honey, if you want to talk murder — why, our best suspects are right here in this room." He pinned each of us with his eyes so hard I felt like shrinking back.

"Of course, you all say you were with someone when Paul died. Except Sam Newman here." The sheriff smiled like he could see through all our alibis. He straightened taller. "And remember, Revonda, if you stir things up too much, you might even get people to wondering about you, honey. Because Paul had life insurance made out to you."

She stared him down. He was taller, but she had more presence. Circe about to turn Odysseus into a swine. "We — were — life — insurance — beneficiaries — for — each — other. Neither — one — of — us — had — anybody — else." She said that like she was spelling it out for a child.

"Two hundred thousand dollars," the sheriff said dryly.

At least *that* insurance wasn't made out to Sam.

"You get out of here!" Revonda began shouting. "Harley Henderson, you're a jackass. I knew it back in school. Harley Henderson, I wouldn't spit in your ear if your brain was on fire!"

Revonda turned to us as soon as he was gone. "I don't know what that man is trying to cover up. But I don't trust him as far as I could throw a house."

Chapter

13

TUESDAY, 1:00 P.M.

The phone rang just as we got to the front door, ready to leave for the church. Cousin Edna came running from the kitchen, shaking her head from side to side as if to say "No, no, not that."

What she did say was: "Revonda, I'm so sorry, Reverend Moore had one of his attacks. Asthma so bad he can't do the service. But Reverend Phillipson will do it for him."

"Phillipson's an old fool." Revonda just stood there in the white doorframe, glaring. "First, that damn fool sheriff, now this."

As we rode along in the funeral-parlor Cadillac, Revonda said, "The killer will be there to watch me while I listen to that old fool preach about how good can come even from evil. He'll preach right for idiots or babies or hypocrites. Not for me."

"How do you know what he'll say?" Ted asked.

"That's all he ever preaches, no matter what he says the subject is. When that nincompoop says God can work through murder — and he will — how can I not get up and scream?" She'd screamed enough.

"Remember, you're not alone," Sam said. "We're with you."

There was a mob at the small stone church a couple of miles down the road. A staring mob. Some people had given up the idea of being able to press into the church. They were standing outside church windows in the hot sun, saving themselves look-in places, waiting for the service to start. One man even had a little boy on his shoulders so the boy could see in the window better. They swiveled around to stare at us.

Revonda was the main attraction. A television reporter with a camera and a backpack spotted us and began to shoot. Was Revonda that famous as an actress? About medium-famous, I'd thought. No, it must be stories going round that brought those people and the TV man. The talk about magic, drugs, Satanism, suicide, or murder.

We hurried in the back door and were ushered through to a front row, reserved for the immediate family. I studied the congregation for a moment or two when we entered the church. I spotted the sheriff and that deputy called Ron, standing up at the back. On the far right Mert in her brown Sunday dress nodded.

Knowing Agnes was just a few seats away. She sure stood out because she had on the same red skirt and unmatching red blouse that she wore when she wandered up and down the road and picked wildflowers. She actually held a bunch of Queen Anne's lace. Revonda's friend Marvelle Starr, all done up in black and diamonds, almost eclipsed Revonda. Revonda stage-whispered: "That Jinx is here." Jinx. The girl Revonda said ran after Paul.

The front of the church was banked with red and white roses.

Revonda, one seat over from me, couldn't keep her hands still. Her right hand kept moving from finger to finger of the left, as if she were counting. There was a small rustling in back of me. The whole congregation was on edge, couldn't keep still. I held Ted's hand to steady myself. I was glad the organ was playing.

Standing up front, the Reverend Phillipson — the one Revonda said was a fool — looked more like an eighty-year-old baby in horn-rimmed glasses. His white hair was soft and fuzzy with the pink scalp showing. His smile was trusting as a baby's. I liked him. But he was as out of place at that service as the heads of the people staring in the open church windows.

"In whatever happens, however terrible, we must find some good for the future." He swept us with his gentle brown eyes, encouraging us to agree. "Paul's death is telling us we need to pray for each other more." I glanced at Revonda. Her jaw was set as if her teeth were glued together.

"Paul was a young man searching for something. Once in a while he talked to me when I was out weeding my garden. He was angry at the world for being so imperfect. That happens to us all from time to time. But he found it extra hard. He needed our prayers. And now he is taken from us violently in a strange way that we do not understand. He is now in the mercy of God, who sees more deeply and understands more deeply than any of us."

He held up a bunch of twigs. Revonda whispered: "The old fool has to act things out."

"This is a bunch of twigs." He took one and snapped it. "See how easily one breaks. We are like that. But when we pray together we are strong." He tried to break the whole thick bundle of twigs. He beamed. "Together, we can't be broken. We must pray together for strength and understanding."

Revonda hissed: "He used that line on the kindergarten." Sam patted her hand.

Reverend Phillipson didn't notice her glare. His gentle smiling face was like a cherub's on a valentine. More rustling in the congregation. His cheerful faith was adding to the edgy mood in that church — I guess they didn't think it fit in with possible black magic. But I thought he made a nice change.

He blessed us all and told us to pray to God for positive thoughts and quickly finished the service.

Revonda leaned heavily on Sam as we walked out. Anne still kept glancing at that eerie black suit as if she'd like to rip it off of Sam and burn it. Not the thing to do in church. Revonda stopped in the back doorway. She turned and looked up at Sam. She stood back and smiled at him. Like he was a long-lost friend who'd just come in the door.

"Thank you for wearing Paul's suit, Sam. It looks right on you." I thought: She's cracked under the strain. Then she repeated back what he'd said to her. "I am not alone." She clutched his arm again. "Sam, you are a son to me now."

Anne watched that with a set face. Like she was scared her face might misbehave if she just let it relax and do what it pleased. I wondered if she was seeing Paul again the way I was. Complete with sneer. Paul asking again, "Where did my mother know Sam before?"

Then Anne came forward and took Sam's other arm and squeezed it, as if to say, *He's on loan to you, Revonda, but he belongs to me.*

And I thought: It's dangerous to love a man with great charm.

Chapter

14

AFTER THE FUNERAL

"I will receive people until three o'clock," Revonda pronounced as we drove back to her house after the memorial service. "I will show them all that I can't be cowed. I survive."

We drove up to her big old Victorian house, still only partway painted, though I noticed Sam had managed to finish the front porch. The rottweilers, who'd been inside when we left, were out on the porch. They both came running toward us, their short ears flapping in the breeze, stumpy tails wagging. They didn't bark because they knew us. "It's all right," Revonda told them and took them inside.

As soon as she freshened up, she stalked over to her jungle-print chair and sat down, head high, ready to take on the world. Her hands were clenched into fighting fists. I didn't like it.

I felt quite sure she was going to do or say something unwise.

Sam went off to get extra ice, which we were somehow lacking, and Anne went out into the kitchen to help put out food and drink. I asked Revonda if there was anything special I could do, and she told me to take her glass and fill it. "Scotch," she whispered. "Anne knows where it is. Don't bring me that nasty iced tea the rest will want."

When I brought the glass back, she said: "Now, go listen to what people say." She didn't need to tell me that. I walked over to the pictures of Revonda's family, specially studying the one of her father. He had a stubborn jaw but reckless black eyes. Like Paul. From there I could watch the front door and pick the people I'd drift near to.

What I was able to hear didn't seem like a help. A large woman with a belly that hung over like a shelf was telling a thin woman, "I'm bringing peach cobbler to the Fourth of July picnic."

A small stringy man was saying, "My tomatoes are doing good, but my corn is looking sickly." Nobody seemed to be gossiping here in Revonda's house. In a way, I was glad of that.

I saw Mert and enlisted her as a who's-who agent. I knew Paul had a girl named Jinx, and I wanted to meet her.

"She'll come," Mert said. "She knows Revonda hates her, but she'll come to any place where folks might talk about Paul. Paul was real mean to that girl. She had it bad, and he didn't. They say she still does."

"Who else is here who might have been close to Paul?" I asked. She pointed out Marvelle, who was just making an entrance in her black and diamonds, and hugging everybody. "Marvelle was Paul's godmother," Mert explained. "Revonda arranged that. They got on so well, Paul and Marvelle — why, that woman in her fancy clothes gets on with everybody. She just loves her neighbors, so they like her. She's vain as a peacock and nice at the same time."

Marvelle the peacock went to talk to a dark-haired woman in gold earrings like coiled snakes. How did she have the nerve to wear them so soon after . . . Mert squeezed my arm. "That woman is a psychologist. They say Paul went to see her. Didn't do much good, if you ask me."

Marvelle went out to the kitchen and came back with a glass of what must have been Scotch. Sam came back, whispered something to Revonda, and took her glass out to the kitchen for a refill.

"That's one of Paul's dinner-theater buddies," I heard Mert saying, pointing to a fidgety red-haired man with a mustache who was standing next to Lady MacBeth. "Paul was in one of those groups that act while people eat dinner. But they only did it once in a while. Revonda said they were playacting boys. Not serious."

The young man with the mustache avoided Revonda's glance, perhaps because he wore a black T-shirt, of all things, with black jeans. The T-shirt said, TO BE IS BETTER THAN NOT TO BE — ASK WILL.

Revonda was all hollow eyes, watching who came. Paul's picture was at her elbow. Somebody had floated one perfect rose in a silver bowl next to that picture. Of Paul, who fought with his mother. Who was cruel to the girl who loved him. Who threatened Sam. Who laughed when Anne walked into a mirror, and sneered at me. Who nice Reverend Phillipson said was lost and needed help. So who was he?

A young woman with tear-swollen face, in a dowdy black dress, came in the front door. She stood at a distance and stared at the silver-framed picture of Paul next to Revonda. Mert nudged me: "That's Jinx."

I thought how pretty Jinx was — with her shining red hair and those wide-set green eyes — even with her face shiny and swollen from recent tears. And how much she looked as if she were waiting for somebody to hit her in the face. From across the room Revonda glared as if she'd like to be the one to hit her. Revonda's hand holding her glass trembled. She turned and nodded at Anne, who took the glass for a refill. Oh, dear, I thought, it's not going to help if Revonda gets drunk.

While my head was turned, Mert had gone to get Jinx and bring her to meet me. When I turned back, there she was. "This is Anne's cousin Peaches," Mert said. "She'd like to help find out what happened to Paul. She'll want to talk to you, Jinx, I know." Mert the Mouth. This was not the time to question this poor girl except to tell her I was so sorry about what had happened.

But Jinx took hold of my arm with a cold hand. "I have to talk to you." There was not enough breath behind her voice. I had to work hard to hear. She pulled me away from the others into the corner near the entrance into the dining room.

"I have something to show somebody who wants to know about Paul." She was one hundred percent intense, quivering like a humming-bird, and still smelling of tears. "Not the sheriff," she said. "He wouldn't understand." I noticed Revonda staring at her angrily. "I don't have to stay here — not if you'll come and see me," the girl said. "Mert will tell you where to find me." She ran out the door, edging past a startled white-haired woman who was just coming in.

Marvelle had moved over toward the hall with the door to Paul's room off it. Moved that way with glass of whiskey in hand. Paul's door was surely locked, but I could see that the door to Revonda's room was open, undoubtedly so guests could use the bathroom. I drifted over near the entrance to the hall, and when I saw Marvelle come back out of Revonda's room, I walked over and stopped her. "When you get a chance, I'd like to talk to you about Paul," I said.

"Good." She reached over and grabbed my arm as eagerly as Jinx had. Except her hand was bonier. Did they think I'd run away?

"Paul wasn't a monster," Marvelle said dramatically. "Some people are unhappy and they don't have any imagination about it. He was unhappy in extremely original ways." She reached out with her free hand and touched the wall, steadying herself. She was a little high. Not quite solid on her feet, but not gone enough so she couldn't navigate.

"When did you see him the last time?" I asked. If she was willing to talk, I might as well find out what I could. We had the hall to ourselves. Behind us was a backdrop of interwoven chatter, like any get-together.

Marvelle let out a long quavering sigh. "I saw him just before whatever happened." She stopped and stared at his black door. "Behind that door." She pointed with amazement. "Because it was just after lunch." Her face contorted into pain, and I half expected bits of makeup to pop off. But she smoothed out her face immediately.

"The day before, he'd asked me to come over to see him." She spoke clearly, like she was reading lines. "He wanted to show me something. But when I came, he said please to go away, he needed to be alone. He needed to think. I believe we each have a right to live our lives in our own way." As she said that, Marvelle's voice broke. "So I left." She took hold of one diamond earring and squeezed hard. "I wish I'd stayed. But he was my friend because I let him be himself." She squeezed her other ear so both hands were occupied. Unbraced, she swayed slightly. "I do not let myself cry over what's done," she said loudly and took off into the living room. I followed, worried that she might trip on the rug and fall, or bump into somebody.

Marvelle stopped not far from Revonda in her jungle chair. She said loudly to no one in particular: "He had a right to kill himself if that's what he wanted." I tried to get to her, to restrain her. But I couldn't get there in time.

The room had fallen silent. "We'd talked about suicide," Marvelle said. "Sure. As the final option when life becomes unbearable." Then she seemed to notice everybody staring at her.

Revonda had heard. "Come here, Marvelle," she ordered angrily. Marvelle didn't move. It was Revonda who stood up there in the center of the room near her favorite chair, holding on to it to keep steady. She turned slowly around to make eye contact with every single person in the room. From Ron drinking iced tea next to the picture of Joan of Arc, to Reverend Phillipson eating a sandwich by the fireplace, to Mert by the window to the porch. The room positively throbbed with surprise and waiting. I thought, Oh, brother! Revonda will give it to them.

She didn't shout or rave like she did at the sheriff. Her voice was low and throbbing and angry and sad. Rather magnificent. "For me to lose . . . what I valued most . . . was unimaginable. But it happened. And I'm still here." Revonda said each word like a separate bead on a string. That's the only way she showed her Scotch whiskey.

Of course, every single person in that room had stopped talking at once. Sam stood over by Revonda's family pictures, silent. Cousin Edna tensed with her tray of sandwiches half-passed.

In that silence, before Revonda could finish, Knowing Agnes in her swearing reds rose up from a corner and strode over and stood in front of Revonda. Her eyes were black and empty, and yet Knowing Agnes was staring, as if something from the great beyond were staring through her. Her skin was leathery from walking outdoors in all kinds of weather, her hair windblown. She still clutched her bouquet of wilted Queen Anne's lace.

Revonda froze with surprise.

Agnes turned to look at each one of us with those empty eyes, as if she were aping Revonda. Then she fixed those eyes on Revonda. "Revonda's son died as a punishment from God," she said in an echoing monotone. "She don't go to church right. She's not saved. Her son used heathen magic. God smote him down. God

140

smites the damned."

Dear God, who said that? Whose words was she repeating? How many people in this room think that? I shivered. Because a part of me thought that. The part that was afraid of jinxes, afraid of curses. Anne, who was coming out of the kitchen with a tray of glasses, dropped it. The crash seemed appropriate somehow. Like a clash of cymbals.

But who would actually say that God struck Paul down because he was damned?

Revonda took the floor. And the amazing thing was — she stopped looking old. Her face was still taut, but with determination. Her head high like the Statue of Liberty in a rage. And this time she swept the room quickly with proud thousand-volt eyes. "You came to stare. All right, stare hard. Because I'm rich. Because my son read books about Medieval magic. Because some of you think that's Satanism, don't you? Because a crazy woman said what you all think. Don't look shocked. Feel sorry for yourselves. You're in danger. A person or persons killed my son. Not the hand of God. I intend to find out who it was. And if you're smart, you'll help. No matter who the killer is related to. Because if a killer is out there — or even in here — and that killer believes he can kill any damned one of us who deserves it . . ." She paused and looked from face to face. "Then who is safe? Which damned one of you is perfect? My son wasn't perfect. And neither am I. And neither are you.

Now get out of my house and go home."

The guests didn't quite stampede out the door. But they sure didn't linger, either.

Chapter

15

WEDNESDAY, JULY 3

Boy, was I glad I'd kept Pop separate from
Revonda. A lady that jet-propelled — even
when bereaved, even right after her son's memorial service — would be a horrible combination with a man that anxious to stir things up.

On the day after the service I went over to see
Pop in the morning to be sure he wasn't in any
kind of trouble. He welcomed me with a tre-
mendous smile, wheeling his chair forward
across the living room to meet me, blue eyes
positively turned to jewels with sheer determination. Bad sign.

"I've got the answer to all your worries about
Cousin Clothilde's little Anne," he said. "And
Mary dropped off a joke for your book before
she left for the beach. Not that you deserve it.
You haven't been by in days, has she, Ella

Marie?" His most excitable young sitter was on duty again, sitting with him at the table.

I'd kept up by phone, but he didn't think that counted.

"Anne was upset because a woman went berserk after the service for Paul yesterday," I told him. "Everyone was."

"Yes, I know," he said. "And so many people think Paul was murdered." For a man who never goes anywhere he sure keeps up.

"So what should we do to help Anne and Sam?" I asked him.

"First," he said with a mischievous twinkle, "the joke." If he has two things to tell me and he's annoyed at me, he always leaves the one I want to hear most till last. He smiled grandly.

"This man and woman were sitting watching television, and the woman said. 'I'm going in the kitchen to get a snack. Can I bring you anything?' "

At least it was a joke I hadn't heard.

"The man said, 'Yes. I want some ice cream, but be sure to write it down.' And the woman said. 'Don't be silly, I can remember that.' "

Be patient, I told myself. It's probably just a line or two more.

"The man said. 'But I want chocolate syrup on it, so be sure to write it down.' And the woman said, 'Oh, come on, I can remember ice cream with chocolate syrup. How dumb do you think I am?'

"Now, let's see," Pop said, "what else was there, Ella Marie?"

"Nuts," she said."The man said, 'But I want

nuts, too, so write it down.' "

"Of course," Pop said. *"And the woman said, 'No. I'll remember. Ice cream with chocolate syrup and nuts.'* "

"Now listen, Peaches," he said. "This is the best part. *In a little while she came back from the kitchen with a plate of scrambled eggs. The man groaned and said, 'I told you you had to write it down. You forgot the toast.'* " Pop happily led the laughter.

"Thank you. Now about Bloodroot Creek," I said.

But Pop said, "Not one word till you write that down for your chapter on writing things down."

And after I'd written down the joke, he said, "I have the answer. This case needs a personal touch. I need your help." I smelled trouble. Pop continued: "I'm going to invite my old friend Revonda over here to dinner, and our cousins, Anne and Sam — and, of course, you and Ted — and we'll discuss magic." He all but clapped his hands with glee. "The radio and the television and the paper all say that some kind of black magic was the reason for Paul Roland's death." What he said was a gross exaggeration, but I could see it made his day.

"Pop, you can't just yank people around at a time like this," I told him, coldly. "Revonda is distraught."

"Nonsense," Pop said. "When Revonda is upset, she takes action. Everybody knows that.

Once, when she was a kid, she stood perfectly still for four hours, waiting till she could shoot the fox that killed her favorite hen. She got that fox square between the eyes. Zingo! Revonda is determined! Now she needs her old friends to rally round her and help her out." He wheeled his chair back around to his favorite table and patted the chair next to him. "Sit down. We need to plan this."

I sat, and I argued. All I could finally manage was to get Pop to agree to put the dinner party off a few days, at least till after the Fourth. The further off the better, I figured. "I'm putting my birthday celebration off," I said. "Ted and I agreed. So you can put off *your* dinner to a time when it'll do the most good."

"Why do that?" Pop glared like I was the whole problem.

"Revonda says the killer will certainly come to the big Fourth of July celebration in Bloodroot Creek. So I need to snoop around. After that, I'll get together with Bessie and arrange a good dinner — but only if Revonda agrees to come." I counted on Revonda not to be so foolish.

I told myself I was lucky — at least Pop wasn't having hallucinations. He had been for a while. Mix that in with some of the stranger parts of reality, and wow! The doctor had adjusted Pop's medications, and at least he hadn't imagined men on the roof with knives or such for quite a while.

Pop picked up the newspaper from the table.

146

He was so blind he couldn't read anything but the biggest headlines, but he probably had had Ella Marie read the story to him so often that he knew it by heart. Of course he watched TV. Perhaps he could see a little of it. And he could hear.

"I like that part about how if just anyone can be killed in a way that fits his sins, we're all in danger," Pop said. "Revonda said that, right? Boy, I can think of some people I'd like to kill to fit their sins!"

Oh, brother! "You'd get killed," I said, "with your nose caught in a mousetrap, from being so nosy."

Pop rubbed his nose and beamed. "I can't think of a better way to go!"

Chapter

16

LATER WEDNESDAY

Somehow, I got myself talked into helping Revonda and Anne sort Paul's things. At the time it sounded like a good chance to find some surprising clue. I was intrigued by the big black red-lined cape in the back of his closet, for instance. My imagination could do things with that. For the first time I noticed a paper knife that looked like a dagger, or was it the other way around? Revonda said it belonged to Paul's great-grandfather. Nothing we found seemed to have the killer's signature. We put clothes in boxes for the Christian Ministry's used-clothing department or the Asheville Community Theater costume collection.

I suggested to Anne that she and Sam come have dinner with Ted and me. A little healing food and conversation. Revonda intended to spend the rest of the afternoon and evening making phone calls. She'd have a sandwich on a tray next to the phone. "I will be too busy to notice whether you're here or not," she told Anne, "and as for answering the phone, I want to do it myself. I want to be positive not to miss anything or fail to speak to every person in this valley. At least one cousin will be here to answer the door. I can't get rid of cousins. They're too curious to go away."

Ted came home about five o'clock, to find me in the kitchen patting rosemary on a chicken. A member of the English Department at the University in Asheville gave me the recipe: Shakespearean Chicken. You know. *Rosemary for Remembrance.* The folks back in Shakespeare's day believed rosemary was an herb that improved the memory. Besides, the chicken is easy and good. Just pat with a little rosemary and maybe a pinch of sage and bake as usual. Serve with a wine and chicken-stock sauce, made with pan drippings, after most of the fat is skimmed off. And if Shakespeare was right — well, we could all use as much memory as we could get.

Sam and Anne ate my chicken as if they hadn't had a bite in a week. We didn't talk a lot about Paul's death. I guess we needed a respite. Sam told us how as a kid he lived on a farm in Pennsylvania. Which is maybe why he likes farm country.

Over ice cream and coffee we did recap the case, and Sam and Anne stayed late. I don't guess they were in a hurry to get back to the scene of the horror. Then their van wouldn't start. Sabotage? When things are going wrong, everything gets suspicious. But it was an old van with lots of aches and pains, Sam said. Could be just something inside it died of old age. Too bad it picked midnight in our driveway to conk out. So we gave them a ride home through the moonlit night. Sam said he'd see about the van in the morning.

As we turned into Revonda's driveway, the moon through the branches of the big trees made moving patterns. I almost missed seeing the odd light in Revonda's house. "That's a light in Paul's room!" Sam cried, just as the light went out. I don't know how he could tell where at a glance. It had been a small light, wavering. Maybe a flashlight. Otherwise the house was dark.

Ted glided us to the house and parked quietly. We heard the dogs barking, and we jumped pell-mell out of the car. Ted called he'd cover the back door, even as he ran toward it. The rest of us spread out in front of the house. I asked Anne to run to the studio to call the sheriff.

The moon had picked this time to go under clouds. We hardly had time to feel our way in the dark when the doors to Paul's room burst open, and someone swept past us so fast that we were unable to grab him. Sam did get hold of a shirt collar, but the man — at least, it later turned out to be a man's shirt — ran right out of it. Must have been unbuttoned. Sam threw down the shirt and ran after him. I rushed into Paul's room, through the wide-swinging glass doors, and turned on the light switch.

No one was there. Revonda kept those outside glass double doors locked just as Paul had. Who had a key? The mirrors on the walls and ceiling winked. I felt like the last flash reflection of a person running had just escaped my eyes. A fallen straight-back chair lay on its side on the floor not far from the small table near the wall. As if the intruder had knocked the chair over when he ran, whoever he was. The rocking chair with the moon face in the center of the room rocked slightly, too, as if the person had brushed against it as he passed.

The door on the house side of the room burst open, and Revonda strode in in her pajamas. "My God, what's happening?" The dogs ran in past her, still barking, and took off after Sam and the burglar or whatever. Revonda was by my side, asking, "What was it?" She'd grabbed my arm and her voice slurred. She had evidently taken a sleeping pill and was having trouble shaking the drug off.

I said, "I don't know. Sam's looking." I wished he and Ted weren't both out in the dark with whatever. But it wouldn't help if I left Revonda.

I heard a car start in the distance. I prayed that didn't mean the intruder was getting away. I hoped . . . prayed . . . Sam was safe. I heard a second car start. Would that be Sam, in Revonda's car?

I told Revonda I wanted to let Ted in the back door so he could search the house. She said she'd let him in herself and be sure the door was locked. But when she did, Ted came straight through the house without searching. He said we'd better wait for the sheriff to be sure we didn't destroy evidence.

Revonda snorted, "Don't count on that fool."

I figured the best thing we could do was calm Revonda and search Paul's room, since our fingerprints and whatever were already in there. Besides, I wasn't sure I should trust the sheriff any more than Revonda did. She knew the man.

Revonda still looked groggy, standing there in her leopard-spot pajamas. I got her to sit down in the moon chair.

At first glance, nothing seemed out of place in Paul's room except the small chair knocked over. Almost everything had been put back the way it was before he died. His narrow cot was unrumpled. The face jug glared down at us from the shelf. But then my eyes were drawn to a mirror on the black floor. It was a small mirror, the kind a woman might carry in her pocketbook, glimmering between the table and the chair. So small you could hardly spot the reflection in all the other mirrors. And it was broken in three pieces.

Revonda said, "Don't pick it up. I'll call Ron. He'll get here before the sheriff since he lives just up the hill." Her voice was still slurred, but her mind was working. She walked unsteadily toward the phone, and when I moved to help, she said, "No, I want to do it myself."

Then Sam was back. "That man got a head start," he said. "I don't know which cove or driveway he turned into."

I showed the others the mirror, a woman's kind of mirror. And I wondered if it was a woman who came in that room, a woman who had a key. Perhaps she'd dropped the mirror and was going to have seven years' bad luck.

"Jinx would have a key to Paul's room." Revonda's voice was still a little slow, but she'd come awake.

I didn't believe the intruder was Paul's sad-sack-but-beautiful girlfriend Jinx. I'd only seen that intruder flash by, but I had the impression it was a man and bigger than Jinx. Still, who can be sure in the dark?

"I should have thought to ask Jinx for that key back," Revonda went on. "That girl is so vague and so promiscuous that anyone could steal her key. I wouldn't be surprised if she belonged to a cult, either. I hear there's sex in those rituals. Those people believe they have sex with the devil." That had her wide awake. She turned and stared at me. Almost as if she thought I had sex with the devil. "You are the one to go talk to Jinx, Peaches." She looked me over like I was a cat she might want to adopt. As if she was of two minds. And then she said, "People tell you things. You look sympathetic." She said that with her mouth slightly pursed and her eyebrows up almost as if it was an accusation.

I didn't like her attitude. I'm a good listener, and proud of it. I used to wonder why people like to bend my ear — me who forgets details. But then I realized people want you to hear the essence of what they say, want you to hear how they *feel*, which is just what interests me. And if they tell you their troubles or hopes, they don't care if you recall it all. In fact, sometimes they're glad you *don't*.

For detection, on the other hand, I jot down notes. For detection, I made up my mind to talk to Jinx at the Fourth of July celebration the next morning. Was Jinx involved in Paul's death? I felt pretty wait-and-see on that. But one thing seemed surer and surer: Paul didn't kill himself.

Chapter

17

THURSDAY, JULY 4

As I drove out to Bloodroot Creek about nine in the morning on the Fourth of July, I kept thinking about that broken mirror. The sheriff hadn't shared any thoughts, though he came in person and summoned a photographer to record the scene.

Who would come into Paul's mirror room to steal a small mirror and drop it on the way out? And where had it come from? The deputies had been over that room with a fine-tooth comb, hadn't they? Or had someone brought it in and left it there as a symbol of God-knows-what?

Jinx had a key. And who else? Marvelle was Paul's godmother, and Mert said they were close. How odd that a man suspected of traffic with the devil should have a godmother. Marvelle might have a key to the room. I'd try to talk to Marvelle, as well as Jinx.

I dropped by Revonda's to see if there were any new developments. Not yet, she said, and asked where Ted was. I said he'd be along.

"The Fourth of July could be our A-number-one chance to trap the killer," she said. "I'll bet my soul the killer is someone who could not fail to go to the celebration without causing raised eyebrows and embarrassing questions. In this valley we celebrate the Fourth of July as a favorite holiday. Even flatlanders have been asked to take part." Revonda smiled at Anne. "I'm glad you are following my advice to go on with the puppet show for the children." She turned to me. "After Paul died, they called and said they'd understand if Anne wanted to drop out, but I told Anne to go and keep a sharp eye out for anything suspicious.

"And don't forget to pick up Marvelle," Revonda commanded Anne. "Marvelle loves to be onstage so much, she'd go right on acting if the theater burned down. She's even thrilled to be leading the Pledge of Allegiance." Revonda traced a tropical flower on the arm of her chair with one red fingernail. "Marvelle needs to be looked at." A little friendly bitchiness perked Revonda up. "You'd think Marvelle had a huge career on the stage, the ways she acts. She inherited money and retired here, copying me. You know where we met? We were doing a toilet paper commercial for television, the low point in my career and the high point in hers. But she'll do the pledge well."

Anne suggested that she and I go to the Bloodroot Valley Community Center together. I figured perhaps she wanted to tell me something in private. "Revonda's in really bad shape," Anne said as we drove off in her van — Sam had found the van's problem was simple to fix in the light of day. "She's afraid to be alone. That's why her cousin Edna is still there." Then Anne explained she had to stop by and get her puppet theater at the church, where she'd done a show for the Summer Bible School kids at Mert's behest.

At the church, the Boy Scouts were putting the finishing touches on their float with the flag at one end and everybody saluting. Several boys helped Anne get the parts of her stage into the van. The stage was black with lots of rods and curtains.

Finally we got to Marvelle's house. We knocked on the door. No answer. If she was so eager to lead the salute to the flag, where was she? Maybe putting the last touches on her makeup? Switching to longer false eyelashes? I liked Marvelle, but her frantic effort to look glamorous was a little comic. Her house was small and painted white and fixed up to the nines, with gladiola and roses and a birdbath with a fountain. But cheerful.

Anne kept knocking, but still no Marvelle. The door was unlocked, so she opened it and stuck her head in and called. Silence. We stepped inside. It was all very decorated with huge cushions on the couch, a shawl on the baby grand piano shimmering with big embroidered red roses. The room was cluttered. Not like Revonda's house, where *House Beautiful* could have come in to take pictures at any moment. The morning paper was out on Marvelle's coffee table, and her sunglasses and some gardening gloves and a bandanna were on a small table by a side door. Anne stood at the bottom of the stairs and called up. Still nothing.

"Maybe she forgot you were coming," I said, "like I might have done."

"Or was I supposed to meet her somewhere else?" Anne asked. "Actually, it's not so far that she couldn't have walked."

We drove to the white clapboard community center, expecting Marvelle would already be there. No sign of her. Not many people there yet. Just children and their pets and the judges for the pet parade. A judge was pinning a ribbon on a little boy who held a chicken in a little straw hat.

We met Sam under a tree and told him we couldn't find Marvelle. "Never mind," he said. "Marvelle's a grown-up. She'll take care of herself." He began to help Anne set up her theater. I'm no good at put-togethers. I admired the crepe-paper Uncle Sam costume on the Wizard and the bonnet that made Me Too into Betsy Ross.

A small girl wiggling a loose tooth watched

Anne and asked: "When does it start?" Not until after the parade and the "speaking," Anne explained. I was glad there'd be plenty of time for me to look around.

Two of Revonda's cousins commandeered Sam to help put up tents for concessions. Anne was still fussing with her scenery. At last I was on my own. The sun shone, the flag whipped gaily at the top of the flagpole in front of the community center. I was supposed to keep my mind on looking for something suspicious. What? There were lots of bouncing kids in shorts and grown-ups with cameras round their necks, beginning to line Valley Road for the parade.

I found a good place to watch in front of a log house with a hedge of shaggy evergreens on one side. I love parades. At least, while I looked for some clue, I could take in this one. And here it came! First, a pickup truck with a huge hand-lettered sign on the side that said: YOUR COMMUNITY CLUB. Must be the club's officers on folding chairs in the back, including Mert. Not one of them looked like a killer. Then came the Boy Scout float. I waved to the boys who had helped Anne move her theater. Then the regional high-school band with three drum majorettes in red, white, and blue, throwing batons in the air. A very enthusiastic short, fat boy played a tuba bigger than he was. I loved the band. The volunteer firemen rode by on their spit-and-polished red truck. A little girl with a snub nose and braids rode by on a black and white horse and waved at every single person, including me. Next came a decorated tractor. Nothing at all seemed suspicious.

After a flatbed truck with a church choir singing "Nearer My God to Thee," there was Ron-the-Deputy in full uniform, riding a big chestnut horse. He waved at three kids sitting on the top of a pickup cab to see better. He waved at two older women on a porch near the road. Then he waved even harder at someone up the road in front of him. It was Anne. He grinned, and winked. Long and slow. Anne blushed.

Then everybody began to press toward the community center. No sign of Marvelle yet. What had happened to her? And I didn't see Jinx.

As I hurried on with the crowd to the patriotic program — the "speaking" — I passed the red-haired guy with the ASK WILL T-shirt, Paul's dinner-theater buddy. Same shirt he wore to the funeral. Otherwise he wasn't out of the ordinary. I told myself some clue would turn up in the community center. Ted had saved me a seat, on a front row next to a family of small girls with red, white, and blue bows in their hair. I looked around. Anne and Sam were standing in the back between a young man and woman each holding a child. There weren't any empty seats. Sam waved.

The M.C. was saying, "Before we get to the

speakin', I want to point out that this is Mary Sawyer's birthday." We all clapped, and a young girl called out: "Tomorrow is Sally Martin's."

The M.C. had a whispered conference with the three other people in chairs on the stage, and then he said: "Does anybody know where Marvelle Starr is?"

Marvelle wouldn't miss a chance to appear onstage. Any stage. That's what Revonda had said. I wished I hadn't thought of that.

The M.C. led the pledge, and we sang "The Star-Spangled Banner." I looked around at Ted when we sat down again, and he was frowning. But Ron, who sat near the door, was smooth-browed and unruffled. He lounged back in his chair with his feet crossed in front of him.

Up on the platform Sally Martin's father told how the Fourth of July was celebrated seventy-five years ago. How they had no fireworks so every family saved scraps of wool and sewed them into balls and soaked them in kerosene the night before the Fourth. They mowed the field close and lit the balls and threw the fireballs from one man to another in the dark. "You didn't get burned," he said, "if you threw them quick enough." I could imagine Sam trying fireballs. He wouldn't be afraid.

The patriotic program ended with the "Battle Hymn of the Republic." Ted and I wormed our way toward the door and so did Anne and Sam. "You haven't seen Marvelle?" I asked them.

They shook their heads, no. "I think something is wrong," I said. We all headed toward Ron, but the crowd was thick with old friends and relatives shaking hands.

Ron stopped to talk with two pretty teenaged girls. Anne had pushed ahead of us and managed to get to him and I heard her say "Marvelle Starr" and look worried and point in the direction of Marvelle's house. I pushed closer and heard him tell Anne he'd check around. Ted said he'd keep close to Ron and see what happened.

Then the loudspeaker announced Anne's puppet show, and she ran off to get it ready. I followed along. Somehow, I felt I needed to keep an eye on her. Something was out of whack on this fine sunshiny day.

Anne's set-up stage seemed great, with the kids sitting in the shade of the tree and one branch bending over the stage like part of the scenery. The kids clapped for the Wizard, dressed up like Uncle Sam, and Me Too in her Betsy Ross bonnet.

When he saw Betsy Ross's flag, the Wizard jumped so high with enthusiasm that a bit of sharp branch hidden by leaves ripped off his Uncle Sam hat and left him bald. Some of the children giggled, and a small boy on the front row screwed his face as if he was about to burst into tears.

Anne flushed. Oh, dear, she was hating herself for being accident-prone. That wouldn't help. But the Wizard seemed to think for himself. "I did that on purpose," he said, extra stern to make up for being bald. "I did that to show you who Uncle Sam really is." He stuck out his red, white, and blue chest and leaned toward the children. "Uncle Sam stands for our country, which is all of us. Me, the Wizard, who knows everything, and also you." He pointed toward a small redheaded boy, still giggling. "And even you. Every one of us is Uncle Sam ready to celebrate the Fourth of July." He sounded downright impressive. He pointed straight to a little girl with braids and a teddy-bear T-shirt. "If you were being Uncle Sam, what would you do to celebrate your country's birthday party?"

Another girl whispered in her ear. Nobody was snickering anymore. They were all waiting to hear. Anne had pulled it off. Now, *that* wasn't being disaster prone!

The girl shouted: "I'd buy cake and ice cream for every person in the whole country!"

Me Too in her Betsy Ross costume jumped right up while the kids clapped. "Me, too!" she shouted. "That won't help the national debt, but make mine chocolate chip."

I wanted to run up and congratulate Anne, but right at that moment I began to hear a buzz and then a hum and then several screams over by the community center. A wave of agitation passed through the crowd as some kind of bad news spread. Sam came hurrying over toward us, and so did the parents of the kids. The show was over.

Sam ran, pale and upset, straight to Anne. He put his arm around her. "Anne," he said. "Marvelle is dead. Ron found her dead. He sent word for us to get back to Revonda quick. First her son, now her best friend. She'll go berserk."

I broke in — I couldn't help it. "Where did he find her?"

Sam's eyes went round with horror, and this was the man who painted bodies frozen under ice! "She was upstairs in her room, sitting in front of her mirror." Sam shook his head like a dog trying to shake off water, as if he wanted to make the picture of that go away. Then he spoke very slowly. "She was in a clear plastic bag. With a spiral over the rouge on each cheek."

When we turned off the light to go to sleep that night, that picture was still in my mind: the vain woman killed in front of her mirror with a magic mark on each painted cheek. "Ted, are you awake?" I asked.

"Umm," he said sleepily.

"I need to tell you something," I said, "or I'll have nightmares all night." He turned on the light and reached over and squeezed my hand.

"The most abominable thing about the killer," I said, "is the way he designed those murders so they stick like cement in my mind. He killed those two in such a damn dramatic way that all anyone who thinks of Paul or Marvelle will ever be able to see in his mind is how they died. He's hijacked all our memories of Paul and of Marvelle, and twisted them to suit himself."

Ted came over to my side of the bed and hugged me. How else could he answer?

Chapter

18

FRIDAY, JULY 5

Pop had arranged his party for July fifth. I couldn't stop him. To get around any this-is-short-notice objections from me, or from Bessie, his housekeeper, he had Laurey's Catering provide a cold salmon with dill mayonnaise and other goodies. (We were spared Laurey's reaction to the short notice.) He had Bessie polish the silver and get out the pretty linen-lace placemats that my mother had saved for best. "Revonda will appreciate luxury," Pop said. "It will soften her up. She always means to have the best of everything." He sent me out to pick daisies for the table and do other errands. "No matter how many airs she put on, Revonda always liked daisies," he said. Boy, he seemed to have total recall! How hot had their relationship been?

Much to my amazement, Revonda accepted the invitation. Anne told me Revonda said it might cheer her up to get out of her house and see a friend from her youth. And she remembered Pop as pretty damned smart. Ted and I came to Pop's dinner on the theory that he might behave worse if we weren't there.

He had invited us for eight-thirty — or about dusk. He said women all looked better in candlelight, which pleased them and him, too. He made Bessie set candlesticks around the living room and turn off the overhead lights.

Revonda and Anne and Sam all arrived together, Sam with an arm around each. Revonda was elegant in a black cotton dress with a wide collar, and her tiger earrings. She still looked drawn, but with makeup so beautifully applied that the circles under her eyes vanished. In the candlelight she looked ten years younger. Even on Ted's face, I could see appreciation.

"You're still a damn good-looking woman." Pop grabbed her hands, and pulled her down for a kiss. They got off to such a good start I caught myself thinking: You don't suppose the old coot would get into his head to marry her at this late date? I went cold and repressed the thought.

Sam was out of his mad-scientist suit, back to T-shirt and blue jeans. Anne wore a white dress with a collar as wide as Revonda's, and a tight belt. She'd pinned a rosebud at the V of the neck. They were cheering themselves up with clothes. Or was Anne trying to make sure Tiger

167

Woman didn't upstage her? Anne kept darting adoring looks at Sam. He winked back. What with Pop's glowing glances at Revonda we sure did prove that life goes on, even after horror.

First, we all sat around Pop's favorite table and had drinks and some wonderful hors d'oeuvres made with caviar and whipped cream cheese.

"Even at such a terrible time, it's good to see an old friend," Pop said, raising his glass of Scotch in a toast to Revonda, who was sitting on his right. "There's one kind of black magic I always approve," he said, "and that's the glamour of beautiful women." He nodded at Anne, who sat on his other side, and again at Revonda.

Gallantry did not extend to his own daughter. And each of the other two stiffened slightly. If Pop mainly wanted to talk about magic, as in doing in Paul, why should they want even a hint attributed to them? But Pop didn't notice.

"It's so good to see you again, Harwood." Revonda put on her Southern Lady manners. "And your clever mind will be an addition to our efforts to find the truth." Ha. We'd see. "The horror of my Paul's death has now been compounded by a second tragic death." She stopped, swallowed, squared her shoulders, and went on. "I'm sure Peaches has told you that the woman we call Knowing Agnes mentioned evil magic when she made that scene after the memorial service. She repeats what people in the valley say. The killer could be some religious fanatic who believes that magic is a sin that has to be punished. My poor friend Marvelle seems to have been killed in a way that highlights her sin — her vanity."

"The same magical symbols that were on Paul's hands and forehead — if that's what those whorls were — were painted on Marvelle's cheeks," Ted pointed out. Nobody commented on that.

"I have called you all here together," Pop said, leaning back grandly in his wheelchair, "to discuss the suspects in these two tragic murders, and the way each suspect may have been involved with magic in an evil way." He stretched out the word "evil" with great relish. "I have asked Ted, who is very good at that sort of thing, to draw us up a list of suspects, their opportunity, and their attitude toward magic. I believe that is the key element here." He leaned back happily in his wheelchair, overjoyed to preside. He paused and looked each of us in the eye. "I am counting on you," he said, "to come up with new information about these people."

"I have made it my business," Ted said, "in the spare time I could save from teaching and correcting all those papers, to talk to the people who might be suspects and find out where they were when."

Sam leaned back and crossed his legs, seeming ready to enjoy a game. Revonda sat straight, ready to pounce. I tried not to look skeptical. Pop loves this suspect-brainstorming business. He's done it before but never discovered a killer that way. Anne glanced around nervously. "Do we have to accuse each other?"

"If any of you knows things about yourselves that the rest of us haven't guessed, I expect you to confess right away," Pop announced pompously. "We all have guilty secrets." Nobody volunteered to confess first, including Pop.

"I've put the names alphabetically," Ted said, "which means that if you go by Peaches' writing name and call her Peaches Dann, instead of Peaches Holleran, she comes first. I come next. For motive, I guess we could be protecting Anne and Sam if we thought they were guilty. Actually, I've been too busy with summer school to murder anybody."

"You're wrong about that list," Revonda said. "Henderson comes before Holleran. Harley Henderson should come first in more ways than one. I think he's mixed up in drugs, and Paul and Marvelle somehow caught on and showed it. I bet you won't be able to pin down where he was at the time of either murder."

"He managed to be vague," Ted admitted. "We're near Asheville, which is a resort. Resorts tend to attract drug traffic. Several people told me Marvelle was a member of Narcotics Anonymous. So suppose she backslid? This could somehow be drug-related."

"Harley believes in money and in power," Revonda said. "And if you don't think that can be just as destructive as believing in devils, you're a damn fool," she said to Pop. "Put our sheriff on the list, Ted. Right at the top."

Ted pointed to the list, "The Justices are next."

"Ruth would lie for Jeeter in a heartbeat," Revonda said. "And I bet his brother Buck would, too. So who cares if they said they were together when Paul was killed. And Jeeter only has his wife to alibi him on the Fourth of July. And he gets violent if he doesn't take his pills."

Everybody nodded. Our jury wanted Jeeter to be guilty.

"And hell hath no fury like a woman scorned," Revonda quoted. "Paul treated Jinx with scorn. He told me he also let that girl look at his magic books."

"She has no alibi for either death," Ted said. He put her near the top of his list.

"Reverend Phillipson is crazy," Revonda said. "Balmy since his wife died. Maybe he's so bound to see nothing but good that his dark side breaks loose and kills. He could have copied the marks from that thing Paul wore for good luck." She sipped her Scotch complacently. "And another good suspect is Mert's grandson Billy. He was one of those kids mixed up with that cult in the high school." Vaguely I remembered news stories of something of the sort. The kids actually stole and slaughtered a goat in some kind of ritual.

"Mert's grandson was involved?" Anne made a rejecting mouth as if she couldn't bear that.

"Of course, you two know that your closeness to the crime puts you under suspicion," Ted said to Anne and Sam. "Anne has alibis, Sam doesn't. He was seen on the Fourth, but not all morning, at least not so anyone can pinpoint exactly when and where."

"I was wandering around," Sam said. "I should have stuck with a witness."

"And just to be thorough, we have to talk about you, Revonda," Ted said. "You were with Peaches and Anne and then Marvelle when Paul died, and Cousin Edna was with you when someone killed Marvelle. Right?"

She agreed.

"It's time for us to eat dinner," I said. They nodded. Ted rolled Pop into the dining room, and we all sat down around the oval mahogany table. On one side of the room my mother's silver service on the sideboard shone, reflecting the candle flames and bits of us. On the other side of the room the windows with the light fading fast behind them turned into dark mirrors, flickering with candlelight. And I remembered something from Paul's magic stuff that I'd rather forget. That's the trouble with a bad memory. You can't count on it. Sometimes it works, even when you wish it wouldn't.

Somewhere in those copies of pages from Paul's books I'd seen one that said that of four men who set out to become magi, one would become an adept and three would go mad. That was the sort of quote that Pop would have loved.

I was not about to tell him. Did Paul think he was an adept? Did he think he could use herbs and symbols, for example, to make magic work? And if he did, how did that cause his death? Did he go mad? And how on earth did Marvelle fit in? I suddenly felt nostalgic for plain old uncomplicated murder.

Chapter

19

SATURDAY MORNING, JULY 6

In the morning Anne called at six-thirty. She knew I was an early riser. "I got up to pick raspberries," she said in a surprised voice. "For breakfast." Pause. "I didn't sleep well. And when I went out, there was a snake." Amazed voice: "I saw a dark something on Revonda's porch steps and it was a dead snake." She was breathing hard. "Sam says it's a copperhead, coiled up — just like . . ." She sounded on the edge of hysteria. I might have been, too. I don't care for snakes.

"Ron is here," Anne said, calmer now. I heard Sam make some remark in the background, but I couldn't catch it, as she continued, "Ron says whoever it was probably walked on the gravel drive and didn't even leave footprints. He's still looking and another deputy is here, too."

"I'll come right over," I said. Ted was swamped with summer-school preparations for second session, and he'd been up working late after Pop's party. He's a night person. I left him a note and set forth.

When I got to Revonda's house, I found her and Sam and Anne peering from the end of the porch while a photographer recorded the snake, artfully coiled to look like one of the spirals that someone marked on Paul and Marvelle. Ugly.

The picture-taking ended. We talked about how strange it was that neither Sam nor Anne nor Revonda heard a thing, and that the dogs hadn't barked. Just as they hadn't barked when Paul met his end.

"We'll go pick some raspberries now," Sam told Revonda. "After this we need a super-breakfast to give us strength." He had some small red buckets in his hand. I almost laughed. Sam had such a way of finding some sunshine even in the midst of horror. Anne held his hand tight. Subdued.

He led us to the raspberries in back of Revonda's house, near the mountainside. They grew in a row at one end of the garden. On one side light green lettuce, dark green New Zealand spinach with pointy leaves, and young beets. On the other a mowed place back to a patch of weeds and wildflowers and a barbed-wire fence and, beyond that, somebody's cow. The cow gazed at us peacefully, as if everything was right with the world. Ha! But the garden was a balm to our snake jitters. It smelled of turned earth still wet with dew.

"A raspberry is about my favorite thing," Anne said. I could see she was trying to convince Sam that she felt better. Her hand hardly shook as she plunked a berry in her mouth. Behind her the sun was shining up over the blue-green mountain, but we were still in shadow. Flatlanders find that strange, that west-side-of-the-mountain people have a sunless morning time.

"My grandmother had raspberries when I was a kid," Anne said. "She'd let me eat nothing but raspberries and vanilla ice cream for a whole lunch!" She managed to smile up at Sam, who beamed back.

In the distance birds tweeted, probably wanting us to go away so they could eat the berries. I watched around me like a hawk. I happen to know that snakes love berries, too.

"Raspberries are like skyrockets," Sam was saying. "I love that flavor-burst."

A young voice said, "They weren't pruned right!"

I turned around quick, amazed somebody got so close and we didn't hear him come. A boy about fifteen or sixteen with wild black hair and a mocking smile stood by the berry row holding a white plastic bucket and wearing dark glasses. And this was 7:30 in the morning with no sun. "Mrs. Roland told my grandmother we could pick," he said. "I'm Billy Holt. You know my grandma."

I had a feeling I'd seen him somewhere, but the glasses threw me off.

"Mert Williams," Sam guessed. "Our favorite person. She has a lot of grandsons."

Silly Billy, I thought. He was all earnestness and elbows and feet and foolish sunshades.

Sam was looking the kid over. "I wasn't here to prune these raspberry bushes. Somebody did that last fall. How do you know they weren't pruned right?"

Silly Billy adjusted his dark glasses, threw a berry in the air, and caught it in his mouth before he answered: "I read a lot. I watch a lot. I see a lot. Do you know I found these dark glasses right by the road in the grass? Glasses make people look smart. My grandmother says you paint pictures." He was what *my* grandmother called "fresh as paint."

"And you don't stake your tomatoes right," the kid said. "You have to prune them if you want them to be big."

Sam kept plopping berries in his pail. "I pruned some tomato plants and I didn't prune some. I don't believe in doing things 'right.' I don't believe in doing them all the same way. That's boring."

The kid stopped picking and just stared at Sam. "Say," he said, "that's kind of interesting. Do people think you're crazy?"

Sam said, "I can't worry about that or I'd be a lousy artist."

"I draw sometimes." Billy wiped his mouth

with the back of his hand. He seemed to be a free spirit, yet he seemed nervous. When his hands weren't busy, he clenched them and unclenched them by his sides. Like a scared grown-up instead of a happy kid.

Something was familiar about him. Something about his general shape. "Turn around," I said. "Let me see all sides of you."

He made a surprised mouth, but he turned obligingly. A willowy kid. Where did that supple form fit? In some recent scene. At the Fourth of July? No. Before that. It'll come to me, I thought hopefully. If I don't force it.

And then I knew. He was the kid I'd seen from Revonda's bathroom window. The one with the black hair that I saw walking across the yard the day we found Paul dead. I'd forgotten all about it. I mean, it was before we found the body, and therefore so ordinary to see a kid pass by, it went right out of my head. So, of course, I hadn't told a soul.

"I like you, Billy," I said. "But I have to tell you that I saw you in this yard the day Paul Roland died. Does the sheriff know?"

"Oh, that wasn't me." I bet that his eyes were wide with fear if I could have seen them behind the dark glasses. He took a deep breath. "Listen," he said, "please don't tell the sheriff what you told me. It's not true. But I can't prove it. I got in some trouble last year. He won't believe me." He took his dark glasses off and looked me straight in the eye. He knew the value of eye contact.

"What kind of trouble?" I asked.

He squirmed. "They thought I was one of a group of kids in some kind of cult thing, some crazy kids that stole a goat. I wasn't. Somebody must be a ringer for me." His whole body leaned toward me, pleading to be believed.

Oh, boy, he was *that* grandson.

"Listen," he said. "You're trying to help Mrs. Roland find out what happened, aren't you? Because she thinks the sheriff is dumb. Well, the sheriff *is* dumb. I hear things. I can tell you things that will maybe help."

"Like what?" Sam asked. Big smile, sparkling eyes. His eyes said he expected the best of Billy. He expected wonders.

"I'll find things." The kid turned to Sam. "I will. I'll be your spy." He grinned, to show he enjoyed that idea.

"O.K.," Sam said right off, "we'll take you up on that."

Anne looked surprised but didn't say a word.

Why was it up to Sam to speak for us all? Except that it took nerve. Sam had nerve, all right. Why did I accept his agreement with the kid and not object? Partly, I think, because I liked the boy. And partly because I'm so bad with forms and faces. I thought he was the kid I'd seen. But I couldn't for the life of me be absolutely sure.

Finally we left Billy picking. We nodded at a deputy still looking around outside, then went in to have breakfast with Revonda in her country kitchen, where the canisters with the herbs painted on them were in an exact line and the copper molds over the fireplace hung exactly straight. We had waffles and raspberries and whipped cream and sourwood honey. Sam fixed the waffles. Because we needed them, he said.

Revonda agreed there was no point in telling the sheriff about the kid, at least until we were sure he was the one. "And maybe we could spy on him while he is off guard pretending to spy for us." She arched an eyebrow. "Mert didn't tell any of you about Billy's trouble, did she? She could never believe one bad thing about that child. She protects him. His father drinks. You can't trust Billy for a minute," she said. "If your father drinks, you learn how to keep secrets, which means telling lies. Billy's father could drink God under the table. Only worse father I know is Jinx's father, that crazy Jeeter."

"I never saw Jinx at the Fourth of July," I said, startled. In fact so much had happened that Jinx had gone right out of my head. Poof! Not a good omission. Obviously my next step should be to go and talk to Paul's girl Jinx. I looked at my watch. Nine o'clock. "And this is as good a time as any to go talk to her. I'll call to be sure she's there."

Revonda laughed. "That girl doesn't have a phone." She drew me a map of how to get to Jinx's cabin. She said Paul's white four-wheel-drive pickup truck would be better on the back roads than my car, so please use it.

I didn't like the idea of riding to Jinx's in the very truck Paul drove just before he died. Jinx must have sat in the seat of that truck beside him. But Revonda insisted, and some of our back roads are a hazard, with sharp grades and deep ruts. Sam offered to go with me, but I was sure that Jinx would be more open with me alone.

"Take a dog," Anne said. "Baskerville is friendly. You'll feel safer."

I did not look forward to asking Jinx the question Revonda had demanded I ask: Was Jinx involved in a cult where they had sex with the devil? Now, how on earth can you ask that politely? Revonda always seemed to suspect the worst and the most dramatic thing.

I certainly wanted to know why Paul's sad-eyed girl had seemed so determined at Paul's funeral to find a chance to talk to me in private. I wished I hadn't waited so long to track her down. Because now, since Marvelle's murder, everything seemed out of control. Anne or Sam or Revonda could be next.

Chapter

20

LATER SATURDAY

As I drove along, the big black rottweiler named Baskerville sat right beside me on the front seat of Paul's truck. A cheerful dog, she seemed to grin. I followed Revonda's map with only one wrong turn, and that was fortunately into a short dead end, so I didn't stay lost.

Jinx, in a neon-orange shirt, was out in her garden next to a little tin-roofed cabin, picking lettuce. Nice garden: in neat hoed rows like a picture in a book I had as a kid. When Jinx saw Paul's pickup in her driveway, she froze. She'd probably never seen it there before except when it brought Paul. Sorry.

I parked under a huge old weeping willow with a gnarled trunk, and Jinx came and met me at the truck, quiet as snow. Baskerville didn't even bark to announce her.

"I'm glad to see you," she said, "though I've got a modeling job in a little bit, so I can't talk long." She had a classic oval Madonna's face and a strange air of seeming dirty when she was plainly clean. Even her hands were clean when she'd just picked lettuce. And why on earth, I wondered, did she choose to wear a bright orange T-shirt with PIKE'S PEAK OR BUST stretched across her breasts, and sexy tight jeans? She led me into the cabin, pointed to a neat cot with a faded flowered spread, and said: "Please sit a while." No place for that but on her bed, where a large black cat was already curled up. A round low table scattered with a few magazines stood in front of the bed.

Jinx put her heads of lettuce in an old white-enamel sink in one corner of that shadowy room. She sat down on the bed to one side of the table. I lowered myself down on the other side, and the bedsprings pinged with our weight so loud the cat jumped off. Those bedsprings must have pinged for Paul, only louder and in more intimate moments. Do bedsprings remember?

"Thanks for coming," she said. "You're trying to figure who killed Paul, aren't you?" She reached smooth childlike hands across the table, between the piles of *True Love* magazines, and picked up a pack of cigarettes and a box of kitchen matches. She kept her eyes on her hands, as she lit up. "Sam told me that you and he and Anne think the spirals on the bodies" — she paused and squeezed her eyes tight —

"must be important."

I did not tell her about the real snake arranged in a spiral at Revonda's. I wanted her story first. "When did you talk to Sam?"

"In the grocery store. He said he was looking for a model." Her voice was hollow, as if she wanted to swallow her words. She looked up straight into my eyes. "I model naked. My father thinks I'll go to hell for that." She threw her head back defiantly. "And if I'm going to hell anyway, it doesn't matter what else I do, does it?"

"Whatever happens to you matters," I said.

"I don't guess Paul thought much of me."

I was annoyed. She had such an I'd-like-to-give-up tone in her voice, a part of me wanted to shake her. But this gal had reason to feel rotten. "Perhaps you know," I said, "that people say Paul was cruel to you." She flinched. Then she flushed. "Men treat me like that." Suddenly her soft voice rose and grated with anger, and I realized I had felt that anger all along. Right under that I-won't-hit-back-if-you-hit-me big green-eyed look. She dragged hard on her cigarette, drank in the smoke, and blew it out toward me. "I've cared for three men. It's always like that. They treat me bad. My father says it's a punishment from God. O.K., sometimes Paul hit me, but that was because he'd been drinking whiskey. He said I chased him. He said I was a slut."

Of course she was angry. Angry enough to

kill? Would she have been physically strong enough to do it?

"I don't think you're a slut." Even in the orange T-shirt. Even with the pout. That wasn't what bothered me.

"But when I stayed away, Paul came and looked for me. He did. And I loved him. Sometimes I think the more he was mean to me, the more I loved him. Does that make sense? Sometimes he'd come and talk to me because I'd listen even to crazy stuff about how people could make things happen by drawing pictures and saying words. I felt like he needed me whether he knew it or not. Do you understand?"

"Not exactly," I said, "but I'm trying. I know you're a person who likes to help. You wanted to tell me something that could help us find out what happened to Paul, Jinx. Isn't that right?"

She pulled a tissue out of her pocket and blew her nose. She reached for something on the table. "The day of Paul's memorial service, I found this." She sighed. "He left it. I guess I put some magazines on top. Later I found it." She held out a floppy green paperback book the shape of a magazine. "It's about spirals."

My eyes had become used to the dim light. Even the cover of that book got to me. Pictures of the wind whirling in spirals around an Asian man. Some of the wind spirals had the heads of animals attached to them, a horse, a fish, an alligator, a giraffe. The man held his hands up together as if he was praying to the sky. The title was *The Mystic Spiral: Journey of the Soul.* How did that relate to murder?

I opened the book to see words underlined in red ink. About how a spiral tendency within each person is the longing for and a growth toward wholeness. *Wholeness?* I turned the pages. Was it Paul who'd underlined a lot of high-sounding stuff? How everything whole goes through cycles. How it starts from a point, expands, and differentiates. Was a spiral supposed to be a picture of that? Each thing contracts and disappears into the point again. That was the pattern of our lives, the underlined part said, and maybe the pattern of the universe.

"Did Paul tell you why he wanted you to look at this book?" I asked Jinx, totally puzzled.

"He said he'd not been nice to me. He actually said that. And this book might teach us how to talk. I thought he was making fun of me. But maybe not. He'd been drinking. But I was so hopeful. And then, the next day . . ." She began to cry.

I patted her hand, but I went on turning the pages. There was stuff underlined about the cycles of the moon and about whirlpools in water and much more. There were pictures of an Egyptian Pharaoh with snakes on his war helmet. *Snakes.* There was a painting by Botticelli that looked like a funnel made of stone walls and was called a spiral cross-section of the pit of hell. Good grief. A Navaho sand-painting of coiled snakes was called a mandala for

186

healing. *Healing!* And what did all this have to do with Paul's death? With spirals painted on him? And with spirals on Marvelle? How about the coiled dead snake today? My head felt like there was a whirlpool inside.

"Paul was more complicated than I thought," I said, and Jinx smiled as if I'd given her a compliment. "May I borrow this book?" I asked. She nodded yes, and I put it in my trusty pocketbook that always hangs over my shoulder.

"There's still danger," she blurted out.

"How do you know?"

She stayed Madonna-calm. "I get feelings. I knew Paul was in danger. I tried to tell him." Such a minor tone of voice, like a sad song. She held the cigarette tight between her fingers as if it were a lifeline.

A shiver waved through me. I knew she meant something more by "feelings" than just sad or happy. "You had no reason but a *feeling* to believe Paul was in danger?"

Jinx had shut her eyes. "Marvelle, too." She blew out smoke, then took a deep breath and the PIKE'S PEAK OR BUST on her orange T-shirt rose an inch. "We're still in danger. Anne and I and Revonda."

Oh, brother!

Paul's dead image came back to me, shimmering in plastic. Then Marvelle's. I could imagine Jinx's orange T-shirt glimmering through a plastic bag. Not a pretty thought.

"Why?" I asked.

Jinx opened her eyes wide. "Paul and Marvelle were like Anne and Revonda and me. We have trouble."

"You mean you *attract* trouble?" I could see Jinx would do that with her T-shirt and no bra, and that don't-hit-me-again-unless-you-really-want-to manner and that give-up voice.

"Like I said, my father thinks I'll go to hell for posing without clothes on. That's got something to do with the danger. I don't know what. He thinks a lot of people will go to hell."

Guilt. I thought. Is that what those people "in danger" have in common? Does trouble smart-bomb its way to the people who feel like they deserve it? Jinx's father was obviously in favor of that idea.

She got up. "I have to go."

"Before you go, I need to ask you some hard questions," I said. "Were you or Paul ever part of a group that . . ." I groped for a tactful way to go on.

"Oh, you've heard that," she said sadly. "That I belong to a cult and we sleep with the devil! It's not true, but I've had letters accusing me of that!"

"Where? Exactly what did they say?"

"I burned them," she whispered. "What would you do?"

Not destroy evidence, I hoped. "And Paul . . . ?"

"Hated to join things," she said defiantly. "He never even belonged to a Boy Scout troop when he was a kid."

"Do you believe Paul was mixed up with a Satanic cult?"

Her eyes widened. I thought: She's scared.

"No." She raised her voice. "I don't care what people say, he wasn't. He tried to talk the kids out of it."

"He . . . What kids?"

"Some of the high school kids. I don't know which. They came and asked to look at his books. They said the devil was the one with power and they wanted power. He told them they thought they were playing a game, but it wasn't a game. They could hurt themselves." Now she was eager. Willing to be late to model. Wanting me to approve of Paul, who had sneered at her.

"Was one of the kids Mert's grandson?"

She shook her head. "Paul wouldn't tell who."

"Do you think Satanism has anything to do with why people are in danger?"

"I don't know."

I was annoyed at her again, which made no sense. Her tone of voice was not going to hurt me. But I didn't like it.

She got the lettuce from the sink and put it in a plastic bag. Semitranslucent. Not thin and clingy like dry-cleaning bags. But I wished it wasn't here.

"I have to go," she said. She picked up a second bag. "I need this job. So I can eat."

I jumped up and followed.

She stood still in the doorway. "I haven't got

189

an alibi. When Paul died, I was here alone. When Marvelle died, I was here alone with the flu." Jinx stood as still as a scared cat. Just three feet away.

I walked toward her, and she backed up. Backed right out the door into her garden. I followed.

"When was the last time you saw Paul?"

"Right here the night before — whatever."

I looked beyond her toward the growing things. There was a row of dill. Still young and short but plainly dill. I went over and picked a piece and felt the feathery leaves in my fingers. I crushed it and smelled the sour.

"There was dill with Paul when he died," I said.

Jinx swallowed and said, "There was dill and another herb Ron said was called verbena." Her voice shook. "Ron went to see my mother. My mother knows a lot about herbs. About the old-timey way with herbs. But I stay away from home. I upset my folks."

"Could I go see your mother?"

"Well, sure," Jinx said. "Go when my father isn't there. You can never tell what he'll do. Sometimes he pretends to take his pills and doesn't. He can get rough." She frowned as if the sun was in her eyes. But the sun was behind her.

"On Monday mornings at about eleven-thirty a friend comes and takes Pa to Bible study and lunch in town. He'll not get back till one or one-thirty. So go see Ma on Monday."

She stopped near an orange lily, reached into the second plastic bag, and pulled out a pair of dark glasses. "Just my things to model in. I'm doing a beach scene. I have a bikini in here." She put the dark glasses on.

They changed her face completely. I almost gasped. With the don't-hit-me eyes covered, she became sophisticated. Her shining red hair was a glory. Her Pike's Peak shirt was witty. Her faded jeans "in".

"I'm late." She ran off to her old pickup. There was room on the grass for her to drive around my truck. She waved and was gone.

Chapter

21

Immediately Afterward

I backed out of Jinx's driveway pondering, first about spirals. And they made me think about Jinx and how she probably *did* tell me more because I'm a good listener. Revonda was right about that. Of course Revonda didn't know I'd written a whole chapter on *What to Do If You Can't Remember What to Say* in my *How to Survive Without a Memory*. You've guessed the answer. I wrote about all the useful flavors of listening including *I understand* (as with Jinx). That answer only works if you've had troubles, but, by my age, who hasn't? And then there's *You're fascinating,* which is not hypocritical like it sounds if you get the person on his best subject. The trick is to discover that subject. Works even on difficult types like *The Detail Addict* who interrupts anything you say to demand names and dates, which then go right out of my mind. Or *The Tunnel Vision* who acts like you are an idiot unless you know everything about his special field. Get those folks to declaiming their own subject quick, and they won't put you down. Except for hard-nut cases like Sheriff Harley Henderson.

Now, I know better than to drive and ponder at the same time, especially on an unfamiliar back road. I have a strong warning about that in my *How to Survive Without a Memory.* But sometimes my pondering just creeps up on me, and by the time I catch on, I'm already lost. I realized that had happened. Very annoying.

I was lost, but not alone. I reached over and patted Baskerville. She was breathing through her mouth, pink tongue lolling out. I noticed how big and powerful her teeth were. But what I evidently needed was a cross between a seeing-eye dog and a homing pigeon, and even that might not help unless the dog was driving the car.

The road had been gravel, but now it was dirt, and always curvy. At the side of the road, young trees were close together. When the dirt track branched, I took what I thought was the best fork and jounced on worse ruts. "Some of the back roads are just logging roads," Revonda had told me. And the narrow track was edged by chunky gray rocks. Not turn-around country. Finally I found a wide, weedy space at the edge of the ruts. The grass and weeds weren't deep enough to bog the track down. That's what I figured. So I backed around. Slowly. But not slowly enough. Baskerville began to bark at a brown-and-white spotted hound on the side of the road. That distracted me.

Suddenly, *bam!* The back wheels went into a gulch. The weeds had hidden it, but, boy, I felt it. The front end of the truck rose, and the back banged, and the back wheels spun in the air. My heart began to bang, too. I was lost, and the truck was stuck in a hole.

I tried to go forward. I tried rocking the truck, going forward and quickly backward and forward again. No luck. I got out and tried to push. The spotted hound sat back in the grass and watched with interest. Baskerville kept barking to get out. The truck wouldn't move.

I let Baskerville out on her leash. The spotted hound came over and wagged his tail. A dog must mean a house nearby. The hound trotted off down a path. Baskerville tugged to follow. I locked the truck, and we ran after the dog.

He stopped once and looked back and wagged his tail, but after that he was not about to slow down. I had to scramble to keep him in sight, even if tree branches caught at me. The path was worn underfoot, but wet branches and briers leaned across it. Plainly we were following an animal trail, faintly marking the shortest way. We kept climbing up one bank and down another. With Baskerville tugging, I almost fell. I let her off her leash, rolled it up and put it in my pocket. We ran up banks of green ferns that smelled spicy when I stepped on them, then down into flat patches of wildflowers. I tried to keep my mind on flowers. That's what Sam would have done. Looked at the beauty. A branch tore my skirt. Another slapped my face. A root almost tripped me. Now how on earth did I get myself into this?

I was following the dog, but I didn't know where I was, did I? We ran over dead leaves, so deep under the trees that no wildflowers poked through. I couldn't see the faint trail at all anymore. I couldn't see a path in any direction. If Baskerville and I didn't keep up with the other dog, we were just plain nowhere.

My grandma warned me about that when I was small. About how if you didn't know how to find your way in the woods, you could wander in a circle for days and starve to death. I tried to remember what she told me. She survived the Great Depression by gathering black cohosh and ginseng in the woods. Grandma said old-timers took a dog to smell out snakes. I wished I hadn't thought of snakes. Well, I had two dogs. Herb gatherers took a gun in case they met a bear. Suppose I met a bear? I stumbled over a fallen branch, but caught myself.

I was out of breath. When I was small, Grandma impressed those lessons on me over and over. Old-timers knew not to wear perfume, not even scent from soap, or the bugs would think you smelled like flowers and bite you.

Bugs were biting me.

The dog who was leading us began to trot faster. I hurried down one side of a gully and back up the other side with my feet slipping and the loose rocks rocketing behind me. And just over a small rise, I found a brook, curling dark around smooth stones and foaming over small waterfalls. "Follow a brook downhill and after a while you'll probably come to a road." Grandma had said that. God bless her.

The dogs came running back and stood with their feet in the brook and drank. Then they raced ahead and vanished. I hadn't followed the brook far when the trees began to thin, and I saw a clearing.

There, in the distance, a good-sized cabin sat in the middle of young corn. This was a fairly prosperous farm, with a big barn and a small shed. Long light-green swords of leaves in the sun. Rows and rows. I felt like crying again. For joy. And I told myself: So I get lost. But I make discoveries being lost. I meet nice people. Think positive.

But this was not a well-kept farm. As I got closer, I saw the corn was full of weeds. The rows were all full of the same weed. Then I recognized the thin leaves. Marijuana.

A man in a red plaid shirt stepped out the door of the house, holding a rifle. At least he didn't point it at me. Think positive.

A dog barked fiercely by his side, a powerful dog with the broad face and shoulders of a pit bull. Pit bulls can kill, quicker than snakes. Baskerville came running to my side again and began to growl. The man let his rifle dangle in one hand, but with the other he raised a set of black binoculars. The lenses glittered in the sun. Pointed at me.

Baskerville and the pit bull both began to bark furiously. I wanted protection, but I sure didn't want a dog fight. I ran back into the woods, calling Baskerville. She followed and we ran so fast the trees, the briers, everything melted before us. I don't know how far I ran. But finally I was so out of breath I stopped. I sat down on a rock, panting. Had I circled around to the same place? Suppose I was lost until after dark?

But no. This was not the same. Near my feet I saw a clearly marked path. A human path? And, amazingly, I was still near the brook. Or another brook. Water was what I needed. I itched and stung. I splashed water on my face and my arms and my legs.

The spotted dog had vanished, I wasn't sure when. But now the path was clear and well worn.

Just as well, since my guiding brook turned an almost right angle and then went into such a thicket of rhododendron I could never have followed it. But my luck seemed to have changed. I came out onto a hillside that overlooked a distant curve of asphalt road. A road! I thought: I'm going to be safe! Finally I came to another clearing, just below me. And there sat a small cabin, not any bigger than Jinx's, with a rusty tin roof. Nothing grew around it except in flower beds near the house. Oh, there was a small square garden on one side that looked like it might have a few tomato plants and some greens. But certainly no place for commercial marijuana.

Two cars were parked in the yard, one old and battered, the other fairly new. I approached the cabin quietly, looking around. Once stung is twice cautious. Nothing bloomed in the flower beds, but plants in different shades of green which had interesting shapes to the leaves. Herbs? I picked a small saw-tooth fuzzy leaf and squeezed it. A pungent lemony smell was so sharp I was startled. There were bits of herb with Paul's body. Not this kind, though.

The cabin was made of logs and weathered wood siding and settled into the earth whopper-jawed. Mint grew by the sagging wooden steps to a small porch. The grass was clipped neatly. I felt there was someone in that cabin I'd like, but I might not have had the nerve to knock if Baskerville hadn't run over to the porch steps. I hurried after her to snap on her leash. I was just leaning over, patting Baskerville and smelling the mint and deciding whether to go up on the porch when I heard the cabin door squeak open.

I looked up quickly and there was a rifle pointed at me. I looked into the glittery eyes of an old man in a battered black felt hat. He said, "I know who you are, girl. You're one of the devil's own."

Chapter

22

SATURDAY AFTERNOON

The gray man stood at the top of the gray porch steps, pointing a long gun right at my head. He had a face like a stone cliff — gray like stone, rugged like a cliff, impassive like a cliff — with a small wary mouth and glittering blue eyes. "You mean to help that snake-temptress," he said. "I've heard about you." A small fuzzy dog yapped beside him.

Baskerville growled. The gun wobbled. The dog kept yapping. I pulled Baskerville close to my heels.

"Revonda Roland tempts young people to the ways of the world as bad as the snake in the garden tempted Adam." His voice boomed out over the barking like a radio preacher's.

The porch door squeaked behind him. A faded older woman came out. "Be quiet," she said to the fuzzy dog, and the dog obeyed. "Jeeter," she said in a tired voice, "here's your pill."

Jeeter! Jinx's father was called Jeeter. He did violent things when he didn't take his pill. I had blundered into him! And suddenly I found myself half-believing that bad-luck stuff — that I was drawn here somehow. Oh, come on!

The faded woman held out a glass of water in one hand and a pill in the other. "You promised," she said. "I know you're a man of your word."

He kept those glittering eyes on me. His radio voice boomed on. "She came creeping, spying. She is from that house of iniquity. Where the devil painted snakes on Paul Roland's hands and feet and forehead, and then stole away his soul."

Did this man paint "snakes" on bodies? He had alibis for the times when Paul and Marvelle died, but just from relatives.

If Jeeter's finger slipped on the trigger, I'd be dead.

"I'm lost." I said it to the woman. She apparently wasn't crazy.

"Jeeter," said the woman, "your brother Buck came to encourage you to take your pills so you can stay with us. We need you."

He kept those glittering eyes on me, but he did lower the gun and reach over and hold his free hand out for the pill. He popped it in his mouth, and then he took the glass of water from the woman, drank the whole thing, and handed the empty glass back. The pill did not stop his words. "We do not know in what form the devil came to Paul Roland, but we do know he will come again to snatch the ungodly."

"Won't you come in? Won't you have a cup of coffee?" The woman said that like I was a neighbor just dropping by for a visit. "I'm Ruth. We're having a bad day today." *Ruth* told the *truth, forsooth.* I certainly knew about bad days, being related to Pop!

Jeeter said, "You come with me. I want to ask you questions." He lifted the rifle again. If the pill was to make him calm, it hadn't worked yet. "Tie the dog to the porch rail," he commanded.

I don't argue with a gun. I tied Baskerville and said, "Sit and stay." She whimpered, but she did it.

Ruth (for *soothe*) politely held the squeaky screen door open for me. I went inside, with Jeeter still pointing the gun at my head.

The light inside was dim, and I almost tripped over a slat basket full of vegetables. "Keep walking!" Jeeter shouted. The basket was at the feet of a man in a rocking chair. He just sat there and looked surprised when I grabbed the arm of his rocker to keep from falling. But not as surprised as I'd be if I saw my brother pointing a gun at a woman.

"Sit there." Jeeter pointed to a chair right across a low table. He sat down on the other side of the table. Jeeter and the other man and

201

me around the table, with one seat left for Ruth, who must be Jeeter's wife (and, presumably, Jinx's mother). Jeeter put his gun down on the table between us. It was in quick-grabbing reach if he took the notion, but at least he couldn't slip and shoot me by mistake.

My eyes began to get used to the dim light. I might learn something useful, right? I tried to keep my mind on that.

The man, who I figured must have been Jeeter's brother Buck, had on a red-checked shirt. Exactly like the red-checked shirt on the man with the binoculars in the marijuana field. He had the same brown hair. I hadn't seen the face well. My heart was pounding as if it knew. But I told myself it couldn't be the same man. That would be too much of a coincidence. There are lots of red-checked shirts.

Jeeter stared at me, but he didn't *do* anything. My eyes took in the room. Spartan. The lightbulb in the ceiling was bare. Almost the only decoration in the room was a bland picture of Jesus, in a white robe, that hung in back of Jeeter as if looking over his shoulder. An old leather-bound family Bible sat on the table by the gun, the same color as the gun handle. Like they were a set. I prayed Jeeter would remember what was in that Bible, about love thy neighbor and especially the thou-shalt-not-kill part.

Red-Checked-Shirt sat at right angles to Jeeter. Behind him was an unpainted wood bookshelf with all sorts of small china animals on the top shelf. Cutesy, not realistic. Mrs. Jeeter's only frivolity? On the next shelf down were books. *Culpeper's Herbal, Goldenseal, Etc., Wild Herbs of the South*, and such. Well-worn.

And, I thought, Ruth-for-Soothe was the one I needed to talk to about herbs. But Jinx had said her mother wouldn't say much in front of her father.

Buck had narrow eyes, like he was used to looking into the sun, and a broad mouth. "Jeeter," he said, "that's a new gun, isn't it? Nice looking, like it'll shoot sweet." He leaned over very slowly and picked it up. He stared through the sight out the window. "I just shot a copperhead," he said. "You and I always was good shots, Jeeter. I hit that snake right in the head."

Was he deliberately getting that gun farther from Jeeter? Was he my friend? Or was he the man who stood in the marijuana field and watched me through binoculars? Did he know my face?

"We have a lot of snakes in these mountains." Buck turned to me. "You get lost, you'll find you a snake by mistake. It's not a good thing to get lost." Was that a threat?

Mrs. Jeeter was handing me a cup of coffee. "I'm out of milk," she said. "Have some sugar." She held out a pretty flowered sugar bowl that glowed white in that unpainted room.

"You're only safe in these mountains if you know what to do about snakes," Buck told me. There was something about his narrow eyes that made everything he said seem like he meant it two ways. If I could snitch on marijuana, was I a snake?

I sipped my sweet coffee. I don't usually take sugar, but after my run through the woods and the shock of Jeeter, I needed fuel.

"We have all kinds of snakes around here," Jeeter said. He seemed to be relaxing some. Buck was putting the gun back down on the table but almost out of Jeeter's reach. Jeeter hardly seemed to notice. "I've seen, the most, copperheads and rattlesnakes," he said. "A rattlesnake can jump eight feet to attack if it's coiled."

Eight feet! I learned back in summer camp that poison snakes have broad jaws and a pointy tail. That's all. Nothing about them jumping!

One side of Jeeter's mouth smiled, though one side was still turned down. He leaned toward me, eyes cold as a snake's. "My uncle Ezra says a rattlesnake can *spit* venom. I never did see it myself, but a big one spit at him, and the venom that hit him made him feel so woozy he couldn't kill the snake."

Buck in his checked shirt laughed. At me or at Jeeter? "Why, you all will scare that girl to death. I've lived here all my life, and no snake has ever bit me." Was Buck going to be my friend? "Nearest I came to snakebite, I was mowing, and something tugged at my pants, and I looked down, and it was a copperhead with his fangs caught in my baggy pants. I just held my snaky leg out and jumped and kicked him away with the other foot. If you're smart, you don't get bit."

And he meant if *I* wasn't smart, *I* would get bit. It was as if they — even Mrs. Jeeter — were conspiring to scare me into staying on the main roads or in the house from now on.

"You need to study on snakes," Mrs. Jeeter told me. "A rattlesnake will give you warning. A copperhead won't."

Jeeter reached for the gun again and put it over his knees. He kept gimlet eyes on me.

I tried to figure how I could get out of that place. I could say I had to go to the bathroom. Maybe I could climb out the bathroom window and run. But they probably had an outhouse. And what would I do about Baskerville?

"A copperhead is an ill snake," Jeeter said, "but a peaceable snake. They wait quiet. Then if you come close, they bite."

He emphasized *bite,* and plainly he didn't mean peaceable the usual way. He meant still. Deadly still.

If I weren't scared of Jeeter's gun and the maybe-owner of the marijuana crop and the snakes between me and home, I might even like to sit and listen to him talk. Some older folks still used words the way the first settlers did, because for so long the valleys had been hard to get to at the end of windy dirt roads. That was why we stuck together so, especially kin. Because once all we had to fall back on was kin.

205

I was sure that Mrs. Jeeter, and also Buck, would stick by Jeeter no matter what. Would even help him hide my body if he shot me.

Even so, I half liked the way those older words like *peaceable* sounded in Jeeter's rolling voice. Kind of hypnotic, except that the doom in his voice made me want to get out of there. I felt like his tone could raise up copperheads in the corners. No wonder Jinx needed to run out and find people to love her. No wonder she didn't know how to find the right ones.

"Snakes have special places where they like to be," Buck said. "There's a shortcut between here and Revonda Roland's place that the rattlesnakes like. Full of sunny rocks. I'd never go that way."

"We're near Revonda's?" I'd blundered my way near someplace I knew! I could make it back to civilization. With luck.

At Revonda's name Jeeter grabbed the gun again. Mrs. Jeeter just patted his shoulder.

"Snakes know when you're afraid." Mrs. Jeeter nodded to herself. "It's like a dog or a horse. They can smell fear. They bite the scared ones. They know when you are safe in the Lord. A snake has never bit *you*." She smiled proudly at her husband. "Even that time when one ran acrost your foot."

Jeeter's gray face creased into a pleased-with-himself smile. "Why, yes. I looked down and there was a copperhead crawling right over my foot." He beamed. "I just stood perfectly still in the arms of the Lord, and it crawled right on where it was going. The ungodly are afraid," he said. "And so they die."

And I thought: Jeeter could be the killer. He feels he has a right to kill anyone who has a reason to feel guilty. So Jinx feels in danger if she's guilty.

I sat up straight, making sure to look as unguilty as possible. "Thank you, for all you've told me," I said, trying to sound in control. "I have to go now, or they'll worry and start searching for me." I figured Jeeter wouldn't like that.

He pointed the gun at my head. "I haven't finished telling you about snakes. Snakes is like sin. You can't get away if you try to hold on too tight. I made a sermon once about the story of the boots."

What did he mean? Would he really shoot me if I ran?

"Because don't think killing snakes is enough," he sang. "You step on the fangs of a dead snake, you get the poison in your blood just the same." That's how Jeeter looked. As if there was poison in his blood. And yet his voice sang. "They's a story about a man who was way out in the woods, hunting ginseng in a pair of fine leather boots, when a great big rattler bit him right through the boots." I could see he had to finish before he let me go. If he did then.

"So when the man who was bit managed to get home, they took off the boots, and they did the things they used to do to get rid of the poison. They cut a live chicken in half and put a half against the bite to draw out that venom. And when he kept sinking, they put hot turpentine in a wide-mouthed jar and pressed that against the bite. Still he died, and they buried him proper, and his son inherited the boots."

I nodded to show I was listening and shouldn't be shot.

"Well, the son had always wanted those boots. Greed is a grievous sin. So right after the funeral, he put on those boots, and the fangs stuck in the boots bit him, and he died, too." Jeeter smiled at that. "So they hauled those boots out to the county dump to bury them with some junk. And one of the men who ran the dump saw those fine boots and pulled them out of the trash and put them on — and *he* died. Sin is like that."

I couldn't see exactly how sin was like that, but I didn't care. I had to leave. I stood up. To my surprise, Buck stood up, too. "I'll get her out of here for you, Jeeter," he said. "I'll get her back where she belongs." Alone in a car with Buck might or might not be worse than being with two others in a house with Jeeter. Anyway, it would be a change. I decided to take the chance.

Jeeter nodded his head. He said, "I'm tired."

At least I had a chance to untie Baskerville from the porch and take her with us. I told myself Baskerville was protection. I took her inside the truck with me. She sat on my feet with her head in my lap.

Buck started the engine and his big brown Ford truck jounced as we rolled down the rutted red clay driveway. He was silent with his eyes front.

"Suppose I did meet a bad snake, what would I do?" I asked.

We crossed a two-board bridge across the creek, one board for each wheel. "You kill it," he said. "No point in keeping danger around." Two meanings again? We swung out onto the asphalt road.

"For a copperhead, the best way is with a hoe," he said. "Stand back and chop off the head with a hoe blade."

I'd want a hoe ten feet long!

Did he hoe marijuana? "And if I don't have a hoe . . . ?" I asked. I didn't exactly keep one in my back pocket.

"Break the back," he said. "A snake can't move if you break the back." We were coming around the bend toward Revonda's. I was so glad I could have yelled hoorah. Maybe Buck was just a good neighbor who never hoed anything more than corn and beans. He turned into the driveway. The old Victorian house looked beautiful to me. Even though it still wasn't all painted.

"Throw a rock or use a long stick to break a snake's back. And keep that dog away from snakes," he added, glancing at Baskerville. "A cat is faster than a snake, but a dog will get bit. And if I were you, I'd stay away from Jeeter. He has spells."

But I stopped thinking about Jeeter, and even about snakes. On Revonda's porch I saw Sam with his arm around Jinx. Anne came out of the kitchen door. That must be a dutch-uncle arm he put around Jinx, I tried to tell myself. But how did Anne feel? Her eyes said scared. Sam was her lover and her good-luck charm. She needed him in back of her now. Did Jinx need him, too? That would be an ugly problem.

I got out of the truck with Baskerville and thanked Buck.

Sam unhanded Jinx and came and threw an arm about me. "You worried us," he said, "when Jinx came and said she hadn't seen you for hours."

"I got Paul's truck stuck in a ditch," I said. "Where's Revonda?"

Sam began to laugh. "She went off on a date. What do you think of that?" He acted like that was a big joke on me. I felt confused.

"Revonda has gone," he said, "to have a drink with your father, wearing her best black dress and real pearls."

Chapter

23

LATE SATURDAY AFTERNOON

It was one of those moments when I needed to be in three places at once. I needed to protect my father from dangerous entanglement with a sexy actress. (So, O.K., Revonda was suffering sorrow and loss, but that probably made her sexier to Pop.) I needed to get home and talk all this over with Ted, and then collapse. But I needed to tell Anne and Sam about marijuana and Jeeter, and show them the book about spirals. I still had that book with me in my trusty shoulder bag that — through thick and thin, lost and found, and even with a gun aimed at my head — never left my shoulder. A durable bag!

Jinx had taken off from Revonda's as soon as Buck had dropped me off. Sam offered to follow in his car to be sure she got home safe, but she said no. If she was going to live in a lonely place, she had to be independent and take care of herself. What a combination: She felt like a target and still refused help.

Sam watched her go with a frown and said, "Inviting fate." He said it like it was the title of a painting. Anne's worried eyes darted from Jinx in her car back to Sam. I said, "Now, about marijuana and snakes . . ."

I told them about the marijuana field and then about Jeeter and Ruth and Buck and their snake talk and how I thought they were trying to scare me. "You know," I said, "in the Middle Ages they had memory systems based on the fact that you can remember something frightening and shocking better than something that's not. And it's true. I could repeat every word they said."

Sam said he thought Jeeter was a good suspect, and that in the future he'd sure steer clear of boots with fangs inside. We all agreed that I shouldn't tell the sheriff about seeing the marijuana farm, since we didn't trust him not to be mixed up with dealing drugs himself. Also, I'd been so lost and turned around in the woods that I didn't know where the place was anyway. I wasn't even sure where I'd left the truck, except that it was on a road not too far from Jinx's.

"Don't worry. I'll find it tomorrow first thing," Sam reassured me. Then he said he had to go check that all Revonda's doors and windows were locked, since she might not be back before dark.

"And then," I told him, "I need to show you the strange book about spirals."

From the studio I called Ted and told him I'd be late but, boy, would I bring news. And God bless Ted, he just said he'd be looking forward to it.

Anne put some soup to heat up and sat down at the table with me. She pulled at a strand of her hair, curled it round her finger, and shifted uneasily in her chair. "I'm sure it's true about snakes." Jeeter's snake stories were still on her mind.

"How do you mean?" I asked.

"Snakes are more likely to bite the people who're afraid. They know. When I think about that, I'm even more afraid and they are even more likely to bite me." She was dead white, almost blue-white in the pale light.

And there wasn't a single snake around. I wanted to say, "Come on, snap out of it." But I knew I should listen.

"You make it sound like Jeeter has my number," Anne said, "like he knows how to make a person afraid of their own fear. And it makes me think about Paracelsus," she said.

"You've lost me."

"I mean," she said, "in that book on magic, Paracelsus said magic came by focusing your mind and will and imagination. What kind of magic do I make when I see pictures in my mind of what I'm scared of? I can't help it. Snakes. Or losing Sam. Or a killer who will spot me as the most scared one. And the most scared one would be the one to kill." Her teeth were actually chattering.

"You stop that!" I said. I couldn't help myself, either. I have a thing about people who give up. I can stand almost anything else and be sympathetic, but gloom gets me.

"Listen," I said, "you see what could go wrong in your mind so you can figure out how to change it. That's the reason. You've got to concentrate on seeing what to do."

I wasn't getting through. "Everything went wrong for me," Anne sobbed, "until I met Sam. Sam is my good luck and my love. He says I'm O.K. And if I lose him, what will I do?" Lucky for her. I thought, that fear almost became her. She was fey like a wood nymph, not like a droopy wet blanket.

"You'd manage," I told her. "But you won't lose Sam."

"Maybe he loved me," she sobbed, "because he likes to help people who have trouble." She sobbed even louder. "And Jinx is worse off than me."

"You have a point there," I said, trying shock treatment. Anne gulped. I handed her a tissue from my trusty pocketbook, and she blew her nose.

"Jinx is the closest I ever saw to giving up," I said. "The worst. She scares me. I bet she scares Sam."

Anne blew her nose even harder. "I ought to

be nice to her." Anne was struggling to be rational. I could see that.

"What kinds of things have always gone wrong for you?" I asked. Facts help.

"Oh, everything." She sighed. "They even had a fire in the hospital the day I was born."

"I'm sure that was your fault," I said sarcastically.

"And I almost flunked the first grade. I never did well in school, except on the out-loud stuff. I was fired once for filing things in the wrong place. I forget things like you do. I learn to spell things and then I forget — which sounds dumb, but I do it. And one time I somehow got turned around and found myself driving the wrong way on a divided road. I even did that."

"Would you be shocked," I asked, "if I said none of that sounds so bad to me as long as you survived it? And you're a great puppeteer."

"Oh, that," she said with a shrug. "That's easy. That's fun."

"Who keeps reminding you about those things you did wrong?" I asked. Anne plainly couldn't remind herself about the fire in the hospital.

"Well, they bothered my family," she said. "They said I better watch out or I'd be like Uncle Fred. Uncle Fred breeds schnauzers and lives with my grandma and is always broke. But Sam thought I was great. And after I married him, I felt great! And now, suppose — ?"

"Be sure you don't imagine bad things that

aren't true about Sam," I said. I went over and gave her a big hug. This gal needed all the hugs she could get. Because I was afraid she had a point. A bully zeroes in on someone who sends out give-up vibrations, right? Wouldn't a killer be like that?

But then, I told myself, Paul had seemed to be angry, not depressed. And Marvelle was downright perky. But the give-up thing bothered me all the same.

Sam came breezing in. Talk about never giving in to gloom. "Now," he said, radiating good cheer and anticipation, "show us the book about spirals."

Chapter

24

Saturday Evening and

Sunday Morning, July 7

Ted was as baffled by the spiral book as Anne and Sam had been. How could it be related to murder? We drank iced tea and conferred at the kitchen table, and were uninspired. Ted was horrified to hear of my blundering near the marijuana farm and visiting Jeeter.

"I wish I could have been along," he said. By which I figured he meant he never gets lost. On the other hand, perhaps knowing about Jeeter and the farm would turn out to be useful. You never know.

"I also wish I felt better about the sheriff," he said. "I talked about him to a source I have, and he said the down-east folks don't trust him, but it may be because of his good-old-boy mountain style." We agreed I wouldn't tell the sheriff about the marijuana, at least for the time being.

Then we took our tea over to the counter and got to work fixing supper.

"The wrong things upset me," I said as I trimmed the broccoli. "Anne and Jinx are both smart, good-looking girls. And they both can act as limp as wet spaghetti. They make me want to scream! That doesn't help."

Ted gave me his wise-professor glance as he dotted the flounder with butter. "So who did you once know — someone who acted that way and it bothered you?" he asked. "Maybe you're reminded."

I drew a blank. "Nobody limp as they are!"

"Did you ever want to give up, yourself?" Ted asked. I thought about that while he made hollandaise sauce to go on the broccoli. A reward, because we'd both had busy days. I squeezed the lemon for him, reaming out the juice with an old-fashioned squeezer I keep for sentimental reasons. It was my mother's. My mother made lemonade after school.

"The lemon squeezer is related to something I need to remember," I said.

"Related to when you wanted to give up?" he asked hopefully.

"Yes!" It came back to me. Ma squeezing lemons and listening to my troubles, and helping me to figure how to cope. Then the time when Ma wasn't there.

"In the second half of first grade," I said, "my mother was gone for a month after an automobile accident. I had trouble learning to read. A bunch of kids ganged up and called me dumb. And some older kids got into the act and I was scared to walk to school, but I had to go. Pop was so upset, because Ma was away, that he was no help. I wanted to give up and stay in bed all day."

"So what happened?"

"Ma came back. She taught me ways to laugh at the mean kids. Do you know the one about, *'I'm rubber, you're glue, everything bad you say about me bounces off me and sticks on you'?*"

Ted said, "No," and cracked two eggs.

"Very effective," I said. "Also, with Ma back I felt better. When you're spunkier, bullies don't pick on you. But it still bugs me to deal with that give-up feeling. I need to help those gals feel spunkier, that's what! I also need to go see Pop." I sighed. "He has a date with Revonda tonight."

"Those two deserve each other," Ted hooted. "But do you think she'd take on an invalid? Never."

That cheered me up. The phone rang, and I answered. A gravelly low voice said, "You keep your nose out of other people's business, or you'll be dead." Buck-Marijuana-Field, I figured. Still, I was scared silly. I also knew that if I told Ted, he might persuade me to *give up* trying to help Anne and Sam. Or he'd worry about me all day. So I did one of the dumbest things I ever did in my life. I told Ted it was a wrong number.

Next morning Ted was bogged down in grading summer-school papers. I went out to Revonda's to show her the spiral book. *Carefully.* I watched the rearview mirror.

I found Revonda sitting in her jungle chair, flanked by dogs, and fuming. Hound growled as I came in, but Revonda said, "It's all right." Then, "What's *not* all right is a big revival on the ballfield next week. To pray for those who are under the power of Satan. I know what that means. They'll pray about Paul, without knowing Paul. He was not a bad person!"

I didn't know what to say. Fortunately, Anne came in at that point and said, "I found out something strange about Marvelle. Reverend Phillipson told me."

Revonda pounced. "That Pollyanna! He told you something useful?"

"He came by to see if we were O.K. and he was talking about how we are all under stress because the murders scare us," Anne said. "So we get fearful and clumsy. Like the way I broke that glass this morning."

Revonda's hands twitched. She hated clumsiness.

"He said people were already fearful before Marvelle was found dead. Even when the sheriff was still sure Paul had killed himself."

Revonda listened one hundred percent.

"He said Marvelle was afraid a man was peeking in her windows at night. She told the minister and the sheriff. No one else. She thought her fear made her look silly. And then, Reverend Phillipson said he supposed it didn't matter now if he told. Marvelle obviously hadn't been silly at all."

"And then?"

"Well, Reverend Phillipson said the sheriff went himself to investigate."

"Stage-struck," Revonda snorted. "He was an extra once in a movie about blockaders shot in this valley. He was impressed with any actress."

"The sheriff couldn't find a thing. Not even a footprint."

"He couldn't find a mad dog if it bit him!" Revonda shrugged. "But Marvelle imagined things. She probably liked to think men would still peek at her." Revonda leaned forward and lowered her voice dramatically. "On the other hand, if there's a deranged killer, he may have watched her from a distance, but she could feel his eyes."

Jeeter?

Revonda turned to me with a charming smile. "Peaches, you can find out about Marvelle by chatting with her psychologist. She'll tell you more than she'd tell me."

So Marvelle was getting help!

"Pretend you're taking a walk," Revonda said. "That woman works in her garden Sundays. Shocks some of the church crowd. Actually Paul went to see the woman once or twice. A while back. Her name is Octavia Morris. Paul said it was a waste of time."

I had my own reason to see the psychologist. I wanted to know if Marvelle had give-up tendencies like Anne and Jinx and hid them. I might find out about Paul, too!

I found the psychologist where Revonda's directions said she'd be — right down the road, pulling weeds in front of a white clapboard house with glorious roses. She was a slender woman in jeans, with short dark hair, yanking grass and stuff out of a circular flower bed around a tree. She was younger than I expected. Maybe thirty-five. Not a woman who minded getting her hands dirty.

I said, "Hello," and started up the gravel driveway.

She stood up. "I'm Octavia Morris." She had remarkable brown eyes that seemed to take in everything about me all at once.

I explained I was Anne's cousin and Anne worked for Revonda, and since I'd had some luck finding out who killed my aunt and such, Revonda had enlisted my help to try to discover who killed Paul, and now Marvelle. This all sounded pretty lame to me, but Octavia Morris smiled and said, "We all want to know that, even young Billy Holt who mows my lawn. That's all he talks about." So Marvelle's psychologist was friends with Mert's grandson. Everybody knew everybody in Bloodroot Creek.

She stepped forward. "I'm just going in for a cold drink. Why don't you join me?"

The house inside was cool and comfortably dark, all natural wood and bookshelves with interesting objects all around. The bronze head of a young woman stood on one side of the mantelpiece. At the other side was a painted wood carving of an American Indian dancing. He wore rows of eagle feathers attached to his outstretched arms like wings, and a blue mask. Arresting.

She asked me to sit in a chair on one side of the fireplace, then went to get us iced tea. I scanned book titles: *The Witch and the Clown, Shadow and Evil in Fairy Tales, An Archetypical Approach to Death, Dreams, and Ghosts.* Spooky.

On the edges of the shelves were small brass and ceramic animals: a white china unicorn, a brass dog with a Chinese symbol on the forehead, a ceramic winged horse, and a handmade-looking green pottery dragon. The dragon, with its horselike head and small batlike wings and pot belly, almost made me laugh. Then I noticed that on each of the handlike claws, on each of the feet, and in the middle of the forehead, were small ceramic spirals. In one claw, the dragon held what was plainly a magic wand. A stick with a triangle at the top and in the middle of the triangle a white spiral. Like the marks on Paul and Marvelle! I sucked in my breath. Imagine keeping that dragon in plain sight after a killer painted spirals on your neighbors! My heart pounded.

"Confront your fears!" She startled me. "Dragon helps my patients to do that about these murders." She had come back from the kitchen and must have seen me staring. She handed me my tea in a sweaty cold glass. Walking casually over to the chair across from me, she sat down and leaned back, so completely self-assured. "This summer is my first time to be questioned about murders. But you've had experience I take it?"

I told her as briefly as I could about the murder of Aunt Nancy and the threats against Pop, and I thought: This is not what I came for.

"They questioned you about Marvelle Starr and Paul Roland?" I asked.

"Yes. I was able to tell them part of Marvelle's schedule before she was killed. She was here at three o'clock the day before."

I felt this Octavia Morris was behind a glass wall I couldn't penetrate. Controlling the way our conversation went. Yet she seemed friendly.

"Was Marvelle Starr depressed?" I asked. "Did Marvelle talk to you about her fears of being watched?"

"I can't talk about the substance of conversations with patients," she said. Still pleasant but on guard. Both sandaled feet were straight in front of her, flat on the ground. Her hands were clasped in her lap.

"Revonda told me Paul came to see you." There was not going to be a way to ask what I wanted except to jump in.

"I really can't tell you about patients." She said it a little louder. "That would be unethical."

"But you hear what people say now about Paul. Some of them say Paul belonged to a Satanic cult. And that maybe Marvelle did, too. I hear there's going to be a revival meeting to pray for those who have been under Satan's influence. Revonda believes they'll say that Paul was one."

She looked up sharply, and I could see by a slight twitching that an inner struggle was going on.

"I *will* say that I don't believe Paul belonged to a cult," she said finally. "I think he would want me to say that much. I told that to the sheriff."

Behind her was a strange picture of a young man turning into a tree — or perhaps the other way around. A symbol for something? It reminded me of my scare in the woods. Yet I liked the picture. The young man even seemed exalted, like Reverend Phillipson when he hoped for the best. But the young man's feet were roots, going down into the ground. His fingers were twigs, with a scattering of green leaves, his bare body like a tree trunk. The picture was a dream.

"There seem to be symbols that have had meaning for our subconscious minds from the dawn of history. They appear in folktales and in dreams," she said. "Paul was interested in those symbols. I don't believe he was a joiner."

I looked back at her bookshelf. In front of a book called *Individuation* was a small sword, probably a letter opener. Not unlike the one in Paul's room.

"Symbols," I said. "Like a sword. Paul's books say a sword was necessary for some kinds of magic. And I suppose a spiral is a symbol like you're talking about?" I asked.

"A symbol can have more than one meaning." Her voice said I was jumping to conclusions. "A sword can be phallic or a symbol of a wand, of power. A spiral can be a symbol of growth or of the way we solve a problem and then come to it again on a higher level to solve again." She kept those brown eyes focused on me. Demanding that I understand. "The important thing is what the symbol means to you. In your dreams, for example."

"And spirals on a dead body?"

"What do you think they mean?" she asked, still guarded.

"I don't know."

"Do you think Paul and Marvelle were members of a Satanic cult?" she challenged. And I thought, wait a minute. Why do I get the third degree?

"I don't know." I felt kind of stupid, but that's how it was.

"Not to know, when you have no way to know, is a very healthy attitude." Octavia Morris seemed pleased. "There are people who can't admit to themselves that they are only human, who can't admit that there's bound to be some evil in every person, including themselves. Those people have to see the evil in somebody else. We call that projection." She was holding me with those brown eyes. "When you see a person who is sure without proof that another person is in league with the devil, ask yourself what the accuser is hiding. Even from himself. Ask yourself if he's unbalanced."

We were straying from the things I came to ask about.

"Revonda thinks Paul might have been killed by a member of a cult who misunderstood Paul's interest in magic," I said. "But I can't see why, unless the killer was a member of a rival cult. Do cults have turf fights?"

"I don't know any members of cults." She raised her voice, the way the television commercials are always louder than the show itself. She dropped her voice again. "I believe people who join cults are looking for someone to tell them who they are. Like all those poor people in Jonestown years back who drank cyanide because their leader said to. I don't believe Paul was like that."

"Was Paul depressed," I asked, "even though he acted angry?"

"I haven't been able to tell you much about my clients," she said firmly.

I started to get up. I was annoyed. "Thank you," I said. I probably sounded sarcastic.

"I'd really like to be helpful. I could tell you something I saw. I haven't told anyone but the sheriff, because I don't like to start rumors. But this might help you." I sat back down quick.

"I drove past Marvelle Starr's house on the morning of the Fourth of July. You remember the Fourth was warm?"

"Yes." My mouth was dry with hope. I took a sip of tea.

"Not far from Marvelle's house I saw a strange-looking woman walking," she said, "a large woman in a big flowing smock, a bandanna, and dark glasses. And I thought: one of those crazy tourists. She must be hot in all those clothes."

"Did it look at all like anyone you ever saw before?" I stood up again. I almost rose in the air with excitement. A great disguise for a killer.

"Anyone could have hidden under all those clothes," she said. "Even a man."

Chapter

25

LATE SUNDAY MORNING

I thought I was going back to Revonda's to discuss the Spiral-on-the-Dragon Lady's news, but I found Anne coming back across the street from Mert's. Jinx's battered pickup was parked by the studio, next to Paul's truck. Good for Sam. He must have found Paul's truck where I left it and brought it back. "I hope you'll come in," Anne said to me, eyeing Jinx's truck like it might explode.

Of course, I intended to come in. I could feel trouble about to come to a head, and it worried me. I was right at Anne's heels when she opened the door at the top of the stairs.

Sam was at his easel, and Jinx was stark naked. Now, I know artists paint people that way. But Jinx had looked naked even with her clothes on. And now she stood balanced on one foot on top of a rickety stool. Without her tacky clothes, even in that odd position, she was more beautiful than she was with clothes on. She was beautiful even in spite of her wide-eyed, half-frowning, off-balance expression. She was gently curved and smooth as the petals of those roses at Paul's funeral.

I turned and glanced at Anne, and what I saw was terror.

I turned back and saw fear spread to Jinx's face. She wavered like she might fall at any moment. Would Sam run to catch her if she fell?

Anne must be asking herself that. She flushed red.

Sam said, "Hi. Jinx has offered to do some modeling for me." Very casual, feet apart, brush in hand, painting full-speed ahead. He hummed to himself, concentrating so hard on his picture he didn't seem to see danger signals.

Jinx said "Hello" in that don't-hit-me-again voice and held her pose. Did she know she was so damn sexy?

Death and danger stimulate the need for sex. I heard that on television. During the Black Death, people copulated in the streets. Was Sam having a little on the side? I could see why Anne wondered.

I tried to defuse the tension by telling them all about the woman Octavia the psychologist saw in bandanna and dark glasses.

Sam said, "So it was someone who would have expected to be recognized." I suspect Anne and Jinx were both so tense they didn't hear.

"Take a break," Sam said to Jinx. "That's a hard position to hold. You look bushed. That's enough for today."

Jinx got down from the stool and wriggled to loosen her naked muscles. "Posing is hard work," she said. I knew she aimed that at Anne and me. "Even if my father does think it means I'll go to hell." She put on her clothes quickly. No underwear, just shirt and jeans.

I went over and looked at Sam's picture. Anne came, too. He was still putting dabs of paint here and there, humming to himself "The Green, Green Grass of Home." The picture showed the rock face of a mountainside with Jinx on a narrow ledge. Naked, of course. Facing us. She wasn't balanced on one foot in the picture, but she had that same unsteadily-balanced-on-one-foot expression with the eyes wide. The picture was just roughed in. But, like all Sam's pictures, it went straight to the pit of my stomach.

I thought: For God's sake, girl, turn and hug the cliff! And however you got there, get down quick. And put on some clothes. Because in the picture her nakedness was like her not holding on. Frightening. Sexy, but frightening.

"I told Jinx," Sam said, "that this isn't a portrait of her. This is a picture of some force that has to do with the murders, a force I'm trying to explore." He smiled at me like we were co-detectives. He stopped painting and stood back and studied the picture. "When I fully understand the force, I'll be closer to knowing who killed Paul and Marvelle."

I put my arm around Anne, who was standing next to me.

Jinx had come over to look at herself on the cliff. She had on her PIKE'S PEAK OR BUST shirt again. She hugged herself. "I feel that way sometimes. I hate that picture."

Sam stood and admired it. So pleased that joy was spouting out of every pore, out of every tangled reddish-blond hair in his head or beard. "Thank you. I want this picture to make you feel. I'm getting it right." He put his arm around Jinx's shoulders and gave a squeeze. I felt Anne wince like she'd been burned.

Jinx caught Sam's joy, and she smiled up at him, softened and warmed like a red-haired angel. Then she glanced at Anne, shriveled, and left. I wanted to yell, "All of you stop and talk this out!" But would that help?

Sam was humming and adding bits of paint here and there to make his naked Jinx even more lifelike. Painting is memory on canvas. So Jinx was still with us.

"When we met, you said you wanted to paint *me*," Anne shrilled. "You've painted Revonda. You've painted Jinx. Why not me?"

Sam put his brush down. The joy shrunk out of him. I wanted to say, "Anne, this is not the way to talk." But she already knew it. Her expression jerked this way and that, like she was trying to control it, but she was too angry and scared. I felt as if little needles of anger were sticking out of her all over.

Sam stood by his easel, beyond the needles. "I'm not ready to paint you." He threw his head back and squinted the way artists do when they want to get the scale of some picture right. "I know you too well, Anne, and not well enough." He said that sadly. Then he turned back to his picture. "You and Jinx are alike in some way. I have to understand that. It's important." He reached out and took Anne's hand. Good! The right move. "I see you, but I don't see you well enough."

Behind Sam, the green leaves on the tree out the window moved gently. Maybe rain would come.

"And what do you see?" Anne challenged.

He winked at me, like he was glad I was there for a witness. "I see gentle hair that does nice things in a small wind," he said, "and hands that act out your words and make them richer, and a tentative mouth that tastes your words to be sure they're just right, and listening eyes with five kinds of light inside."

Some of the stiffness went out of Anne.

"And those wonderful eyebrows that lift and lilt at the edges like the wings of a seagull in flight."

He shut his mouth and let go of Anne's hand. His eyes had that faraway look, like he'd retreated so far inside his own head he forgot we were there. "So why do I want to paint you wrestling with a ghost? Wrestling with a white smothering thing? Wrestling with a white glob of wind?"

"So that's how you feel! You don't want to paint me in any way at all, or else you'd do it." The screech in Ann's voice was back. Oh, dear.

He started and looked at Anne as if he really saw her again. "You know," he said, "I think part of what is wrong is that you're not sure of yourself. You get lost. Why Anne, you won't even write home unless I fix your spelling, and then you feel dumb."

Anne flushed. She bent her head as if she didn't want to see him. Why on earth was Sam bringing up spelling — of all things — at a time like this? Sometimes I thought he was a little crazy. But he wasn't about to stop.

"I saw this article in the paper about dyslexia —"

"So you think something is wrong with me, too! Just like my family! There's nothing wrong with me! I manage fine!" Anne was shouting.

And then Sam laughed, and I was afraid Anne was going to haul off and hit him. Maybe I should have left. But I wanted to know what would happen next.

"Of course something is wrong with you," he said. "Something is wrong with everybody." He threw his arms wide as if he was ready to hug everybody. "Ask Peaches!"

He went over and ruffled through the scraps of this and that. "I clipped this today." He grabbed something he'd torn out of the paper and held it up. "This is about a Dr. Zimmerman who specializes in dyslexia."

"I don't have to have it just because it's in the paper!"

Sam wouldn't give up. "Here. Read this. It tells how some people keep feeling like they fall in black holes. This Zimmerman just moved here from California."

"I am not some kind of a nut who doesn't know where I am!" Anne shouted. "You're just changing the subject so I'll forget to be mad with you about Jinx. I don't need to go to this Zimmerman from California."

Sam stayed reasonable. "You could be color-blind," he said. "You could be mean. You could have no sense of humor. Why, you could be stupid or self-righteous. You could be dull. But you're not. You've got to have something wrong, or how can you be human?"

"So what are you, Sam? How are you human?"

"They tell me I'm not practical." I almost laughed. "But it doesn't bother me." He shrugged. "And whatever is wrong *does* bother you. Go see Dr. Zimmerman. Why not?"

"What does all this have to do with why you don't want to paint my picture?" I felt the porcupine quills zoom back out. Sam actually stepped back as if he felt them, too. Stepped closer to the canvases stored against the wall. "I tried," he said "I tried to paint you holding a bunch of zinnias. With all those bright colors for the way you get enthusiastic. But they turned to black and white and began to whirl." He laughed a sheepish laugh as if she'd caught him at some silly naughtiness.

"Where is the picture? I want to see it."

"No, you don't. It's just a study. It turned out wrong." He moved even closer to the canvases by the window, as if he wanted to protect them.

She pushed past him and began to look.

"Please." He followed her over. "I can't hold you down and prevent you from seeing that picture. But in the stage it's in, it will hurt you to see it. I don't want to hurt you, Anne." He threw a look of appeal to me. "Ask Peaches. You shouldn't look at something that will give you wrong ideas."

Anne kept looking. Mostly Sam painted what was wrong with the world. I thought, Good Lord, what has he painted?

The picture was the next-to-the-last in the row. Anne pulled it out, and a wild sound came out of her, half gasp, half moan.

"Anne, for God's sake, I told you that picture isn't right. I'm searching for what's right." Sam was yelling as if a shout could make her hear. But he didn't grab the picture. He let her study it.

I angled around to see. The draft was rough, but there was no way to mistake that the girl looking out from the canvas was Anne.

She stood staring straight in front of her, almost trance-like. Eyes huge, like when she was scared. Bull's-eyes were painted on her in bold black and white. One target was in the middle of her forehead. And a smaller one on each hand and foot. I sucked in my breath.

Sam had painted a picture of Anne, jinxed. That's how it was: There was a girl named Jinx, a girl he was painting. She had the name, but Anne had the real thing. Anne, who was double-scared because Jeeter said that snakes bit the ones who were afraid of them. Who remembered that Paul's magic books said visualizing a thing with strong emotion could make it happen. Who visualized all the things she feared, even losing Sam.

Sam took the picture out of her hands. He didn't try to hug her or apologize or anything like that. He was dignified, like someone at a funeral, even in his jeans and SAVE THE WOLVES T-shirt. I remembered him wearing Paul's suit in the pine church banked with roses. That seemed so long ago.

"I am going to destroy this picture." He tucked it under his arm with the ugly part toward his body. He went into the kitchen and took the box of matches next to the two gas burners. He grabbed a few old newspapers and stuck those under his arm, too. He came back and took Anne's hand in his free hand and asked us both to come with him. Anne looked so in shock that I'm not sure she could have followed without his guiding grip. I followed down the steps out into the yard. He led us across the gravel driveway, around Revonda's big white house, and to the stone barbecue grill in the backyard. He removed the iron grill and balled up newspapers in the fireplace.

I thought: What on earth would some cousin think if she came to pay a visit on Revonda now and what she saw was us, burning this ghastly picture.

Sam said, "I don't quite believe in magic." I knew that had to do with the picture. The picture of Anne jinxed. He took some kindling from the pile by the grill and arranged it over the crumpled paper, tepee style.

Then he turned to Anne and said, "But there's a power in images, for good or evil. I'm sure Paul's magic books are right about that, or I wouldn't paint. We'll get rid of this image." Then he lit the fire and put the canvas on top. I wished he'd put it upside down, but he put it right side up.

We watched Anne burn, the orange flames curling through the canvas at the feet first, then the rest fast with a loud crackle and an ugly oily smell. We stayed until nothing was left but ashes and the empty charred wood frame.

Sam stood triumphant, holding Anne's hand. "There. That's the end of that!"

But Anne's eyes were still wide and scared.

I found myself thinking of a foolish expression my friend Lottie the messy poet used to say: *If a messy desk is the sign of a messy mind, what is an empty desk a sign of?* That's the kind of dumb stuff I remember.

What was an empty picture frame a symbol of? Anne's eyes were asking that.

Chapter

26

I went back up to the studio with Sam and Anne. Sam kept glancing at me to be sure I was coming. Anne kept holding on to my arm. Maybe they were so upset that they didn't want to face each other alone. We had tuna-fish sandwiches and coffee, sitting at the round table. (Revonda was off eating with a cousin.) My efforts at conversation sounded phony, so we ate in silence.

Then Billy showed up, complete with ever-present dark glasses. He handed Anne a platter with a big golden-crusted pie. "My grandmother sent you this. It's peach." Mert was cheering us up, with a pie fit for Sunday dinner.

Billy waited as if he was hoping for more than Anne's "thank you." He had a paperback book in his back jeans pocket.

Sam finally said, "Won't you come in and have some pie with us?" The kid beamed his "yes." Anne cut us each a piece of the juicy pie, which was totally delicious. Billy ate his slowly and toyed with the last bite, like he was putting off something.

At last he turned to Sam and said, "I'm scared." He swallowed, and his Adam's apple bobbed like he might choke. "I have to talk to somebody who thinks it's O.K. to try things. And maybe" — he turned to me — "a detective person is O.K., too." He took the book out of his pocket, hesitated, then thrust it at Sam. It was a small black paperback with a picture on the back of a hypnotic-eyed man and strange symbols.

Anne's eyes went round. Get that out of here, we have enough trouble, they seemed to say. But I was sure we needed to find out what Billy had to tell us, however frightening.

"My friend got this book when he was out in California," Billy said. "And I read it because I like to find out about things." He turned to Sam and took off his dark glasses as if he wanted to see Sam better. "Do you understand?"

Sam nodded.

Billy's eyes were extra wide, and there were circles under them. He reached out and took the book back and opened it to a page that was all underlined. Then he gave it back to Sam: "Read that."

While Sam read, Billy helped himself to an-

240

other piece of pie — gulped it down like he needed the strength. He kept swallowing even between bites, and his feet kept wiggling, very uptight.

Sam took a long time reading. Anne made a pot of coffee and poured us each a cup. She dropped a cup, broke it, and cleaned up. Finally Sam turned to me, not to Billy. "The man who wrote this book was upset when terrible things happened — like murders and gory accidents, and people said, 'It was God's will.'" Sam stopped and considered the book, and then added, "He saw this as deception and hypocrisy. Hypocrisy is the hook."

"Yes." Billy's eyes burned angry. "I don't like it when people act like that. Like, if some kid's father goes to church and acts so holy and comes home and gets drunk and beats up the kids. Or even acts so great in church and outside just acts mean. I hate that."

Sam nodded strongly. "I hate that, too." Sam turned to me. "This book says that members of other religions say one thing and do another, but that Satanists do exactly what they say." He turned to Billy. "And you liked that?"

"Yes. And I wanted to know if spells and stuff could work. I wanted power." Billy grinned and squirmed so much when he said those last words that his slat-bottomed chair creaked. "It would be fun to say a spell and have money or girls or even revenge. That's what I figured. I like to try things to see if they work." His dark eyes, naked without the sunglasses, shot a hopeful glance at Sam for sympathy on that one, then at me. Anne's eyes were cast downward onto her hands, like she didn't want to hear.

"So we started a group," he said, "me and some friends and this older kid who said he knew about this stuff, and an older man he knew. But they didn't do it right!" He raised his voice, and his eyes were surprised and mad. He took the book back and turned the pages and pointed: "Right here it says that a Satanist uses the power of spells, so he doesn't need the things you get addicted to, like drugs. But those kids had a big drug party every time we met. I don't want to be smashed like my father. I hate that. That older kid kept saying how Satanism meant we should indulge in natural desires. Then we'd have no frustrations that could hurt us or hurt our friends and folks. But it wasn't like that."

Billy kept swallowing. He laced his fingers together palms up and stared at his hands. The skin was fine, mottled pink and white and damp with sweat. A sensitive kid, stressed-out. But they were strong-looking hands all the same.

"Those guys said I couldn't quit or I might tell and if I quit they'd put a spell on me." He hardly moved his lips, like the words scared him. "I kind of believed that stuff." He twisted and pulled a lock of hair near his ear. "Mr. Harder, the principal, found out about us, and they put a spell on him, and he wrecked his car."

"He might have wrecked his car anyway," Sam said.

"The older kid — well, he was really a man, about twenty-one — said they'd been nice to Mr. Harder — they didn't put the worst kind of spell on him, the kind that would kill him. They all said they'd put the bad kind on me if I left." Billy was breathing hard.

I wondered what I'd do if I knew somebody deliberately put a spell on me. I guessed I'd be scared to death. I'd try to be logical, but that would be hard.

I could see just listening scared Anne silly.

"Well, what I'm getting to," Billy said, "is that to do the spell on the principal, so as to have enough power, they caught a funny little dog and killed it. I like dogs." Billy had turned light green. I was scared he might be sick.

He turned the pages of his little black book again and thrust it at Sam: "Read that. It's about making a spell for somebody to die."

Sam read it out loud, slow and surprised: It said a proper human sacrifice was anyone who had deliberately and unjustly wronged the sacrificer. It said that such a person would have asked by their actions to be cursed. Sam ran his finger down the page. Therefore, the book said, you had the right to symbolically destroy that person. And if the curse resulted in his death, you could be glad. Sam looked up. "It says 'symbolically' destroy. That means not actually kill, doesn't it?"

Billy was shivering hard. "It wasn't symbolic

when those kids killed the dog. I didn't read that book right. I didn't finish it before I joined those kids. I don't want to decide who ought to die! And suppose those kids thought that Paul . . ." He choked.

Sam put the book down on the table. "Are you saying that this group of kids could have killed Paul and Marvelle as part of a spell?" His voice rose with wonder. "This group of kids?"

Billy put his head down on his arms and began to sob in great gasps. Sam put his hand on the kid's shoulder. When the sobs let up a little, Sam asked, "What are you going to do?"

Billy pressed his hands into fists, wiped his eyes, and said: "I'm going to make them stop." I almost laughed. He sounded like single-handed he was going to be Superman.

He sat up straight, and his eyes flashed. "I wrote all their names on a piece of paper, and I put it in an envelope. I told those kids I had a way for that envelope to be found if anything happened to me. I didn't tell them how, or they'd just steal it. I told them if they let me leave, I wouldn't tell who they were. But if something happened to me, people would find out." He sat up straight and squared his shoulders and smiled. "I outsmarted those kids."

And then a sob took hold of him again. "But if they kill people and I don't tell, I'm part of it, aren't I? An accessory or something? I'm scared. But if I do tell, what will I tell? I don't know what they did."

"We are all going to try to find out who did the killing," Sam said. "It's not all up to you. You're part of a team."

"We want you to be safe," I said.

Billy nodded, as if he'd been about to get to that. "I need somebody besides me to have this list of names," he said to Sam. "I need those kids to know somebody else has a copy of the list. So if they find my list I have hidden, they still won't dare hurt me."

He handed an envelope to Sam and said, "Please promise not to open it unless something zaps me."

Anne looked up with terrified eyes. "Can't we give the list to the sheriff?" she asked. "I know Revonda doesn't trust him and thinks he's mixed up with drugs, but . . ." Her voice trailed off.

Billy shrugged. "The sheriff knows who the kids are. Same ones as before. He just doesn't have proof."

"There's no real danger unless the cult kids are killers," Sam said, "and if they are, they aren't going to like us anyway." He held up the plain white envelope. "I won't even tell you where I'm going to hide these names," he said. "I won't tell anybody. I trust you not to tell anybody I have them." Billy and Sam shook hands, dead serious. Billy grinned and relaxed a little and ate the last piece of pie. Sam put the names in his back pocket, waiting to find a hiding place, I figured, until we weren't looking.

"Did the kids use herbs in spells?" I asked.

"We've never solved the riddle of the herbs in the plastic bag with Paul's body."

"The older kid used herbs," Billy said. "He said they made strong spells and were easy to get. But I never learned about how to do that because I left." He reached over and put his dark glasses back on, and immediately he looked like a trickster.

He stood up and went over past Sam's easel to peer out the window. "I have to see if anybody is watching this place," he said, grabbing the empty pie plate and sneaking off dramatically down the stairs.

"I'll go see Jinx's mother, who knows about herbs," Anne volunteered. She said it angrily, like a challenge to Sam. Maybe she wanted him to worry about her. He nodded unhappily.

"I'll come, too," I said, "tomorrow when Jeeter goes to his prayer meeting in town. I wouldn't go near that place again when that crazy man is there. But when he's gone, I bet his wife could tell us about all sorts of things, even aside from herbs."

I stood up. I thanked Anne and Sam for sharing their meal with me, and I said, "We're all stressed out, but we all need each other. Believe me, that's true!" I meant: "Listen, you two. Make up!"

Chapter

27

LATE AFTERNOON

"I deserve some time to smell the roses," I told Ted. He'd finished preparing his stuff for class. We sat out on the terrace, and one rosebush by the corner of the house was in bloom, fragrant in the late afternoon.

"Someone keeps calling us up and then hanging up when I answer the phone," Ted said. "Very odd. Like a threat. I hope you're being extra careful."

I promised I was, but I was tired and I changed the subject. "I forget how distinguished you look," I said, ignoring the way his hair stands up like antennae, especially after he's been working and running his fingers through it. So he's a distinguished Martian. Just my type. Next to him on the glass-topped table was a book called *Good Magic* and another called *A History of Magic and Folk Cures*. "Are you taking over from Paul?" I asked.

"No," he said. "One of Revonda's cousins dropped these books off, with a note from Revonda that says they show that magic can be used for good purposes. She said Paul had these two in his collection, so she asked her cousin to get us copies." He laughed. "Revonda will go to any length to prove Paul never ever did anything wrong."

"I don't intend to think about Paul now," I said. I swirled my iced tea so the ice clinked, my favorite summer noise. "Thank goodness our house is our fortress," I said. "I feel safe here."

"Actually," he said, "we have a weapon on hand. I thought we'd gotten rid of every plastic bag in the house, just to be safe. But when I took the glasses out of the cupboard, I happened to look up on the very top shelf, and there's a plastic bag around the gold-rimmed china that your mother got from her grandmother. Up out of reach."

"Oh, well." I sighed. I didn't want to get up and go remove it. Who would know but Ted? We ignored it through a wonderful leisurely dinner and coffee, and then for some reason that bag on the high kitchen shelf began to prey on my mind. Our kitchen stepladder wouldn't reach, and the outdoors ladder was broken. I admit, I ran over it backing out of the driveway. I'd been meaning to buy a new one. Never mind, a chair on a table would give me a handy perch. I climbed up while Ted was watching CNN. He doesn't approve of improvised ladders, but heck, they work. Maybe just to spite me for improvising behind Ted's back, I slipped. Not with dishes in hand, thank goodness. I had them unwrapped and back in place and the plastic bag dropped to the floor. As soon as I felt unsteady, I jumped, so I wasn't hurt, but I knocked the chair over with me and made a *thump, crash.* Ted came running. I tried to look as calm and pulled-together as possible. I stared at the chair as if I were surprised to see it there, lying on its side on the red tile floor. It reminded me of something.

"It's not safe for you to climb up like that," Ted said unhappily. "You'll break something." He meant some part of me, of course. But a picture came to my mind. A broken mirror on the floor and a chair lying on its side by a table.

With a start, I remembered the chair in Paul's room, lying knocked on the floor next to the small table. Yeah, reenactment is a good way to bring something back to mind. I'd thought the burglar knocked Paul's chair over when he ran away. But now I remembered there'd been a thump. And if we could hear it at all outdoors, it must have been a loud thump like I made when I hit the floor. In a flash I saw that the burglar who broke into Paul's room had been climbing on that chair to reach something near the ceiling. What on earth?

We could have called Revonda, but Ted said

we ought to be with the first searchers for what-ever it was. I agreed. I won't say I'd stopped trusting anybody else, but I'd stopped being sure who had what to hide. I stuffed the plastic bag in the garbage, and we put that in back of the house in the outdoor can as we set forth.

"Something is hidden high up in Paul's room," I said as soon as Revonda came to her door. That got her attention. We told her about the chair and table reenactment.

She gave us her Oh-come-on smile. "What could we still find? After the way the police searched?" But she called Ron.

He came right down from up the hill, off duty in an old plaid shirt and jeans. We all trooped into the mirror room, plunged into Paul's flashing world when Revonda turned on the electric light. I scrutinized the wall near the place where the chair had fallen. My heart began to beat hard. I was pretty sure I saw the high-up hiding place. Most of the mirrors on Paul's walls were odd shapes pieced together, but one was square and about the size of the door of a bathroom medicine cabinet. I bet it was just that, sunken flush with the other mir-rors. "Look!" I pointed.

Ron seemed to spot the mirror door at the same time I did. He climbed up on the seat of the ladder-back chair and pried at the square mirror, which came open so suddenly that he started to fall and jumped. Just like me. Just like the burglar?

Inside, there was nothing — or that was my impression. Just a white-painted shallow cabinet with two shelves and nothing more. But Ron climbed back up, examined the inside, and flashed us a grin, excited. "Here's a razor blade down in the bottom," he said, "and a plastic straw." He took his index finger and wiped it on the bottom of the medicine cabinet and held it up with white powder on it. "We have us a find. I think this is cocaine."

"That's ridiculous," Revonda said.

"Folks who use cocaine put the powder on the mirror, take a razor to line it up right, and sniff it with a straw, Revonda. So it seems like Paul did that," Ron said. "That could be why he didn't always think straight."

Revonda had sat down in the chair with the face. For once she was without words. All the lines in her own face drooped.

"So the burglar knew Paul used cocaine," I said, "and knew where he kept it, and broke in to get it?"

Ron whistled. "That burglar may know who killed Paul."

"Paul was killed over drugs?" I didn't believe it. Everything about Paul was too fantastic to be that simple. "And Marvelle was killed over drugs, too?" I didn't believe that, either.

Ron laughed a shallow bitter laugh. His teeth were bright white. He bit at his words: "Drugs are everyplace."

Behind him was the closed door to the living

251

room, and I was glad Revonda had taken down that magical figure on the door, of a naked man spread-eagled in a star. The face jugs with candles in them were gone from the bookshelf. Paul's room was like a largely empty cave of ice. But that mirrored room still felt dangerous.

"Listen," I said to Ron, "something may have happened to me — or not. Related to drugs. But I'd better tell you about it." Somehow, I trusted Ron more than the sheriff. I told him about the man with the binoculars in the marijuana field. How he could be Buck, who was at Jeeter's house and gave me a ride home. But that I couldn't be sure. I said I hadn't told about coming across that marijuana between the corn because I wasn't positive that's what it was. Furthermore, I didn't know where the field was. But, I said, "the worse part is I'm getting threatening calls." Ted chipped in about the calls where someone hung up as soon as we answered.

Ron listened carefully. He took notes.

"We'd have heard if there really was a marijuana farm nearby," Revonda told him scornfully. She glared around her. "You're certainly going to find that any drugs in Paul's room were a plant."

We didn't wait to hear what Ron said. We said good night and made a quick exit.

"I wish Sam didn't have Billy's secret list of the cult members," I told Ted on the way home. "Of thrill-seeking kids. Or drug dealers. Or whatever. And something about Sam scares Anne," I said unhappily. "And why isn't Sam himself more afraid?"

"Let's go home and forget our worries in a little light reading," Ted said. "We can case the books Revonda sent and find out what kind of magic she wants us to think Paul believed in."

Chapter

28

MONDAY, JULY 8

When I arrived at Sam and Anne's studio on Monday, I heard laughter upstairs. Silly laughter with squeaks. The upstairs door was open, and Anne stood by the kitchen counter with a lighted candle in her hand, which was rather strange at eleven o'clock in the morning. On the counter was the book titled *Good Magic* and also *A History of Magic and Folk Cures*. So Revonda had sent them the books, too! Anne was giggling. Thank God. Sam and Anne must have made up.

"I like the one," Sam was saying, "where you can be safe from sorcery by spitting in your right shoe. Those old spells have tradition." He saw me, grinned, and winked. "I also like the one," he said, "where you light a banquet with candles made from the semen of an ass. By the light of those candles, all the guests have the heads of asses. Say, that might be kind of fun," he whooped. "Half the deputies who come around here already look like jackasses to me."

Anne blushed. Because he meant Ron? "I bet you like the one," she said, "where a naked virgin touches you with her right thumb to cure epilepsy."

He winked again. "Too much is made of virgins. A naked wife would suit me fine."

She shrugged at me like: What can you do? and put down the candle. She grabbed a grapefruit off the counter, threw it at Sam, and missed.

He grabbed it up and threw it back. Obviously they had the sillies. Best thing in the world when you're too tense. Anne caught the grapefruit against her hip.

"Unfair magic!" he shouted. "Catching my grapefruit with your right hand at eleven A.M., near a clove of garlic, at the time of the waning moon."

"And with the wind from the west — the wind should be included." Anne threw the grapefruit back hard and missed again. "Damn," she said.

Sam stopped laughing. "Actually," he said, "those spells that make you think about exactly where you are in the world and in the universe make sense to me. Like when you're supposed to pick a certain herb with your left hand while facing north under the dog star or the full moon or whatever. The knowing-where-you-are part feels right. I do that to paint."

Anne grinned. "You mean I'd have to stop mixing up left and right and going east for west, or all the spells would work backward?"

Sam was back to whooping. "Jackasses would look like deputies!"

I looked at the lighted candle, still on the counter. "Were you going to try a spell?" I asked Anne. "Was that candle part of it?"

She shrugged. "I thought it would help me not to feel so much like a target. But Sam's been razzing me. Now I don't have time, anyway." She blew out the candle.

"The strange thing about these spells," I said, "at least the ones in the modern books Revonda sent us, is that some are listed just as historical curiosities, but the ones that are advertised as workable are a lot like the tricks I use to remember things."

They both turned, surprised, and waited for more. It was an odd connection. "One way to remember," I said, "is to turn something that makes no sense to you — like a name, say, Bill Cunningham — into a visual image. And the more that image is funny or punny, or shocking, the easier it is to remember. Like, you could picture an irate bill-collector, handing a bill to a clever and cunning ham. The more thoughts you hang on that image, the better you remember. And from Albertus Magnus in the Middle Ages to modern memory books, they all agree on that."

"How is that like a spell?" Anne asked, pulling

out a chair for me and then sitting down at the table herself.

"From what I've read," I said, "in magic you make a strong image and even act that image out. Maybe you want it shocking so it's more memorable and that's part of the reason for the naked virgin and the ass's semen and touching a dead man to get rid of a mole. In one of those books I just read, it tells how to act out the image of what you want in a lot of ways at once — even by the stage of the moon and the direction of the wind. You send your mind a strong picture — well, more than a picture. You use all your senses."

"And so," Anne said, "if you kept sending negative messages, you might lose your mind."

"I never said that!" I was at a loss. I wished Sam would say something funny, or that Anne would throw the grapefruit at me.

Sam walked over to the counter and picked up a book called *Exorcism*. "And that fits with what this book says." I hadn't looked at that one. Revonda hadn't sent it to us.

"It says that strong emotion plus visualizing a thing can make it happen. Can even put on a curse or remove a curse."

I looked down at the prickle on my arms and realized I had goose bumps.

Anne swallowed. "Then you could even put on a curse by mistake!"

That seemed like half psychology, half black magic. It felt ugly. There was a weight in the pit

257

of my stomach. I wished Ted was there to say something sensible.

At least I could bring us back to why we'd been looking at the magic books to begin with. "I wish we knew enough about Paul to know if all this strange stuff helped cause his death. But we *can* find out what the herbs with his body meant."

"Give me your right shoe, Anne," Sam called out. "I want to spit in it for protection. It's much pleasanter to spit in someone else's shoe than in your own. Right?" Back to the sillies to break the gloom.

"Anne and I need to go," I said. "To be sure we are at Jeeter's house while he's out."

Sam turned serious. "Before you go, Revonda told us about the traces of cocaine in Paul's room. She said someone planted it there. Is that true?"

"Ask Ron or the sheriff for details," I said hurriedly. "I only saw Ron find it. We have to go."

Sam picked up his brush and went back to his painting. Anne glanced at his watch, which was lying on the counter. I wondered where hers was. Mine, alas, was home by the bathtub. But, by feel, I knew it was getting late. Even Baskerville, who Anne brought along on a leash, seemed in a hurry.

"What time was it?" I asked as we came out into the driveway.

"Twenty of twelve," she said. "Time to go, quick. Jeeter is due home at one."

I saw Revonda picking yellow lilies in the circular wildflower garden. Nobody else around. "Good morning," she called, and then, "My mother loved these."

Good, at least Revonda was recovering. I waved to her and called back, "We've got to hurry over while Jeeter is out. It's already twenty of twelve."

We walked up the hill, toward Jeeter's long rutted drive.

Mrs. Justice was out on the narrow wood front porch, hanging dishtowels on a line just under the roof. They waved like worn-out flags.

She was as pale and wispy as I remembered. "Good morning," she said to me. "No snake stories today." Was she laughing at me?

"This is my cousin Anne," I said. "Your daughter tells me that you know a great deal about herbs, and how they're used in these mountains. She said she believed that if we came on a Monday you would tell us what you could."

She hesitated with arms up to the clothesline. Her voice was wooden: "I haven't seen my daughter in a while."

Keep talking, I told myself: "Of course you know there were herbs found with Paul Roland's body. The sheriff doesn't seem to be doing much to find out why. Not that we can discover. We thought it might help us know what happened if we found out what those herbs meant, maybe help prevent more killing."

"Deputy Ron talked to me." She lowered her arms but didn't invite us in.

"Did he ask you about the herbs?" I asked.

She sighed. "You can come in, but please tie the dog on the porch, and you have to be gone before my husband comes back."

She opened the door slowly as if she was tired and led us over to the bookshelf. The books were almost the only color in the whole dimly lit room. What a place to grow up. I tried to picture Jinx as a child in this gray room. Jinx, who inspired Sam to hug her. I hoped Anne wasn't thinking about that.

The only furniture in that room other than the bookshelf was the low table Jeeter had laid his gun on when he tried to scare me, and a few assorted chairs. His gun hung on the wall now.

"When I talked to Ron, my husband was here," she said. She fingered an old leather-bound book on the shelf. "Jeeter doesn't like me herb doctoring. He says only faith can heal. But I figure God made the herbs, too. I didn't tell Ron much. Just that those herbs do grow around here. Most anybody with a sharp eye could find some. I told him Paul came to see me to ask me where wild herbs grew. Some only grow on south slopes. Some want sun, some want shade." But dill was one of the herbs found with Paul — and dill isn't wild.

She pulled an old book out of the bookcase and stared down at flowers and leaves embossed on the leather cover. She stroked the book like it was a pet. Her hands were worn shiny with work. Large hands for such a small woman. "My husband was glad to see Paul come, at first. My Jeeter thought he might save Paul. But Paul wouldn't be saved, and Jeeter decided all herb doctoring was the devil's work."

She opened the book and leafed through the pages. "After they found Paul, I was curious myself," she said, "and I looked in this book that tells some of the old lore about herbs. I found this." She pointed to a picture labeled "Verbena officinalis." I pulled my sketch of the herb that had been on Paul out of my pocketbook. That was it. She handed me the book, and I began to read the quaint old type. Boy, did verbena have a lot of names: verbenacaea, enchanter's plant, herb of the cross, holy herb, Juno's tears, pigeon's grass, pigeonweed, simpler's joy and vervain, blue vervain and hyssop. And lots of uses. Good for eczema or skin conditions, had been used for whooping cough, dropsy, jaundice, liver and kidney problems, and to heal wounds. Once thought to be a cure for the plague. But Paul didn't have those problems. Certainly not the plague.

Mrs. Jeeter ran her finger over the picture of the spiky flower. "Some people call verbena 'herb of Grace,' " she said. "They say it grew on the mount of Calvary, and stanched the wounds of the Saviour. They say it has the power to protect."

I looked down the page: Albertus Magnus

said verbena was a love charm. Why would Paul need a love charm when his girl ran after him? Nicholas Culpeper in the seventeenth century said you could mix verbena with lard to help pain in secret parts. A sexy herb.

"Maybe this is what you want," Mrs. Jeeter said and pointed to a couplet down at the bottom of the page:

> *Vervain and dill*
> *Vervain and dill*
> *Hinder witches from their will.*

Vervain and dill! Exactly the herbs found with the body. To protect Paul from *witches?*

"There are witches in the high school," she said. "Jeeter says it's one sign the end of the world is coming."

Was Paul afraid of the cult of kids? Were they afraid of Paul? That was a weird thought. Did the person who killed Paul, or more than one person, put the herbs with his body for protection from him? From maybe a curse as he died? I shuddered.

"I couldn't tell Ron about this with my husband here," Mrs. Jeeter said. She glanced around the room nervously, as if she expected Jeeter to be hiding in a corner. "You understand, don't you?" she asked. "You saw how he can get. And yet he's a fine man with a great faith until the sickness makes him misbehave."

She found a flyer for some carpet-cleaning

service. "Lord knows I don't have a carpet," she said. She wrote the lines about vervain and dill on the back.

I put the verse in my pocket and promised to get it to Ron. I turned the shiny old pages of her herbal to dill. Nothing about magic there. Just said that infused with water or white wine, dill was good for the stomach.

"Paul saw this book?" Anne asked.

"Yes, he surely did." She bent her head as if she felt she'd helped to cause his death by letting him look at the book.

I was trying to think of something helpful to say when I heard Baskerville begin to bark. Mrs. Jeeter turned white. But it couldn't be time for Jeeter. I glanced at my wrist — and remembered. I'd left my watch by the tub. I took no chances. I ran out on the porch and undid Baskerville from the porch rail, fumbling at the knot in the leash. By the time I got it loose a car was coming into sight around the bend.

I pulled open the screen door, ran through the house with Baskerville, and out through the back door, which Mrs. Jeeter was holding open. Anne ran with me, both of us breathing too hard to speak. I heard the front screen door slam, high pitched and flimsy compared to a real door, but it must mean Jeeter was in reach of his gun. Maybe this isn't one of his bad days, I told myself, but I didn't believe it. I ran for the nearest opening in the weeds around the mowed part of the backyard, praying I'd find the shortcut there, and thank God I stumbled onto a path formed mainly from chunks of flat rock — uneven, but I could run on it. Anne being younger ran past me like a frightened wood nymph in her long paisley skirt and white blouse. "Hurry," she called. Briers caught at her skirt. She stumbled, but quickly righted herself. Baskerville ran just after her. A gun boomed behind us, and I almost tripped on a rough part of the rock. The path had grown narrow with weeds at both sides: The briers leaned across and grabbed at us.

Suddenly Baskerville stopped ahead of me. I tried to slip around her and see the trouble. Right across the path there'd been a rockslide. On one side of us was a cliff, too high and straight up to climb. On the other side were high weeds. Covering the path, and jutting out into the weeds, was a huge boulder and a bunch of small rocks that had evidently broken loose from the face of the cliff. Thank God they hadn't fallen just as we were passing. Anne was struggling through the weeds. Was Jeeter just behind? The boulder leaned toward us. We couldn't possibly climb over it. I plunged after Anne.

I let out my breath with relief when we came to the path again on the other side of the rock slide. My foot slipped on a rock, and into a crevice between two rocks. Ouch, my ankle turned. My whole leg cried alarm. I listened. No more gunshots yet. I limped onward, after Anne and Baskerville.

A stone floor stretched five to six feet wide, even wider in some places. The midday sun shone down into this corridor of rock from high above. A pine tree grew out of a crevice on the cliff side of the rock path, as if to say, "You see, I can grow anywhere."

Baskerville began first to growl and then bark. Anne tried to shush her. We didn't want to remind Jeeter where we were. The hair on the dog's back got dull black as it stood on end. Anne stood stock still. Stopped by a snake.

Right in the middle of the path, about ten feet ahead of us, a snake was stretched out in the sun. At least six feet long, with the wide ugly jaws that meant poison. Poison. Before I could even be sure that was a diamond pattern on its back, the snake coiled back, raised the tip of its tail, and began vibrating.

"Rattlesnake!" I called to Anne. "Stay back." She had already frozen.

Baskerville barked louder and crouched as if she was about to lunge. I threw my weight against Baskerville's leash, wrapped the leash around the pine tree, and tied it in three knots. Dern, I turned my ankle worse. I held the dog's mouth shut. I said, "Be quiet," then remembered what Revonda said, and added, "It's all right." Baskerville was a well-trained dog. She barked no more except for an occasional whimper.

Meanwhile, beyond Anne, the snake had moved to coil itself into a shallow mini-cave in the rock wall on the mountaintop side of the path. That cold metallic rattling was too even and shrill to seem like it came from a live thing. I felt the hair on my spine stand up like Baskerville's. I sat down. My ankle throbbed. "We can't go back," I said. We couldn't go forward past the rattler, either. In front of us, the path narrowed. "And I've sprained my ankle," I told Anne. "I'll do what I can, but I can't move fast. Above all, stay clear. I hear they can jump eight feet."

"How can we kill it?" Anne asked. She gave the snake a wide berth, but she didn't run. I was surprised how calm she was in a real crunch.

That coiled rattler was thick as my arm, thick in a way that said "power." Those bulges at the back of his triangular head made him look cruel, as if he enjoyed being poison. He watched us with alert eyes set under bony ridges, and the tip of his tail vibrated so it blurred and the ugly sound of the rattle went on and on. One brier grew out of a crevice on one side of his ugly coil.

"You can throw a rock to break a snake's back," I said. I noticed a flat rock near the bluff. Anne began to pry it up.

She picked up the rock, stood very straight, and took a deep breath. "I want to be the one to kill the snake," she said. "You can tell me how."

I was amazed. "You're not afraid?"

"I am terrified of snakes," she said, lifting her chin. "And that's why I'm going to kill this one. I'm going to send my mind a strong image, of me being brave. I'm not a target. That will be my magic."

Good Lord, I thought, that's what I get for spouting forth my silly theories about magic. I started to say, "Just get a good-luck charm." No, that wouldn't do.

"You have to break his back," I said.

"Yes," she said. "I'll throw this rock with all my strength."

There weren't but a few loose rocks I could see. Anne had to hit him just right. I thought: The gal who can't even *thunk* a two-hundred-pound husband with a grapefruit in the kitchen wants to try to hit the snake.

I wanted to say, Look: I know how to do this. Even if I'm scared sick. Even if I have to hobble on a bum foot. Why, you can't hit the broadside of a barn.

But I knew I would sound just exactly like Cousin Clothilde. Like poison. Just what Anne had heard all her life: You can't. Anne certainly didn't need to hear that now.

The rattler watched us with those small round eyes with yellow slits in the middle. Pitiless eyes.

"I know you can do it, Anne," said the part of me that feeds stray cats and hugs kids.

The rest of me went cold and thought: What does a rattlesnake do if you attack it and miss?

Chapter

29

MOMENTS LATER

"Stay at least ten feet back." My voice quavered. I think watching Anne was worse than trying to kill that snake myself. She had to throw that rock from a distance and at an odd angle, throw a curve to hit the snake square and hard.

She raised the rock and threw with all her strength. There was a loud *thunk*. She'd nicked the side of the snake's little cave and that took the force from her rock. The snake curled back tighter and rattled louder. Coiled in a spiral. Like the marks on Paul.

"Almost!" I said.

She looked around for another rock, but the stone floor of the path was solid, the top of a buried ledge. All I saw was a dead piece of tree limb which must have fallen down from high above. The dead limb might not be strong enough to kill the snake.

On the other side of the rock slide, there'd been a lot of stones. On this side on the stone floor of the path, nothing loose.

"There's a ledge above us," I said. The side of the rockwall up the mountain was at a steep slant, but there were cracks and crevices in it here and there. About halfway up was what looked to be a fairly wide ledge. "Rocks could be up there."

In fact, when Anne started to climb, I noticed the crevices arranged themselves nicely for easy toe- and hand-holds, almost to the ledge but not all the way. She reached up into the unknown. Her hand came down with a good-sized rock. Thank goodness. She dropped it down to the path below for ammunition. Baskerville let out a low growl. I held my arm around her. "It's all right."

Anne put her hand back and pulled down another rock and something clear. It was a folded-up plastic dry-cleaning bag!

I sucked in my breath. Somebody was hiding his murder weapons here. Or some group was doing it. In this snaky place where nobody wanted to come, Anne reached again, but I called, "Leave what's there. The sheriff will need to see." I hoped no one could hear me.

"More plastic bags," she called. "They were under the rock." So they wouldn't blow away, of course. She put the first bag in the pocket of her India-print skirt.

We had to get past the snake before the killer or Jeeter joined us. And the killer might be Jeeter. Anne climbed down. Pale but determined. I wanted to say "O.K., now let me try to hit the snake." I didn't really want us to be found dead with a plastic bag in Anne's pocket. But I knew how important it was to her to kill that snake. And I'm not the best shot in the world myself.

I said: "You'll get him now."

But with the snake farther under the overhang and as much in back of the brier as he could get, the aiming would be even harder. Anne got down on her knees and tried to skim a rock in. It hit the brier, which must have been tougher than it looked, and the rock shunted to one side. The snake went on rattling. The next stone had the same fate. I felt sick.

Now what? Anne came back and picked up the dead branch. It was about the length of a hoe, but twisted rather than straight. She would have to get close enough to hit the snake directly. The stick might break in her hands if she put force on it. But she'd have to put force to break the snake's back.

She walked toward the rattler, leaning forward so that her arm plus the stick put as much distance between the snake and her body as possible. With the tip of the stick, she pushed the brier-cane aside. I could see the snake coiled under the overhang watching us. He moved his head from side to side above the coil of his body, as if positioning himself to strike. She shoved the stick at him quickly. I prayed she'd break his back against the stone with the thrust. The stick broke. She jumped back. The snake was still moving. But the noise of the rattle had stopped. After my heart stopped thunking, I managed to pull myself up with the help of the tree and hobble over to look. Anne just stood there, a little stunned, I think. The stick still lay where Anne dropped it, holding the brier down so I could see Mr. Snake, coils pushed lopsided, head no longer held above them. I picked up the broken stick-half nearest me and threw it at him. His coils moved feebly. He did not rattle or try to strike.

I put my arms around Anne. "You did it." I laughed. "We're safe!" Well, more or less.

I undid Baskerville, and Anne helped me hobble down the path, past the snake, now definitely harmless, through a long patch of woods, through the edge of someone's pasture, and out into a pasture with three cows. I knew where I was when I hit the road. Just up from Revonda's. Hoorah!

But as I got my bearings, I saw flashing blue lights ahead in Revonda's driveway, through the trees. "Something's wrong," I told Anne. "What now?" My stomach turned over. With Anne's help, I hobbled as fast as I could, down the road toward the lights, and turned in the driveway. I told her to go on ahead, but she wouldn't do it.

We pushed our way through a knot of neighbors, not even stopping to ask what was wrong, and hurried toward Sam, who was standing on the porch talking to Ron and another deputy. Sam looked half sick, leaning on the porch rail. I also saw several men in uniform by the springhouse.

"I need to talk to you alone right now," Ron said to Anne. He took her arm, even before she could hug Sam, and pulled her through the kitchen door.

One of the deputies told me. "It's that girl named Jinx. She's dead."

I saw the sheriff and hurried over. "Where have you been?" he asked accusingly.

"Is Jinx dead?" I asked. He said yes, but that he was the one asking the questions. So I told him as briefly as possible where we'd been. When I finished, he looked at my swollen ankle and said, "There's bound to be trouble when amateurs get mixed up in these things." I bit my tongue. He softened slightly. "I guess we're lucky to find those plastic bags. These were pretty handy to the perpetrator, weren't they? Why, you could be at that shortcut from Revonda's place and back in five minutes if you ran, and most of the way you'd be out of sight. I'll send somebody to look at the scene right now.

"I reckon you want to see the body," he said. *Want* was not the right word. "Well, you can't," he said.

"I bet I can tell you how you found her," I said

sadly. "In the springhouse, since your photographer just went in. And it must be in a plastic bag, and I'm sure poor Jinx is naked." He gasped. I could see I was right.

"She felt guilty about her body," I said. "This killer goes for guilt. What kind of marks were on her?"

He blushed. The marks. I was sure, would be related to her sex. Because that was the seat of her guilt.

Chapter

30

The sheriff gave me permission to wait for Anne in the studio. "I am her nearest relative now here in the continental United States," I told him. He did believe in kin. I watched through the window as his men searched the place. Finally Anne came out of Revonda's house, almost staggering. Ron held her arm and walked her over to the studio. As soon as he left, she threw her arms around me and held tight.

She sat down at the table, eyes not quite focused, stunned. "They think it's Sam. It's my fault. What if it was Sam?" Her voice was flat.

I sat next to her and took hold of her icy hand. "You've got to tell me about this," I said. "I can't help if you don't."

"It's about the time." She almost choked on the words. "You remember I looked at Sam's

274

watch. It said twenty of twelve."

I did remember because we had to be sure to get to Jeeter's house while he was gone. Much good it did us, but we tried.

"When Ron asked me about what time we left, I told him because I had no reason to lie. That I knew of."

"Of course not," I said.

"Ron asked me was I absolutely sure of that time, and I said we knew we had to go see Mrs. Jeeter and get back while her husband was still gone to prayer meeting. So I'm sure I remember right. And Revonda saw us go."

"You told me what time it was, and you told her," I said. "Two witnesses."

"Ron asked me when I'd seen Sam after that, like it was some big deal. But I had to tell him, the first time I saw Sam was after we killed the snake and came home just now. And Ron said 'Jinx is dead,' like that's connected." Anne took a great breath, as if to pull in strength. "He said Billy found Jinx in the springhouse. Dead. In a plastic bag. There were those spiral marks. On each nipple." Anne put her hands over her own breasts and shuddered. "And like a target with an arrow — down there." She was so devastated just telling me that it took her a while to go on.

Markings of Jinx's guilt, as she and her killer saw it.

Finally Anne was able to speak in a weak and wondering voice. "Ron said that at quarter of twelve Jinx had stopped at Revonda's and left a picture of Paul she'd found on the last roll of film in her camera. Revonda and her cousin Edna were there, too, and saw her." She breathed deeply several times, as if that gave her strength to go on. "At about quarter to one Billy came to get springwater and found the body." Her voice became angry. "Revonda and her cousin and Billy all swear to that. So he knows Jinx was killed between those times." She twisted her hand and squeezed mine tight as if she needed something to hold on to. "He says Sam swears we were with him at noon. Sam says we were actually with him till twenty after twelve. He says he looked at his watch right after we left and was worried that we were so late."

"Have you talked to Sam?" I asked. "A madman killed Jinx. Sam isn't a madman."

"No, but I don't think Ron would have lied. Why would Sam lie?" Her eyes grew dark with terror. "I know what Ron thinks. He thinks Sam killed Jinx — and that means . . ." She put her hands over her face. She massaged her face as if she could rub those words away. She took her hands down and clamped them together.

"I'm not good at most things," she said, "but I've always been good at picking people. But maybe I only thought so. Because why would Sam lie? Why?"

"There must be an explanation for all this," I said firmly. "You *are* good at picking people. So am I. And I don't believe for a minute that Sam did that."

I said that to buck her up. But the truth is, my biggest fault as a sleuth is that I tend to like people, at least at first, and see their good sides. If I'd met Jack the Ripper, I would probably have been impressed by how nice he was to his dog.

But in Sam's case I felt rock-solid sure. He was much too charming to be a crazy killer. "What motive could he possibly have to kill Jinx?" I asked Anne.

"I don't know, but Jinx is dead and Sam lied about what he was doing at the time she was killed. Sam has no alibi, and Ron knows it. All because of me. How could I be such a fool," she demanded, "as to think that if I killed a snake I'd know I was O.K.? Jeeter kills snakes, and look at him. He's a nut."

"Yes, but a nut with an alibi," I said sadly.

Chapter

31

Revonda had asked us all to come over and brainstorm because none of us believed that Sam had killed Jinx. Yet Sam stuck to his story, saying that we were with him at noon whether we knew it or not. How could he be so stubborn?

I sat on the couch next to Ted. Revonda sat next to her vase of yellow lilies. Sam was at his easel, working on her portrait even while we talked.

I got up and hobbled over and looked over Sam's shoulder at the portrait. Under his brush, Revonda was both beautiful and elegant, because her bone structure was good, her chin was firm, her brows were high and arched. Her black silk dress was a subtle backdrop for her diamond necklace. Perhaps that's why she liked the

278

picture. But I studied the anger in that face, so subtle I could hardly see how Sam put it across except in the tenseness at the corners of the mouth, the brilliance of the eyes. There was fear in that face, not too obvious, but it came across, maybe in the same tension that held the head high like a queen's. To me, it was a disturbing picture. Almost a hypnotizing picture. The eyes grabbed, the way Revonda's eyes did in real life. It was a face with charm in the small smile, but, underneath the charm, no hope. I'm not sure how the paint strokes showed a quality that wasn't there, but they did. If I had been Revonda, I would have wanted Sam to burn that picture, like he did Anne's. Revonda probably didn't know about Anne's.

But I figured Revonda must have some hope left. She kept talking about how we were going to find the killer. She had hope of being avenged.

Sam said, "O.K. That's it. I'm finished." Revonda got up and went over to admire her picture and talk about how talented Sam was and how she'd help him gain the recognition he deserved as soon as we found the killer.

Revonda turned to me and raised an eyebrow. "How do you like it?"

I said I thought Sam had an amazing talent for catching the essence of the subject of a picture.

"Then don't look so sour," she commented. "It doesn't become you."

At least Sam hadn't been formally charged yet. That was something. We sat in a rough circle and tried to add up what we knew. Now, at least, we knew where the killer had kept the master supply of plastic bags even after the sheriff had made sure there were none left in the valley.

We added to Ted's list of people and time and alibis. For Jinx's death, Anne and I alibied each other. Cousin Edna had been in the house with Revonda. Billy had told us he'd been at his grandmother's. Not that she'd ever admit if he wasn't. We didn't know about the kids in the cult yet.

Revonda talked about all the artists Jinx worked for and how artists were not very stable people, except, of course, for Sam. And how Jinx had almost asked to be killed. By living off by herself, by wearing those provocative clothes, by associating with the wrong people.

Those words brought out the cruelty in the lines around Revonda's mouth. I kept seeing her as she was in Sam's portrait. I wanted to believe her when she said one of Jinx's artists must have killed Paul out of jealousy, Marvelle because she saw something, and Jinx in a rage. Artists, she said, have the imagination to find power in spreading terror. The killer, she said, "is the most powerful person in this valley right now. He has us all afraid. We expect horror. When Billy came running to my door, so scared he didn't even scream, I expected the worst." I saw the fear in her eyes glitter, just like in the picture, only more so.

Before we could say a word more, the doorbell rang. Revonda jumped up out of her chair and said, "You go, and if it's someone I want to see, I'll come out. I'm going to my room." She strode off through the hall to her bedroom while I went through the living-room to the front door. I opened it to Reverend Phillipson. I greeted him loudly. Revonda certainly wouldn't want to hear him talk about how good would come from evil. Or see him try to break bunches of twigs to show that we have strength when we stand together.

Sam said he had jobs to do. Ted said please to excuse him, he had to help Sam. Anne and I stayed.

Personally, I felt comforted by the Reverend, even as he stood there in the doorway. He really did have the face of a happy baby, round, innocent, with fine skin, blue eyes beaming kindness. His white hair was as fine as dandelion fuzz and circled his bald dome like a monk's. He reached out and touched Anne's hand lightly. "I have been thinking of you and hoping for the best." He turned to me. "And I'm so glad you're here with Anne. How can I help?"

It was a pleasure to be with someone who didn't seem a bit afraid. He smiled gently, like he believed in Santa Claus all year round — not for him, but for us. His ears were baby pink. His small pink hands were peacefully folded in front of him.

We sat down in three carved rosewood chairs near the front door. "Can I tell you things you won't tell anybody else, not even the sheriff?" Anne asked.

"I might advise you to tell the sheriff," he said. "But rest assured, I won't tell him myself."

She had lowered her voice, and he lowered his, too. I realized he'd inadvertently picked the chairs farthest from Revonda's closed door. She wouldn't be able to hear.

Anne gave him a pleading look: "I'm afraid."

He nodded. "That seems natural. We're all afraid right now."

"But I'm afraid of everybody. I'm even afraid of my husband. I'm even afraid of myself. I'm afraid of being afraid."

Too bad, because she had seemed so bold facing the awful reality of that snake.

She told the whole story of her relationship with Sam, beginning with Boston, including the fact that she didn't really have any way to know anything about Sam except what he told her and her gut hunch, which had been that he was the very best thing in her life. "But now . . ." She swallowed and took one of those I-absolutely-won't-cry deep breaths. Then she told the Reverend with his pink hopeful ears how Sam seemed to tell a lie. How there were witnesses that what he said wasn't true. "I know in my gut he wouldn't lie. But I'm not sure I can trust my gut."

He put his hand over hers. "Trust is a great

gift," he said. "Why don't you trust yourself?"

"Things go wrong for me," she said. And she told him about the time she took a turn and thought she was going the right way down the road, and suddenly she was going the wrong way, against the traffic. "Things like that are always happening to me."

"Traffic is different from a gut hunch," he said. "I would trust you with a gut hunch. I bet Peaches here does, too."

I nodded.

"I wish," Anne said, "that I hadn't read Paul's magic books. Because one kind of magic in Paul's books makes sense to me. And that's if you concentrate one hundred percent on visualizing a thing, with strong emotion, that's the way to make it come true."

The Reverend frowned like he didn't agree.

She explained faster, "I mean maybe you could change things in your own life."

He sat perfectly still, hands clasped. And nodded. "That sounds a little like prayer, if there could be prayer without God."

"The trouble is," Anne sobbed, "that I can't help visualizing what can go wrong, visualizing the things I fear, like me dead in a plastic bag. So maybe I'm making bad magic against myself. And the more that scares me, the more I can't stop."

He stopped patting her hand and got up from his chair. He wandered over to the whatnot shelf where Revonda kept the little sewing basket I'd

never seen her use and the pearl-handled re-
volver, which must have belonged to her
grandfather. He picked up the gun and weighed
it in his hand. How odd. And I thought, suppose Revonda is right? Suppose he's crazy?

He took a small brown paper sack out of
Revonda's sewing basket with the red satin
lining. He shook something out of the sack into
the pink palm of his hand: a bullet. "Most
people don't know Revonda keeps bullets
hidden in her sewing kit," he said. Calm as ever.
"I found out one day when I was waiting for
Revonda and a button came off my jacket. I'm
going to load this gun," he said, in the kind of
warm melodic voice he might have used to say,
"What a lovely baby."

"My father taught me how to do that," he said
sweetly. "He collected guns. You never forget
those things." He turned around and I heard
clicking noises of bullet going into gun. I was so
surprised that I froze, staring at the back of his
humbly bent head. Suppose we'd escaped Jeeter
and the rattlesnake and the marijuana farmer
only to be shot by a preacher who looked like a
cross between a monk and a Kewpie doll. He'd
been so one-sided good he'd gone crazy — that
was it. Yet we'd trusted him. So much for *my* gut
hunch. I heard Anne laughing. She sounded
hysterical.

He turned and aimed the gun at her head. I
wondered what to do. You don't want to startle
a madman. "This gun is magic." He nodded to

himself, as if approving his own wisdom. His small mouth curved in a gentle smile. He kept the gun aimed. "Paul talked to me about magic. Most people wouldn't talk to him about that. He used to come by when I was working in my garden. Don't move away," he ordered me. Anne sat perfectly still in her chair. Stunned?

"My father taught me to hit the target." The Reverend turned to Anne. "I'm a good shot. I could hit you right between the eyes. Are you visualizing that?"

I was. Even seeing the headlines: INSANE MINISTER MURDERS PUPPETEER. How could I think about headlines when I needed to be defending us? Somehow the whole situation seemed unreal.

"This gun is Paul's kind of magic," the Reverend repeated. "Aimed at your head because that magic means thinking it's all up to you to do things exactly right, to visualize exactly right. You are alone."

I remembered a charm in the stuff Sam copied from Paul's books that said the devil would drag you down to hell if you got it wrong. I could see what hell it was for Anne, being scared of her own fear.

"If I killed you and put you in a plastic bag in a way that showed what I thought you ought to be punished for, that might be black magic," he said. I figured he was even crazier than Jeeter. He needed pills, and no one knew it. So was he saying the murders were some kind of magical human sacrifice? He still looked as kind and gentle as a baby. The gun was now pointed at Anne's heart. What on earth could I do?

"Don't you see, each of these murders can be a kind of cruel magic to make the people of this valley focus their minds on a wrong idea: that each of us is alone with his sin, alone with his guilt." He was beginning to use his singsong sermon voice. I wondered if he'd shoot too quickly if I tried to hit the gun out of his hand, and decided he might.

"There is no good magic but love," he sang. "Love is God's magic."

Then all of a sudden he lowered the gun and beamed and raised his voice to a friendly triumphant bellow: "We are not alone with our sins. We are never alone when we can pray."

He turned to Anne. "You were certain I would shoot you. You saw it. But you saw wrong. It was your fear you saw, not your future."

He went over and put the gun back on the whatnot, just as casual as if he hadn't almost given me a heart attack. I still felt weak. He strode back, eyes flashing joy. "I believe these terrible murders can teach us that lesson. They're dramatic enough so the whole community, and maybe eventually the whole nation, will finally learn that lesson. That would be a blessing." He was radiant, arms raised.

I was glad Revonda wasn't there, or she would have choked him in a rage.

Anne's mouth was open in amazement. I thought: He's so wrapped up in his lovely ideas he doesn't even see us. He doesn't know what he just put us through, making his point. He came back and took Anne's hand. She stared at her hand in his as if it might explode.

"You believe that, if you visualize your death in fear, that will help to make it happen."

"Or losing Sam," she said tentatively. "Or anything I'm afraid of."

"But you see," he said, beaming, "God has the last word. So visualize God helping you. Have faith." He hugged Anne. "You're going to be all right. I'll see you soon. Give Revonda my love." He came over and hugged me, too. And with that he left.

I sat. I felt like I'd been picked up by a tornado and put back down again. Anne looked dazed. "He does have faith," she said, "gun and all. I'd like to have that kind of faith. But I'm still scared."

His words were still whirling round in my brain, but I did have the gumption to say, "He's right about your intuition, Anne. You've got to trust it."

Chapter

32

MONDAY, 8:00 P.M.

I walked Anne back to the studio, through the early evening cool, just at the time when the light begins to get blue. I was still favoring my ankle. We found Sam at his easel, painting furiously, seeming isolated in an island of bright electric light. He was humming cheerfully to himself.

"Reverend Phillipson pointed a loaded gun at me, Revonda's pearl-handled pistol," Anne told him in a flat voice.

"Umm," he said. He was entirely focused on his picture. He didn't even say "Hi" to me.

Anne repeated the gun bit, somewhat louder. He glanced up. He laughed. "He was illustrating some noble truth, right? He is a character." Sam hummed louder, wiggling his bare toes and dabbing paint. He could have acted a little bit concerned. This was the evening of the day a young woman he knew had died. And he was the prime suspect. So who was the real Sam?

"The Reverend scared me a lot." Anne hugged herself, and I thought: She wishes he'd hug her in one of his great bear hugs.

"He likes a good image," Sam said, hardly looking at Anne. "He got your attention. Religious shock treatment." He kept right on painting sixty miles an hour.

"You don't intend to let anything upset you, even a pearl-handled dueling pistol. Loaded and aimed at your own wife. If you think you've got a picture right, nothing else matters to you, does it, Sam?" Anne's voice rose harshly. "Not even me."

He looked up, eyes wide with surprise.

I walked around behind him to see what kind of picture had grabbed his whole attention like that.

The picture under his brush was glimmery, reflective, but warmed by touches of red and green. Pretty. But I'd learned never to trust my first glance at one of Sam's pictures. Beneath the pretty colors I always suspected booby traps. I kept studying the canvas, and suddenly it sorted itself into a crucifix . . . under ice? Very odd.

Then, like a hit over the head, I understood what I was looking at. I saw Christ on the cross in a plastic bag tied shut with Christmas ribbons. Sam was just dabbing more red on a ribbon. Anne let out a gasp so loud I was afraid the sheriff's men would come running. She'd seen it, too.

"Sam! You can't paint that!"

He turned and looked at her, feet apart, head back, and those bushy eyebrows up. "I *am* painting this." He actually smiled.

"You've got to get rid of it. Someone from the sheriff's department might come in here and see it."

"I'll tell them I'm painting it for them." He grinned so broadly his beard wiggled. He winked at me.

"Oh, Sam, don't joke," Anne begged. "Three people are dead from plastic bags."

"You've got to understand." He had turned around and was giving us a lecture. "I explore things in paintings. This painting probes the killings. Otherwise, the very thought of them would drive me mad. I think I know the essence of what's wrong. I have it here even if I don't have the details yet." He was actually bouncing on his toes with satisfaction.

"You mean you don't know the details of who did it and why?" Anne sounded scornful.

He completely missed her sarcasm. "No," he said. "I don't have those details quite yet."

"You don't have an alibi for any of the killings, and we're flatlanders, and you're a suspect. You're a fool." I had never heard Anne so bitter. She was rigid with anger.

"I have to finish this picture." So he was going

to be a mule. Too bad.

"My God, Sam," she exploded, "you're in the Bible Belt. Jinx's father would lynch you if he found this picture. Even Revonda, who loves you so, will think you're crazy. Unless you get rid of this quick, I'll think you're crazy. If the sheriff wants any further excuse to arrest you, he'll think this is it." Her voice came out sharp and raspy.

"I can't get rid of this picture." He crossed his arms. He sounded hurt. "I have to explore further. Also, I think this is one of the best things I've ever done. Someday this picture will make me famous."

"Famous in the electric chair!" Anne yelled. "You're pigheaded. You'll never change."

Should I leave? I asked myself. Should I try to mediate? Curiosity got the best of me. I listened. But I said, "Better keep your voices down."

"Don't you even care about the people who are dead?" Anne whispered.

"I care." He didn't even lower his voice. "Just like I care about you."

Anne opened her mouth and shut it. She hugged herself harder. "All right," she choked. "What does this picture mean? What does it prove?"

"It's about having to hide what's ugly," he said. "About having to cover agony and pretend it's something else: a Christmas present. About how something in us always sees through and knows the agony is there but can't face it. That's what's wrong with the world. It's worse wrong with somebody here in the valley." He was waving his arms, full of himself. Anne wasn't going to be impressed.

"If we can't find the killer, that's all bullshit!" she yelled.

Sam drew himself up, dignified. "I believe that if I keep working on this picture, I'll know who the killer is," he said. "I intend to keep working." He raised his voice angrily: "If you want to change somebody, then change yourself."

Oh dear. He needed to hug her, not say that. But something had hold of him. I hoped to God it was his muse and not some hidden inner demon.

"My mother and father were right about you!" Anne yelled. She turned to me and said, "I need air."

And I thought: Good. A cooling-off period. That might help.

We walked up and down the driveway in the half light. Revonda had turned on the outdoor lights, and the last daylight and the electric mixed, making the leaves on the trees vibrant green.

"I hate Sam," Anne seethed. "And I love Sam. He must he crazy. But he's what I count on." Her voice rose with surprise at that. "I know he told a lie about the time. But I want to trust him. I'm so confused. I feel like there's no central me to tell all the other parts how to behave or what to think."

"There is a central you, and you have to be very still and listen for it," I said. "That's what works for me. Sleep on this."

We walked round and round and finally went back inside. We found Sam still painting like there was no tomorrow. "I think I'll work all night. I feel as if I have a deadline." He sounded frightened.

"I'll be back in the morning," I said. Something was out of kilter between these two, about to run amok. I wished I could stop it. But I couldn't spend the night. I hadn't been invited, and I needed to get back to Ted.

Love needs to be nourished and cared for. I couldn't bear to see Anne and Sam ignoring that, so I went home to nourish and care for my own.

Chapter

33

Tuesday was a day when nothing fit together. It began with a dream. I saw a spiral just like the spirals painted on the bodies, except this spiral stood alone in the air. It began to revolve and a voice said, *"Clockwise."* Then the spiral turned the other way into a vortex, a whirlpool. I fell into it headfirst and was sucked down, struggling while the voice said, *"DAB is BAD."* I opened my eyes, and it was morning, and I was tangled in the sheet.

I struggled loose and sat up. Ted was awake, too. "Nightmare?" he asked. I told him about it. I said, "Dab is what Sam does with paint." I threw myself over next to Ted and said, "I want people to love each other. I can't help it. When they do love each other a lot, and then it looks like they may stop, I almost can't stand it."

294

We loved each other a lot, and that helped. "Thank God I trust you," I said. "To care this much for someone you didn't trust would be awful."

"Likewise," he said.

"I wish I could find somebody *besides* Sam to confess to three plastic-bag murders quick," I told Ted at breakfast as I stared out the kitchen window at the rain. He pointed out that it was always possible Sam was guilty. That made me feel so sad I could have cried. At least we hadn't had any of those strange hang-up calls this morning.

After Ted left for the college, my car just naturally found its way to Bloodroot Creek. The rain was lifting. Clouds came and went. Mist clung to the mountaintops. I met Knowing Agnes in her mismatched reds, walking along the road picking wet wildflowers, and on a hunch I stopped the car in a wide grassy spot by the road and offered her a ride. After all, if she repeated word for word what she heard, here was a whole source of information we hadn't made the most of yet. After Paul's funeral something had triggered Agnes to repeat what she heard about Paul. She didn't just say gibberish. We couldn't ask her questions, but maybe I could find some way to guide her talk.

She stood near the door I'd opened on the passenger side and peered at my face as if I was a sign she couldn't quite read. "You can't come in," she said. "We don't let anybody in our house now except our kin."

I smiled in what I hoped was an encouraging way and held out my hand. "We never used to lock our door," she quavered, "but now we don't know who to trust." A tear rolled down her weather-beaten cheek.

So the murders had made her less welcome. I supposed even Agnes could kill, at least in theory. She could have a plastic bag in that big battered red pocketbook, hanging over her shoulder just like mine. She felt rejected. I reached in my pocketbook and took out a chocolate bar, insurance that if I'm lost I won't be hungry, too. I patted the seat in welcome and held out the candy. She took the bar and handed me her bunch of wildflowers. "All our sympathy," she said. She climbed into the car, gave me a glowing smile, unwrapped the chocolate, and took a bite.

I noticed how her nails were cared for, how neatly her skirt was mended where it must have been torn by briers and such. Somebody loved Agnes enough to take good care of her and leave her free. She sat back in the car seat and made herself comfortable.

"Revonda Roland," I said to her. "Anne Newman. Sam Newman." She took another bite and licked her lips. "Marvelle Starr," I said. "Paul Roland." I paused a while between names, also between first and last names in case she only knew the first. "Sheriff Henderson," I said. "Ron Brank, Mert, Octavia . . ." I couldn't remember Mert's or the psychologist's last names because I hadn't given them my *How to Survive Without a Memory* treatment. Never mind. "Jinx Justice, Jeeter Justice, Buck Justice," I said.

I guess I hoped it would be a little like seeding clouds to get rain. I'd drop a subject, and it might pull out more. But Agnes quietly finished the chocolate bar, and then she seemed restless. How could I jog her mind before she left me?

Words wouldn't work. I'd try reenactment. The couch cover I meant to take to the dry cleaners was in the backseat of the car. I reached back and got the middle seat cushion cover that is shaped a little like a short plastic dry-cleaning bag. Shirt model. I put it over my head. Any sane person who'd come along would have been sure I'd lost my mind. But I'll try anything

Agnes cried out, "No! No! No!"

I pulled the cover off quick. She was reaching for the door handle and wrenching it open. She jumped from the car. I figured I'd blown it. But then she turned and made a pronouncement. "Nobody will ever suspect me."

The killer had said that. I was sure! Who'd care what Agnes heard?

She left me in a hurry and took off in a flash of red down the first driveway. I hoped she found a welcome.

I sat there in the car and pondered. Whoever felt above suspicion had someone to confide in. Or it could be someone who talked to themselves out loud. So it could be almost anybody.

Except Sam! So he wouldn't have said "nobody will ever suspect me."

Wow! I could tell Anne why it couldn't have been Sam! I'd felt so bad about that girl. I wanted to bring her hope.

I set right out for the studio, singing to myself. Things are going to be better, I told myself. They are. Outside the sky opened up again and cried in a steady light rain.

Chapter

34

Immediately Afterward

The sheriff's car drove into Revonda's driveway just ahead of me. I followed him in to see what was up, crossing my fingers. He parked in front of the house, got out of his car, and when he saw me get out of mine, too, he waited for me on Revonda's front steps. "I was hoping you'd be here." Nicest thing he ever said to me. It wasn't mutual. "I want to talk to the lot of you." He seemed pleased with himself. If you could cross a steam shovel and a grinning Halloween pumpkin, that was him. Still wearing those fancy cowboy boots.

Anne met us at the door, and the sheriff strode over to Revonda's chair. He was really in luck if he wanted all of us together. Anne and Sam were sitting in the living room, drinking coffee with Revonda. One on each side of her, pointedly not looking at each other.

"Revonda, honey," the sheriff thundered, "you need to be sure that anybody who works with you lets me know right away about anything like a threatening phone call or a marijuana field." He said that straight to Revonda, implying the rest of us were deaf and blind and under Revonda's thumb.

Hey, he meant me! "I told your deputy," I said. "I didn't tell him right away, because the calls were so vague, and I wasn't sure where the farm was, or if that really was marijuana." That sounded pretty lame, and his shrug said he didn't believe me, but it wasn't really me he stayed mad at. It was Revonda. He glared at her like it was her fault that I fell short.

"Since we heard, we've been tracing calls to your number," he said directly to me. "Some came from a farm in the area where you say you got lost and then saw marijuana between the corn rows."

"So what are you coming to tell us?" Revonda demanded. "Why are you beating around the bush, Harley? Making my friend stand here like a school kid." (I wasn't sitting because I didn't want Man-Mountain looking down at me.)

The sheriff kept grinning. "I went with my men to that farm yesterday morning, Buck Justice's place. Jeeter's brother."

So. It was Buck.

The sheriff turned to me and raised his voice. "But we didn't get there soon enough. No marijuana growing there."

I kept my mouth shut and waited. What was he about to spring?

"We did find traces of leaf they left when they pulled it up." His grin turned into a grin of rage. His voice went higher. "Somebody warned Buck. Now, which of these folks did you tell before you told the law?" he asked me. "Somebody saw to it that Buck knew before we got there." He swept us with a triumphant glance.

"Evidently," said Revonda, "Buck had the elemental intelligence to know that if you had a hint of where the farm might be, you'd have a plane in there searching before breakfast. Even you would be smart enough to do that, Harley."

"I was smart enough to find a lot more than marijuana when Peaches Dann here finally gave us the facts." He pointed a finger so close it almost jabbed me. "We went to that farm and we found cocaine in the house — two pounds, hidden good. In a shed out back, we found black candles and feathers and bones and a knife." He said that like it was what he'd always wanted to find, and like it proved me guilty.

"We also found a list of high-school students. Kids who got in trouble a while back. We've brought them in for questioning, and some of those kids admit they were members of a cult that met on that farm and helped distribute drugs. What do you think of that?" I thought it was amazing we hadn't heard about it. He must have scared the families into silence, or Mert would have picked it up on the grapevine.

I wondered where Sam had hidden the list of cult members that Billy gave him. Sam, sitting there next to Revonda, kept his mouth shut tight.

"Now, what I came here in person to say is that, this time I'll give you the benefit of the doubt about deliberately withholding information. But if it happens again, I will arrest every one of you for obstructing my investigation."

With that he stomped out, still grinning like he had the best of us and meant to keep it that way.

I felt sorry for Mrs. Jeeter and almost sorry for Jeeter. I bet they hadn't known they were related to the man behind such ugly goings-on. I also felt like another shoe was going to drop. Certainly the sheriff would send someone over to question me further. And maybe the others. I still worried he might arrest Sam. Suppose they found the list of cult members Sam had hidden goodness knew where?

"That Harley is full of himself," Revonda said. "I could have told him Buck Justice was no good."

"I have some good news," I said and told them about Knowing Agnes. But Anne wouldn't give up being mad with Sam. And as I say, Revonda didn't look well. We were not a lively group.

"What did you discover by painting your picture last night?" I asked Sam. "Did you sort out your intuition while you painted? Did you find any answers?"

He perked up. "Partly." He put his coffee cup down on the little table that held Paul's picture. "The killer is getting desperate because he can't control things. Because he can't commit the perfect crime." Sam began to expand, almost glow. Anne watched him coldly, Revonda with interest. "Whoever is killing isn't doing it for normal reasons — not for greed or lust or revenge," Sam said. "So any one of us could be the killer and not show a sign of those passions." He glanced at us eagerly, like we might enjoy a chance to confess.

"Is that all that came to you from painting that picture?" Anne asked. Her scornful eyes said "crazy picture." That wouldn't help.

"Yes," he said. "If the world ends it will not be for greed or lust or revenge, either." He said that like an added inspiration. "It will be from self-deception."

Poor Anne wanted to throw something at him, I could tell. Theorizing about the end of the world while we had to deal with a real pickle. So I shouldn't have asked him — but I was intrigued.

"Why self-deception? I think that's a pretty tame sin. I indulge in it myself, sometimes."

"Think about it!" he cried. "The greatest realistic greed still wants the world to exist to enjoy possessions in. Same with lust, same with revenge. But if you pretend the world can't end, then here comes the end of the world."

"This is a hell of a time to worry about some

end of the world," Anne snapped. "We might be killed today, before we find who's dangerous here."

"A killer who deceives himself is the most dangerous." That rolled off his tongue like one of the Reverend's sermons. "So I'd like to suggest we stick together in twos or threes. I may get arrested at any moment," he said, "because nobody will believe that you-all got the time mixed up yesterday, and I did have an alibi." He said that rather casually, as if it didn't matter in the long run.

Anne looked at her feet.

"Even you can be wrong, Sam," Revonda said, "but that doesn't mean you're guilty. Maybe your watch was wrong and you forgot you reset it."

"My watch keeps excellent time!" he announced. "I never reset it. But let's talk about the future, not the past." He sure didn't help the people who wanted to believe he had a future.

"And since we're sticking together," he said, "Peaches and I can both go with Anne to her puppet show. I hope you didn't forget it, Anne. Because it's nearly time now." He glanced at his controversial watch.

Puppet show! I was amazed. In the middle of all this?

Anne said, "Oh, dear. That. I'd like to forget it. But they called and reminded me. I signed a contract for a family reunion. The descendants of James Norwood. Now I think they want me especially because I'm notorious. I'm on the news. When they called up yesterday, they offered to pay a bonus if I'd still do it."

Revonda put her hand over Anne's. "Those Norwoods are related to Jeeter's wife. You certainly ought to look them over. This may be an opportunity."

"Come on," Sam said to Anne. "We need to get the puppet stuff in the truck." She didn't answer him, but she got up to go.

Good, I thought, this'll get us out of this house before somebody shows up to give the third degree. Why hadn't the sheriff told us to stick around? Did he think we'd lead him somewhere?

I sat down next to Revonda, patted the dog, and tried to sort out my thoughts. "Is this Hound or Baskerville?" I asked. They were so alike.

"Hound," Revonda said. "Sam took Baskerville to the vet yesterday. She was throwing up."

One less protection for Anne, I thought. Baskerville had attached herself to her since Paul died. I didn't trust Hound. "Even Hound is acting oddly," Revonda said.

Sam came back and said the puppet stuff was ready, and we set out, three of us together in the van. Anne still glowering at Sam.

We hadn't gone far when we saw flashing lights from the sheriff's department car in our rearview mirror. The car zoomed up behind us and blinked us over to the side of the road.

When two deputies took Sam, that shook Anne out of her anger. She hugged him goodbye like he was more valuable than gold. He seemed to take this all in his stride. "I expect you to find the real killer," he commanded us grandly.

I offered to drive, since the tears streaming down Anne's face would have made it difficult for her to see the road. We agreed that returning to the studio would be more depressing. We had directions to get to the Norwood family re-union, but we got lost. Unfortunately, I'm good at that. So is Anne. And I'm sure we were more prone to it because we were upset.

This wasn't a good day to get lost. Someone was following us. I noticed that almost as soon as we were on a totally unfamiliar stretch of road. The houses were few and far between: a small clapboard cabin, glimpsed down a drive with a big bushy dog barking as I passed; a pink trailer with no car in sight. If I turned into a driveway to ask for help and nobody was home, we might be trapped. I mustn't panic. But that blue car reflected in the rearview mirror fol-lowed every turn we made. Suppose . . . ? Stop it, I told myself, trying to keep my mind on the road. But the car kept following. Way far back. When I slowed down, it slowed down. When I speeded up, it speeded up.

And as we drove along, I found myself won-dering: If the cult killed, why hadn't they killed me when I found the farm where they met? If they knew the sheriff found their list of members there because of me, what might they do to get even now? Or was the cult a diversion, and the killer was out there, totally unknown?

Anne turned and looked behind us.

"Pretend you don't see that car," I said.

If I kept turning uphill, maybe I'd get to the Blue Ridge Parkway, which tended to be a high road. If I got there, I could get my bearings.

Chapter

35

EARLY TUESDAY AFTERNOON

The car behind us vanished around the curves as the road wound up and up. Then we began to descend. I guess God does look after fools, drunks, the USA, and me. Thank goodness, we came to a TO-THE-PARKWAY sign. Perhaps I could get out of sight around a curve before the blue car came close enough to see whether I went left or right. I whisked past two young men on motorcycles.

I was going way over the speed limit, but I sure didn't care if I got arrested for speeding. In fact, I thought of jail as a nice safe place. How fast would I have to go to be hauled in on the spot? My tires squealed on a curve. I hoped our follower wasn't in hearing distance. A side road went downhill from the Parkway. I turned down. The more turns, I thought, the more I can hope to lose the blue car.

Suddenly houses were closer together. The road straightened and ran along the side of the mountain. That ominous car came back into view, then curves hid him again. I began to look for a driveway I could zoom into and hide behind a house. But on the steep hillside, most of the driveways were in front of the houses. The road straightened again. No hiding place once he got to the straight part. He could see my every move.

I saw a sign in front of a house on the down side of the road. "There's a great drive!" I said. "It goes around in back of the house. And that building has offices in it. Someone is sure to be there. We won't be trapped by ourselves."

I zoomed into the driveway, trying to slow down bit by bit, but the wheels squealed again. I parked in back and was pleased to see there was a back door. We jumped out of the car and hurried over. The sign on the door there was smaller: RONALD ZIMMERMAN, PH.D. SPECIALIST IN DYSLEXIA AND OTHER LEARNING CHALLENGES.

"Zimmerman," Anne said. "That's the man Sam told me to go see! The one he said helped people who did dumb-seeming things and had trouble in school."

"Don't just stand here," I warned. "Let's get inside."

We went into a dim hallway, but I could see that the brass doorknob inside had a little turnable piece in the center. A knob lock. I latched it behind us. The narrow hall ran from back to front. We followed it to a brightly lit room with a reception desk, and a woman behind it, who looked like the universal grandma. White hair, glasses halfway down her nose, pink cheeks. She smiled and said, "Oh, one of you must be Marcia Albert. We were afraid you'd forgotten your appointment for an evaluation. You're late."

I pointed to Anne. "This is the gal you want," I said.

Anne blinked, but then she followed the receptionist. Well, after all, if Marcia Albert wasn't coming, why waste the doctor's time? What better place to hide? Wasn't it fate that we ended up where Sam said to go? I bet that's what Anne thought. The receptionist said the basic evaluation took two hours. I asked to use the phone. I called Revonda and told her where we were and that I needed the name and number of the people with the family reunion. She didn't know it. I called Ted. No answer. Anne might know, but I wasn't about to disturb her appointment with Dr. Zimmerman. The family reunion would have to amuse itself with speculation about why we vanished.

I almost tripped over a lamp cord that snaked out into the room. Some hyper kid with an earlier appointment must have pulled it out. Part of me noticed, but most of me began thinking about loose ends. Good old one-track-mind.

I made a list of all the odd pieces we were trying to fit into the puzzle. Someone that no one would suspect, in a bandanna, a loose smock, and dark glasses. Someone near Marvelle's house, near the time she was killed. A large enough person so it could be a man. Jinx had favored dark glasses, but she was dead. Billy wore dark glasses even in dim light. He said he found them by the road near Revonda's house. Which could unfortunately point to Sam, since he lived in the studio.

Revonda had an alibi from Cousin Edna for the time of Marvelle's death. Cousin Edna was pretty vague. But Revonda would *never* have killed Paul, and besides she was with us at the time he died. The psychologist wore snake earrings and flaunted a dragon with spirals in the same spots they'd been painted on Paul. Very odd. The sheriff definitely had it in for Revonda. How could I find out more about him?

Jeeter was certified to have a mental illness, controlled by medication, except sometimes he didn't take it. If the Reverend Phillipson had flipped out after his wife died, as Revonda thought, he was not certified and not on medication. None of that particularly fit with what the sheriff said about a cult.

Ron was definitely taken with Anne, but I didn't think he'd go far enough to try to frame Sam, and besides, there was no need. Sam spent every free moment framing himself!

No matter how I tried to fit the pieces together, I couldn't get a picture. I got up and wandered back down the narrow hall and looked out the back window. A blue car was parked next to Sam and Anne's van. No person in sight. Now what?

Finally Anne came out. I never saw anyone glow with happiness so in my whole life. "Hey, there's a reason," she cried, "a real reason why I do things wrong. Like when I get lost or perceive things backward."

"So that's good?" I asked, surprised.

"Not bad luck, and not that I don't try. It's not that I'm lazy or mean. It's something real I can even do something about. I feel so relieved. It's great!"

Dr. Zimmerman had come out, too. He shook my hand. Maybe he thought I was Anne's mother. "And you have a talent," he said, turning to Anne. "So often, we find a special creative talent. That's why you have those puppets you told me about."

"That goes with the problem?" I asked. "What *is* all this?" Wasn't one of them going to tell me?

"Anne has a perceptual problem," the doctor said. "The term most people know is dyslexia. But each case is different."

"That's where you read words backward, right?" I asked.

"What you see," the doctor said, "is a smart girl who has trouble in school. Who has to work to read. She needs a special way to learn. And yes, sometimes she does read a word backward."

All of a sudden I remembered my dream. "I must have known it in my gut. I dreamed about that," I said, amazed. But why? My whole mind is on trying to solve three murders. Why would I . . . ? And then it hit me with a jolt. "In my dream someone said, *'Dab is bad.'* " I heard my voice screech with excitement. Anne, the doctor, and the receptionist all stared at me.

"If you could flip a word," I said to Anne, "you could flip a clock, couldn't you? See it backward, so to speak?" I was so excited I could hardly get the words out.

"Yes," the doctor said, eyeing me like I might have flipped. "I had a patient who did that."

Light dawned on Anne's face. "Twenty *of* could be twenty *after!* I saw Sam's watch wrong! Sam didn't lie!"

The doctor blinked and turned to one of us and then the other, totally confused — especially when Anne rushed over to throw her arms around him, tripped over the stray light cord, and she and the lamp fell to the floor with a loud crash.

The front door burst open, and Ron rushed in. Ron?

He had a gun in his hand, and it took him a minute to figure out there was no one to point it at. I introduced Dr. Zimmerman. I explained that nothing was wrong except someone had been following us.

Ron acted embarrassed. "I followed you," he said. "Heck, it's my day off, and I can do what I please, and I was scared maybe Sam was not the perpetrator." He flushed. "I didn't mean that like it sounds," he said quickly. "Mrs. Holleran here gets herself in jams," he said. And remembering the rattlesnake, I couldn't argue. "I was worried about Anne. Heck, I don't like to see any more pretty girls get killed. We never have enough of those."

"Would you write a letter that says I might see a clock backward?" Anne asked Dr. Zimmerman. Of course she had to explain to him what this was all about. He said he'd be delighted. In fact he said this was the most unusual case in his entire career.

"Would you take me right to the sheriff?" she asked Ron. "I want to tell the sheriff what happened. And I have to tell Sam I'll always trust him from now on, no matter what."

That was going to be exciting, I bet. But then, Anne was a playwright. Whatever happened would be grist for the mill.

Chapter

36

TUESDAY AFTERNOON

After Anne left with Ron, I asked to use Dr. Zimmerman's phone again and called home. Ted was off teaching. But I had a hunch that, with events moving so fast, I should try my answering machine. I have a special code for picking up messages.

The first message was from Pop. "Peaches," he said, "I want you to be sure to take Revonda's advice. She says she's going to be the first one to figure these murders out. I told her I thought you were close to figuring who did it, but she said she thought that she'd be first." That was all. No explanation.

The second message was from Octavia-the-Psychologist. "I have something you may need to see at the first possible moment," she said. "I'll be here all day." I called her back. No answer. Strange.

The last message was from Revonda. "I've made an important discovery about the murders," she said. "Get back to me." So I called her immediately, and she said to be at her house at three o'clock. "The time is important." Dr. Zimmerman's round clock on the wall said 2:30. When I asked Revonda what was up, she said, "I have a friend with me," in that I-can't-talk-now tone of voice. "The front door is unlocked," she said. "Come right on in."

I called my answering machine again and left word of what Octavia and Revonda said for Ted. "Revonda seems nervous about something," I said. "That's not like her." I asked him to meet me at Revonda's as soon as possible after his class that ended at three o'clock. Of course, he might have conferences with students. He might not even check the machine till quite late. I also left a message at the English Department Office, but he might not check that, either.

I figured I had time to get to Revonda's comfortably. But I was held up ten minutes in back of a fender bender while a tow truck hauled a smashed Honda out of the way, then I had to honk at two teens who were leaning out of their car windows, talking in the middle of the road. By the time I came to Octavia-the-Psychologist's house, I was running late. She was out weeding, saw me coming, and waved. When did that woman see patients? At midnight?

"Wait just a second," she called. "Billy gave

me a picture he said he wanted you to see. He said not to give it to anybody else. He'd have asked his grandmother to give it to you, but she's off somewhere. He wouldn't tell me why it was so important."

Why didn't Billy leave whatever at Revonda's? Or get it to my house? But perhaps he didn't know where my house was. Anyway, this was ridiculous. But I waited a minute and she went inside and came back out bearing a white envelope, which she handed to me. Billy the envelope boy. I took a quick peek, even late and annoyed as I was. Some sort of group photograph at a picnic. And most of the people were squinting in the bright sun, but Revonda and Mert were both smart enough to have dark glasses on. No note. This didn't make sense. I'd ask Revonda about it.

A car I didn't recognize stood in Revonda's driveway, an old red Volkswagen convertible. Dashing but battered. Why had Revonda asked me over? I had just stepped up onto the porch when I heard barking and screaming. The front door was unlocked as advertised. I opened it and heard Revonda's voice, outraged and frightened: "You'll never get away with this!"

The Persian rug hid the sound of my feet as I slipped in to find out what was wrong. I passed the shelves with all the mementos on them. A brass bowl of pennies teetered on the edge. Old coins, no doubt. No time to worry about that. My eye fell on the small pearl-handled gun.

Loaded! That fact had gone right out of my mind from the moment Reverend Phillipson had put the gun down. How could I forget a loaded gun? Thank goodness no kid had come along and shot himself by mistake. But the gun might be useful now! I'd never shot one. I hoped I wouldn't have to. I took the gun and slipped it in my skirt pocket. The door to Revonda's bedroom was half open, so I could hear but not be seen.

"Where's the money? Paul owed me money. You admit that, and I mean to have it. I'll use this knife. I'd enjoy using this knife on a bitch like you." The man's voice was hysterical.

I peeked through the crack near the door hinges. The man's back in a black T-shirt was toward the door. He had red tousled hair. Revonda sat at her desk, turned sideways toward him, in a red pants suit and lots of gold. The dog by her side was growling but not advancing on the man. Why not? Revonda needed help.

I backed up from the crack. *Thud!* I'd knocked against that derned bowl full of pennies. They fell on the floor and rolled in all directions.

The man sprang to the door and opened it wide. I recognized him. Paul's dinner-theater buddy. Who wore his TO BE IS BETTER THAN NOT TO BE T-shirt, of all things, to the memorial service. He had it on now. While his back was turned to Revonda and before I could even think, she reached in the drawer of her desk, took out a black pistol, and with both hands aimed the thing at his head. "Drop that knife."

He turned back around and dropped an ugly hunting knife with a clunk. Revonda nodded toward a roll of package tape on her desk, the brown shiny kind that's so hard to get off when you're opening a package. "Put this around his wrists," she said to me. She kept her gun on the young man.

"March him over to the closet," Revonda ordered. "He'll be safer in there till we get help. Now tape his ankles together."

The looks he shot me were as poisonous as tarantula bites. While I taped, he went on yelling at Revonda.

"Why did you call me and tell me to come for the money? You never meant to give me that money, did you? Why in hell did you call me here?"

The dog kept growling but sat quite still.

What he said didn't make sense. "You must be the one who broke in last week," I said.

"Paul gave me a key, and I want what's mine!" he yelled. "The cocaine or the money. I didn't find cocaine, and this bitch used the money to lure me here." I put the roll of tape down. Something was definitely wrong.

"Did you ask him to come here, Revonda?"

"That's not enough tape," she said. "Put some more." She shook the gun at me. "Go on, or I'll shoot."

I caught my breath. Billy had tried to warn me. That dawned on my thick brain with a thunderclap. Revonda was the one who dropped the dark glasses. He found the picture and recognized them! But I didn't. And me with my bleeding heart — I had to help Revonda in trouble. I'd thought I was helping the mother of a murdered son. But she was using me. I mustn't let the hot anger that surged through me trip me up.

"Put tape over his mouth," she ordered. "Put more. Now push him in the closet and shut the door. Now, put your hands up." Revonda stood so she could watch my every move. "He's going to die, but let him die ignorant of what becomes of you." After I shut the door, I could hear him making moaning noises through the tape.

With eyes and gun still on me, Revonda went to her desk. Holding the gun in one hand, she pressed or moved something on the side, and a small compartment came open. Two markers clattered to the floor and a piece of paper fluttered down. She pulled out a plastic dry cleaning bag and put the other things back. The thin plastic glimmered in folds of liquid ice.

"You're the killer!" My voice squeaked. I began to back up slowly. With her hawk's eyes fastened on me, I couldn't reach down into my pocket for the gun. She followed me. The dog followed us both, as if we were a small parade. Revonda shut the door to her bedroom, blocking out the young man's moaning noises. I backed through the dark of the small hallway into the light of the living room, past Revonda's childhood pictures framed on the wall. Past her father holding up a snake. How appropriate. If I turned and ran, she'd certainly shoot. We were like a silent movie, without a piano player.

Just as I stood near the front door, someone knocked. Ted! I thought in hope and terror. "I'll shoot if you scream," Revonda hissed. "And I can shoot through the door, too." Then, more loudly, she called, "Come in."

The door opened and Anne backed in calling, "Thanks for the ride, Ron. Thanks for trying to help." My heart sank as I heard a car drive off. If I called out to Anne, one or both of us would be dead. She came all the way in, before she looked up and saw Revonda and the gun. "Both of you keep your hands up and stand together," Revonda commanded. She wanted an easy target. She walked over to the door and locked it. "We don't want to be disturbed. Keep moving. I don't care for all these windows. We'll go in Paul's room."

She stood sideways, keeping the gun on us, and opened the door to the mirror room. "Go ahead of me," she said. "And don't bother to run for the French doors. They're locked."

We went into an ice cave, stripped of Paul's magic things now. The face chair was still there, and Paul's cot with a white throw. But the face jugs, the candles, the books were all put away somewhere by efficient Revonda. The room which had felt like it hid demons was now just icy cold as death.

Anne seemed speechless. And what could either one of us say? But Anne rose to occasions. At least she'd risen to the occasion of the snake. And she moved with more assurance now than she had then. If we kept our wits, we might survive.

"You'll never get away," Revonda said. "Why fight?" She laughed, and red Revonda with her red lips laughing was reflected in the ice around us. "As for you, Anne, you told me yourself you have bad luck. You might as well get this over with." Her eyes were hypnotic, the white large around the blue, the blue darkened like a storm, the pupils growing large.

Anne stood tall and straight, still silent. Stunned silent? Or quietly gathering force?

Revonda held the plastic bag in front of her, glimmering, gun in one hand, bag spread between the two hands, bag moving in the mirrors, almost mirror colored. Ice colored.

Anne and I had to divert Revonda. God willing, help would come. Yet if Ted or Sam came and didn't suspect Revonda, they could be trapped with us. If Anne was here, did that mean Sam was out of jail? Billy must suspect Revonda, or why the picture? Would anyone listen to Billy? Who would he go to for help? If we could divert Revonda, I might get the pistol out of my pocket and shoot quick.

Suddenly there rose into my mind a picture of that day when Revonda said to me, "People tell you things." She'd looked at me in that strange way, half admiring, half something else. I couldn't figure out what that something else was. It was fear. My heart began to beat faster. I *was* good at listening, and all at once I knew why that scared Revonda. Because she needed so desperately for someone to listen. She needed to justify herself.

Around her, the mirrors glittered cold, even with me and Anne and Revonda, all reflected in them. Her life was like that. Self-justification was the nearest thing she had to warmth. And, therefore, precious to her.

"You've fooled everyone," I said as we backed farther into the cave of mirrors. "You killed Marvelle and then Jinx, and nobody even suspected you. Did you kill Paul?"

Her eyes widened. She clenched her hands tight around the gun and the bag. "I was a good mother!" That was a cry of pain. I was almost sorry for her. Her face of pain reflected all around us.

"Listen," she said, "everything I did was for my son. I got away from this place where everyone treated me like the daughter of a man who drank himself to death in a privy. That was the first step. I became the sort of woman who could someday bear a happy child."

Anne backed against the face chair, and the grinning face went up, down, up, down reflected and rereflected the mirrors. And the bouncing reflections still made me a little dizzy. But this time I thought that strange carved face was laughing at Revonda. Laughing at the good mother of the happy child. I almost laughed. I steeled myself. Don't get hysterical.

Revonda still held herself like a queen. "I married a rich man and he helped my career. I was a star." Her voice thrilled at the word *star.* "I came back here, and nobody treated Paul like they'd treated me. Nobody. He had a chance to be whatever he wanted to be, and he threw that away. All he could do was this." She waved the gun at the mirror room, which gave her back a hundred waving guns. "I've fought so hard to be what I am. The fools in this valley are not going to put me down. I would not let them say that my son killed himself. He was all I had. All I cared about. And then I found him dead like that. With a terrible note."

She shut her eyes, but opened them so fast that I couldn't take advantage of the moment. " *'Better my own self dead than your puppet alive. You are a witch.'* He wrote that to me. His mother." Revonda tossed her head back like an angry horse, and all the reflections tossed. I felt woozy. "He was never my puppet. I tried so hard to help him be what he could be, but he would never listen."

I saw Anne start to speak and then restrain herself. Her eyes were angry.

A witch. In my head that strange jingle from Mrs. Jeeter's herb book read itself out loud: *Vervain and dill, vervain and dill, hinder witches from their will.* I saw Paul's body with those herbs showing through the plastic, and the strange whorls painted on it. He was crazy. But he was crazy in a logical way.

"I did what I had to do!" Revonda glared at us. "I hid that note in my desk. Fortunately, the sheriff is too naive to look for anything as simple as a secret compartment. And with the note I hid the markers Paul used to paint those crazy marks on himself. I should have thrown the note away. But somehow, I couldn't. Not his last words. Although I hated them." Her voice wavered. Then she stiffened her spine and began to move toward us.

The dog, by her side, let out a low growl. The dog's eyes followed us, and I felt like now she was just waiting in case Revonda needed help. I was the one who needed help. I wished to God the dog in the room was Baskerville, who loved Anne, instead of Hound, who always obeyed Revonda.

"I knew what I had to do." Revonda moved closer. We backed a few steps, but there wasn't far to go. I knew my listening face turned toward her was keeping us alive. That and her need to be heard. "I had to prove Paul was murdered." Her voice rang with drama. "I had to prove to the people in this valley that they were wrong about me." She spit the words. "They said my grandfather killed himself, my father drank himself to death, my husband drank and killed himself in his car. They weren't going to say my son was a suicide, too! That I was a black widow. No." She raised the plastic bag.

"So why did you kill Marvelle?" Keep her justifying. She was an ice witch, not a tiger.

"That cruel Marvelle told me Paul had told her he wanted to die. He opened up to that show-off, not to me, his mother. I needed someone else to be killed just in the way he was. To prove we had a serial killer, not a suicide."

"So you disguised yourself," I said, "in dark glasses and a bandanna and a big floppy dress, not your style. And took the nye way, mostly cross-country, to get to Marvelle's and back as quick as you could."

She laughed, and that tinkly-ice-cube laugh in this ice room was wildly eerie. "I knew I had to do it during Edna's favorite TV program. Nothing pulls that old fool away from that. I even told her to feel free to take the phone off the hook, that a half an hour wouldn't matter." That splintered laugh again.

Anne clenched her fists. Oh, dear, I thought, Anne's going to let fly and lose her temper, and perhaps our lives. But she stayed frozen.

"Then Jinx came to me," Revonda said solemnly, "with some crazy idea about how the marks on Paul's body meant personal growth. Which was like that terrible note from Paul which said death was the only way he could be his own self. That fool girl talked about how Paul had been depressed, had threatened to kill himself. She couldn't keep her mouth shut. She'd make my son look like a coward who couldn't face life. So I killed her." Revonda became clearer. "Besides, serial killers keep killing, don't they? That's why a serial killer will put you both in plastic bags, marked with the fingerprints of that stupid young man in the closet. And he'll be dead because he attacked me." She raised her eyebrows and smiled in a knowing way.

"Our serial killer will put Anne here in a bag with a broken mirror, a well-known symbol of the bad luck she's so proud of."

Anne erupted. "You're telling me I'm such a fool I'll almost help you kill me. Is that right?" Anne's voice was strong and angry. She held her head high.

"Yes," Revonda said. "Now."

"That's like a curse."

"Yes," Revonda said, "you can call it that. You know you're cursed. Something is wrong with you."

"I know something is wrong," Anne said proudly. "And therefore I can figure out how to get around it. That's more than I can say for you!"

I kept expecting Revonda to pounce, but she didn't. She seemed unsure. Surprised to be challenged.

"You also told me what Paul said about curses," Anne went on. "That if the intended victim refuses a curse, it goes back on the sender. You believe that, don't you?" Anne raised her voice and threw the words at Revonda: "I refuse your curse!"

I caught my breath. Of course. Anne knew first-hand. If you let yourself believe you're jinxed, then you are. Could she turn what she knew into a weapon to save our lives? It might work. Combined with every other way, we could fight back.

The dog growled again. Her eyes were still on us, ears pricked.

Revonda stopped dead still, as diverted as she'd ever be. I reached down for the gun in my pocket. The time had come when I had to do the best with it I could. But before I could do more than get my hand in position around the cold metal, Revonda turned to the dog and yelled, "Sic 'em!" Anne screamed in terror. I raised the gun, aimed as best I could, and pulled the trigger. There was no bang, only a sick click as the dog bounded forward and arched into the air. The Reverend Phillipson had only loaded words. Even in terror, a part of me almost laughed. I should have known!

A scream and a crash!

The dog had lunged at Revonda, not at me or Anne. Revonda lay on the floor near the table, quite still, with the dog holding her down. As I tried to sort that out, there came a pounding on the French doors. Anne ran to open them.

And there were Ted and Sam and the sheriff, and also Billy — a mob. And I'll tell you, a mob of moral support was just what I felt we needed. Now that the threat was over, I was shaking. I hugged Ted. Anne hugged Sam. We were like the last scene in an operetta. Except for the sheriff and Billy, who were staring at Revonda on the floor.

"I told you I suspected her," Sam said to the sheriff, over Anne's shoulder, "but it took Billy and Ted both to convince you to come see. You were sure pigheaded at first," Sam scoffed, "not even letting Anne see me." He hugged her extra tight.

It was the first time I ever saw the sheriff look humble. "I never thought Revonda . . ." He stared at her hard. "You know what, she's breathing. She's still alive!"

I knew she would hate that anticlimax. She would prefer to be dead.

"Is this dog dangerous?" the sheriff asked no one in particular.

"Of course not," Sam said, with a huge self-satisfied grin. "Anne, call off Baskerville. It was Hound I took to the vet. I don't trust Hound. I figured that was one way I could stack the odds for Anne in case I was arrested."

Baskerville bounced over and began to lick Anne as soon as she called. Baskerville, who jumped to protect Anne when Revonda threatened and Anne screamed.

The sheriff leaned over Revonda. "She's hit her head," he said. "On the table, I think. She's knocked out. But she's breathing." In fact, Revonda stirred and moaned. The sheriff pulled out a pair of handcuffs. He sighed. "I guess she's a dangerous woman," he said. I was surprised to see tears in the sheriff's eyes. "But she was a lovely young girl."

I was glad he remembered that. Because even for Revonda I felt some pity. A woman that proud would find worse than hell in prison. Execution, if it came, would be a reprieve.

Poor Pop. He'd feel bad. But not so bad that he wouldn't be thrilled to have been in the middle of the action. The boyfriend of the killer. Pleased as pie that with a little help from his friends he'd trapped the Bloodroot Creek killer, before she killed me in some appropriate way.

And do you know? I was just a little bit disappointed. I would never know how Revonda would have done it: what she would have thought was my most dramatic sin.

Chapter

37

A YEAR LATER

Ted was standing by the table near the front door, looking through the mail. He picked up the *Citizen-Times*. A headline said: MAGIC MURDER TRIAL BEGINS TODAY.

"But it wasn't magic that killed Paul and the others and destroyed Revonda," I said.

Ted raised both eyebrows, which I knew meant: *What wild conclusion have you drawn now?* I'd been trying to digest the whole Revonda-and-Paul thing, mostly out loud.

"Magic," I said, "was the symptom. Paul was looking for a way to believe he had some kind of power, some way not to feel overwhelmed by Revonda. He picked a way that made things worse, that cut him off from most of the people around him." I thought of his ice-palace room and shivered.

Ted put the paper down on the table and began to go through the envelopes. "But it did seem that the curse Revonda wanted to put on those around her came back and zapped her." Logical Ted said that! He picked up a heavy ivory envelope and began to rip it open.

"Revonda has a desperate need to be in power," I said. "So when Anne refused to be controlled, Revonda lost her cool. But we wasn't really dealing with magic as such," I said, "unless imagination is magic. We were certainly dealing with sick imagination."

"Hey, look at this!" Ted handed me an ivory card.

The True Spiral Gallery
invites your presence
at the opening of an exhibit of
the paintings of Sam Newman

Including a collage incorporating news stories
of the murders in Bloodroot Creek
and excerpts from a speech on the U.S. Senate Floor
denouncing the artist as well as praise for the artist
from a sermon
by the Reverend G. O. Phillipson
of Bloodroot Creek

Friday evening, August 15, at 7 P.M.

The True Spiral Gallery
will be representing Sam Newman

332

"Well," I said. "That should help Sam to become famous. Just like Anne always said he would be. Talk about imagination — Sam's got it in spades! And maybe the right kind of imagination *is* magic," I said, "in art and music, and writing, too."

"And you even use imagination in order to remember." Ted shook his head and grinned. "Some of the ways you use to remember are beyond anything I could possibly dream up. Would you please tell me why you have an upside-down soup pot in the middle of the dining room table, and a stack of books on top of that, and a ceramic tiger on the very top?"

"Certainly," I said. "The tiger stands for Revonda. When I go to set the table at six-thirty, that's exactly the time I need to call Pop and remind him to see how they cover the opening of Revonda's trial on television. Pop begged me not to let him miss it. He wants to write Revonda a note and tell her she looked lovely on television. Which, knowing her, I'm sure she will. He says they'll both be condemned to die. Revonda by the state, and Pop by Father Time. So they need to cheer each other up."

I wandered over to admire my wild tiger assemblage. "You've heard of Found Art," I said, "made of whatever comes to hand. Well, I call this Temporary Found Art, and it's a great

memory-jogger. Because you can't miss it —
right? And the surest reminders are the ones you
can't miss, even if you try."

The employees of G.K. Hall hope you have enjoyed this Large Print book. All our Large Print titles are designed for easy reading, and all our books are made to last. Other G.K. Hall books are available at your library, through selected bookstores, or directly from us.

For information about titles, please call:

(800) 223-1244
(800) 223-6121

To share your comments, please write:

Publisher
G.K. Hall & Co.
P.O. Box 159
Thorndike, ME 04986